Christmas by C

by

Ruth Saberton

KPBE6

Copyright

Published by Millington

Copyright © 2020 Ruth Saberton

All characters, organisations and events in this publication, other than those clearly in the public domain, are fictitious and any resemblance to real persons, living or dead, is purely coincidental.

The opinions expressed in this book are solely the opinions of the author and do not represent the opinions or thoughts of the publisher. The author has represented and warranted full ownership and / or legal right to publish all materials in this book.

The moral right of the author has been asserted.

All rights reserved. No part of this publication may be reproduced, stored in a retrieval system or transmitted, in any form or by any means, without the prior permission of the publisher.

November 2020

Dear Reader,

Before you begin *Christmas by Candlelight* I want to say a few words about this book and how it came to be written. It's been an absolute joy to write and an escape during a very difficult time. I really hope it will also provide solace for all who read it. *Uplift lit* is apparently an industry buzz word right now and I think it's a term that fits the Polwenna Bay novels beautifully. I certainly laugh out loud and feel uplifted when I write them!

Who could have imagined what 2020 would bring? As I write this note it is November and we are still in the grip of the Covid 19 Pandemic. The UK is in a second lockdown and Christmas looks as though it will be very different this year. The world is certainly a very different place to how it was twelve months ago, and it feels almost odd to think there was ever a time when we didn't need to wear facemasks while shopping and could meet our friends and loved ones easily. Some of us haven't been able to see family members for many months because of shielding or regional restrictions, and that's been so hard. This week there has been news of a potential vaccine and a glimmer of hope. I'm tentatively looking forward to a time, hopefully not too far away in the future, when everyone says wonderingly, "Do you remember that?".

When I turned my attention to starting the next Polwenna Bay novel I had a dilemma on my hands. Readers often email or write to me about this series and I knew it offers a wonderful escape to so many people, and I include myself amongst that number. Returning to the village, and the people who live there, feels like catching up with old friends. The world of Polwenna is the world of summer holidays, ice cream, Cornish seaside escapes and sunshine. It's a place where locals chat at the bar, squabble over raft races and plan village weddings. It's a melting pot of artists, fishermen, locals and holiday makers and a place like no other - a state of mind as much as a location. I actually think this sums up Cornwall. The county is a much a character in the books I write as any other that may appear. When a reader picks up a Polwenna Bay novel I want them to immerse themselves in that world because each book is a holiday in your hand and a respite from reality.

This led to a quandary: did I set the new Polwenna Bay book in our current Covid world or did I keep it very much apart from all this? This was a problem lots of my writer friends were also facing and in our (socially distanced!) online forums we discussed it at length. Setting a book during the pandemic would date it, and Polwenna is a timeless place, and my own personal feeling was I didn't want to write, or read, about the pandemic. It's become quite enough of an intrusive and worrying part of daily life already. Reading and writing have played a huge role in keeping my spirits up when things have been hard - especially when I was shielding earlier in the year. Did I want Covid 19 to encroach on this?

I asked my Facebook Author Group some questions to find out what readers thought about this issue and the overwhelming response was they would prefer the world of Polwenna Bay to continue exactly as it always has. The consensus was that Polwenna is a place to escape to so masks and hand gel and social distancing could stay in the real world! I was pleased about this since the next Polwenna Bay book would be set over Christmas and feature Jules and Danny's wedding - I couldn't help thinking Jules would be secretly relieved to have a small and socially distanced day. That wouldn't have afforded me much of a plot!

So, without further ado, here is *Christmas by Candlelight* - a magical and festive novel which grew from the original novella because I was loving writing it so much. Thank you to my editor, advanced readers and proof-readers who have all worked so hard at a difficult time to polish it so the book could be published before Christmas.

Dear readers, I really hope you enjoy this book and that it transports you, for a few hours at least, to a carefree and magical place.

Looking forward to brighter times ahead.

x Ruth x

Chapter 1

Saturday 19th December

Although it was long past five o'clock on the last Saturday before Christmas, Truro's town centre bustled with people brave enough to battle the cold, crowds and full carparks in their quest to finish their festive shopping. The narrow streets lacing the old cathedral to the High Street thronged with well-wrapped folk weighed down by bulging carrier bags as shop tills rang out as joyfully as the cathedral bells. Dusk bloomed beyond the soaring spires but the wintry darkness was cheered by splashes of colour from lights strung above the busy pavements and rendered magical by the twinkling bulbs of the city's enormous tree.

The whole city sparkled and for a few blissful moments Jules Mathieson forgot how dreadfully stressed she was. Lost in the delicious wonder of her favourite season, all worries about her imminent wedding were briefly and blissfully erased. Christmas was the most hopeful time of the year. It was a season filled with goodwill and love. If she could just focus on this rather than seating plans and difficult family members then all would be well.

Wouldn't it?

A brass band played carols on Lemon Quay and a huddle of pretty wooden chalets had been erected for the Christmas Market. Even late in the day these were doing a roaring trade. Vendors called out to tempt peckish passers-by with slithers of cured meats, olives glistening in chilli oil, and crumbly hunks of local cheese. It was usually impossible for Jules to resist these samples and in the past she'd indulged herself by trying the most peculiar flavour combinations. Last December she had brought home mint chocolate chip cheese, which she was certain had tasted totally different when offered from the tip of a cocktail stick

beneath a fairy light strewn awning. Unsurprisingly, this purchase hadn't held *quite* the same appeal when she'd offered it to her fiancé, Danny. Undeterred, Jules served up this epicurean delight with crackers and wine at the next church meeting only for Big Roger Pollard to spray his entire mouthful over Sheila Keverne's neatly written minutes. Apart from sending St Wenn's verger into a near meltdown, Big Rog had claimed to suffer stomach pains all night and called the local GP out. Although trapped wind rather than cheese poisoning was Dr Richard's unglamorous diagnosis, Jules had admitted defeat. She chucked the cheese out of the vicarage window for the seagulls but even they left it to turn stale on the grass. Polwenna's orange beaked thugs usually mugged Jules if she so much as dared to think about eating her lunch in the garden and they were infamous for their ability to spot an open bag of chips from even the most distant chimney pot.

She should have gone for the chilli chocolate cheese. There was bound to be some of that here today and the pickled red onion one was calling her too. And the garlic cheese was to die for!

The problem was Jules wasn't meant to be eating cheese. With under a week to go until her big day, she was still a fair few pounds short of her self-imposed target weight. Cheese, mad flavours or not, was well and truly off the menu along with salami, taster chunks of Christmas pudding and big cups of hot chocolate topped with whipped cream and marshmallows. Eating mince pies when out and about on parish business was not helping either when there was a wedding dress to fit into. Her wonderful fiancé, Danny deserved to have a slim(ish) bride walking down the aisle to meet him and to this end Jules had been diligently counting calories, avoiding the biscuit section in the supermarket and stomping over the cliffs. There was no way she was falling at the final hurdle, Jules told herself as the rich scent of hog roast and fried onions made her mouth water, not when her beautiful wedding dress was hanging up in the spare room and she was already planning to double Spanx. Maybe even triple?

"Jules! Come on! The stall I was telling you about is over here!"

Mo Carstairs, Jules's soon to be sister-in-law and self-appointed wedding planner, beckoned to her impatiently. Mo often looked impatient, not many people moved or thought as fast as she did, and even at seven months pregnant she'd stomped her way through the busy streets twice as fast as the others in their small group. Summer and Alice had given up and headed for a tea shop hours ago. Jules would have loved to join them but there was no way Mo would have this. Not when there was serious wedding business to attend to.

"Come on!" urged Mo, almost pawing the ground like one of her horses. "Some time this year would be good!"

Her tone suggested she was finding Jules something of a trial today, and Jules didn't blame Mo for being frustrated. She should be filled with excitement about her wedding. After all, wasn't this what most girls dreamed of? The big white wedding in a beautiful church? All her nearest and dearest gathered? A huge reception at an exclusive hotel? And best and most importantly of all, she loved Danny Tremaine with all her heart and couldn't wait to be his wife. Jules had absolutely everything anyone could ever want so what on earth was the matter with her? It must just be pre-wedding jitters, that was all.

"Come on! We've still got lots to do!" said Mo, setting off again at a pace which even former soldier Danny would have thought twice about. "Stop dawdling!"

Jules wondered what remained on Mo's long and very detailed list but knew better than to argue. She was no longer naïve enough to think getting married just meant a ring, a white dress, and an hour in the church followed by sandwiches and cake in the village hall. She could almost laugh at the version of herself who'd actually believed she and Danny would have a small and simple affair like that. Back in the summer, when Mo had first delivered a stack of bridal magazines, Jules had scorned the kind of woman who woke up in a cold sweat because the wedding flowers might not match the groom's waist coats but fast forward six months and somehow she'd morphed into that very person.

How on earth had it happened?

Oh happy days when all she'd had to worry about at the Christmas market was what cheese to horrify her fiancé and her parishioners with, Jules reflected as she followed Mo through the press of winter coats and carrier bags. Last year she hadn't needed to fret about matching ribbons or wedding favours or who sat where and at what table. This seemed liked another life, and a very simple one too.

"Oh my God!"

Mo stopped so abruptly several shoppers had to slalom to avoid her and Jules, cannoning into Mo's waxed jacketed back, was alarmed.

"What's wrong? Is it the baby?"

"The baby? No, of course not. I was looking at that. Isn't it amazing?"

Mo pointed across the bustling market. Following her gaze, Jules saw a gleaming trap pulled by a handsome pair of horses. Of course. Mo was bonkers about all things equine. Jules wasn't quite so keen on horses herself, especially after Mo's daughter Isla's pony christened the church floor during a pet blessing, but she did her best to sound enthusiastic.

"Lovely."

Mo whipped out her mobile phone.

"I'll give them a call, shall I? We haven't got a wedding car organised yet and the Pollard's quad is lethal."

Jules's stomach plopped into her boots, a sensation she'd become very familiar with over the past six months. She'd first experienced it when Danny pointed out how the residents of Polwenna Bay and his family would be really hurt if they really ran away to Gretna Green or had a small wedding. Jules had hoped for an intimate affair with just her closest family and friends, but she understood this and had shelved her reservations. She was the village vicar and Danny was a Tremaine; it only stood to reason that their wedding would be a key event in the village calendar.

She'd experienced the sinking sensation again a few weeks later on when Alice and Jonny St Milton offered to pay for the wedding reception and host it at the Polwenna Bay Hotel. This was a hugely generous gesture and Dan had leapt at it, especially once his chef brother Symon volunteered to take care of the catering while his wedding planner girlfriend sorted out the logistics. How could Jules have refused when they were all so keen to help out and so very generous? Of course she'd agreed and if her dreams of a small meal for close family and friends evaporated like sea fret in sunshine, then this was surely a small price to pay for making everyone happy? Marrying Danny was what really mattered.

Looking back, Jules realised she ought to have known keeping quiet about what she'd really wanted was a recipe if for not disaster exactly, then certainly a wedding that would run away with her like the harbour fish cart with the brake left off. Her modest wedding had morphed into the highlight of Polwenna Bay's year and had become something of a competition amongst the villagers for who could help the vicar the most. This was practically an Olympic sport now and when she somehow managed to include Sheila Keverne amongst her bridesmaids Jules realised her initial inability to let anyone down was becoming an issue.

Jules felt utterly overwhelmed. As much as she was longing to marry Danny, she was also growing increasingly nervous. She'd tried several times to tell him how she was feeling but he was so excited, and Jules hated to be the one to burst his bubble. Besides, what good would voicing her concerns do at the eleventh hour? It was far too late to put on her brave pants and admit she was terrified of the scale of their wedding and desperate to tone it down. Taking place at St Wenn's on Christmas Eve, the big day was just a week away. The reception was booked, the menus chosen, and Symon was already preparing the food. Patsy Penhalligan from the village bakery had baked an enormous cake, the Pollards had offered to decorate their quad to drive Jules and Danny to the reception and the primary school choir had been practising Ave Maria for weeks. Scores of their friends and family had made travel arrangements and booked their accommodation and her curate was even cutting short his visit to his family on the Isle of Mull in order to conduct the ceremony. There was no way Jules could say anything now; all she could do was pray hard her Boss would help her to overcome her nerves.

"Hello! Earth to Jules! Have you been drinking those artisan gin samples?"

Mo waved her hand in front of Jules's face, snatching her out of her reverie and plopping her back into the heart of the Christmas market. It was almost a shock to find herself surrounded by stalls selling wooden toys and artisan candles rather than in the vicarage, staring at a colour chart as she tried to choose between aubergine and plum for the ribbons that would hold the order of service together.

"What do you think? Shall I book it as a little present from me and Ash?"

"It's a lovely idea but the Pollards have already got our transport to the reception sorted," Jules said quickly, crossing her gloved fingers behind her back and hoping her boss would forgive this half fib. Although Mo was just desperate to get horses involved in the wedding Jules was standing firm on this matter. Mo had already tried valiantly to persuade her to ride to St Wenn's side saddle and Jules wouldn't put it past her to pop a bow on one of her event horses and sneak it in as an extra bridesmaid.

Mo huffed out a disbelieving breath.

"The Pollard quad rather than a carriage? You can't be serious?"

"I'm totally serious. Big Rog and Karenza are really excited. They've sprayed the quad cart white especially and are decorating it. I can't let them down."

"You're utterly mad," said Mo, shaking her head as she slid her phone back into the pocket of her Barbour. "It's not that long since the parish council banned them from running the luggage taxi after they nearly killed Keyhole Kathy."

"They didn't nearly kill Keyh— I mean Kathy Polmartin. That's a vast exaggeration. Little Rog caught her hessian shopper bag on the wing mirror and just towed her along for a couple of feet. He couldn't have been going more than five miles an hour."

"Hmm," said Mo, unconvinced. "Well, that's not what I heard, and Granny Alice said they kept bashing into her flower tubs. Jonny nearly had his foot squashed too. You won't ride Dandy, but you'll travel with them? Really?"

"Really," said Jules. Although the Pollards had been lethal with their luggage taxi, and were hopeless at maintaining the church and vicarage, they generally meant well and you had to admire how they always bounced back with a money-spinning idea, even if these tended to be a little dubious. The last one, *Polwenna Ghost Tours,* was proving popular with holiday makers and if nobody local had ever heard of the resident phantoms this didn't seem to deter the customers or their *creative* tour guides. Keen to give Mousehole a run for its money in the Christmas illuminations stakes, Big Rog had also taken sole responsibility for this year's Polwenna Lights. If the village lit up at night like one of Heathrow's runways, it was at least cheerful and one less thing for Jules to try and organise. Inspired, Big Rog was also smothering St Wenn's with fairy lights especially for the wedding and Jules was touched, if a little nervous about the electricity bill.

Hmm. Touched in the head to let the Pollards anywhere near the church's ancient electrics, but it was a sweet gesture and just one of many such from her parishioners, all of whom were determined to make sure their vicar had the best wedding Polwenna Bay had ever seen. She really must try harder to be grateful and get into the spirit of the whole thing, Jules reflected as she trailed after Mo who was heading full steam ahead for a stall selling ribbons and lace. This was vital apparently, although Jules couldn't think for the life of her why. She'd never worn a ribbon in her life.

While Mo sifted through ribbons, Jules told herself sternly that she needed to relax and enjoy the run up to the wedding. This was a special time and she ought to make the most of every minute – she'd certainly attended enough weddings to know the day would zoom past in the blink of an eye. Dresses, guests and competitive villagers would all fall into place and if Danny was running the entire operation like an episode of *SAS: Who Dares Weds* it was only because he was excited and wanted their special day to run smoothly.

"I want everything to be absolutely perfect for you," he'd said yesterday when insisting upon yet another recce of the Polwenna Bay Hotel's dining room complete with seating plan manoeuvre. As he worked out where to place each guest, and checked with a ruler to ensure all the tables were the right distance apart, Jules felt like clicking her heels and saluting. Since when had Danny, her outdoorsy and easy-going fiancé, cared about such things?

"I don't need it to be perfect. I just want to marry you," Jules said, quietly and from underneath a table.

But Danny had been far too busy studying his table plan to hear a word.

"Is that one and a half metres exactly?" he asked, frowning down at his clipboard. "Make sure, sweetheart. Otherwise we can't fit enough tables in, and people will be left out. I'll get this sorted. I promise. Nothing is going to spoil your special day."

Jules appreciated Dan wanting to make their wedding run without a hitch. It wasn't his fault she never enjoyed being the centre of attention. Jules had never been any different. Her fleeting appearances in primary school nativities had never featured tinsel haloes or a starring role as Mary because Jules was more likely to be wearing a tea towel on her head or moving props before being ushered in with the ensemble to sing Away in a Manger. Not much had changed over the years; she was far happier wearing a cassock at the altar than a big white dress. Not everyone wanted to be the star of the show.

But Jules loved Danny with all her heart and she wanted to celebrate this. She couldn't wait for the whole world to know just how much she adored him and how very proud she was to be marrying him. Making their solemn promises in St Wenn's, before God and their closest family and friends, was all she cared about in terms of their wedding. The rest of it was immaterial and fast becoming something of an ordeal.

She sighed. What was the matter with her?

"You don't like this colour? I suppose it's a bit bright. What about this one?" asked Mo, scrutinising a roll of plum velvet through narrowed blue eyes. "Does that look to you as though it will match the bridesmaids' dresses? We don't want the tie the posies and buttonholes with the wrong colour."

Not for the first time in the run up to her big day Jules experienced a sensation of total blankness. Oh Lord. What colour were the bridesmaids' dresses again? Some kind of plum? Or was it dark red? Claret? Something wintry anyway for a December wedding and which had matched the velvet cloak she planned to wear over her wedding dress to prevent her from freezing to death in St Wenn's as well as hiding any stubborn pounds which refused to budge. The aroma of pork was very tempting. What Jules wouldn't have given to be meandering through the market with Danny, munching a floury bap crammed with juicy meat and scalding apple sauce…

"Maybe it's more like this?" Mo, happily sifting, wasn't really wanting for an answer as she brandished fistfuls of deep burgundy velvet. "That's closer to the colour of those carnations Perry showed us. It will match the dresses, don't you think?"

"Mmm," hedged Jules who really couldn't say. It seemed a lifetime ago she'd sat down with Perry Tregarrick to choose the wedding flowers. As for picking the bridesmaids' dresses - the trauma of frock shopping with Sheila Keverne and Mo was so great it was hardly surprising her mind had attempted to blank it out completely. Sheila had wanted them all to dress like nuns while Mo was merrily channelling her inner strumpet, all heaving Nell Gwynne bosom and creamy bare shoulders.

"You may as well be in your underwear, young lady. If you ask me it's indecent, baring flesh in God's house," Sheila huffed when Mo had suggested a strapless design. She pulled a high necked and long-sleeved number from a rail and held it against her. "This is far more modest and appropriate."

"We're bridesmaids! Not extras in the Handmaid's Tale!" Mo parried. "Are we wearing chastity belts as well? Not that you'll nee—"

"How about this style? It's a lot like the one Pippa Middleton wore when Will and Kate got married. Simple and stylish," Summer said quickly, holding up a waterfall of plum silk. Scooped necked and with capped sleeves, it offered the best of both worlds and pacified Mo and Sheila. Since Summer would look good in a bin liner and little Isla was three and wearing pink anyway, Jules had leapt on this compromise, thanking her Boss for the diplomatic Summer and doubly thanking Him her mum was safely living in Tenerife. Jules shuddered to think what Linda Mathieson would have chosen. Probably something even Katie Price would baulk at.

Jules still wasn't sure quite how Sheila had managed to become one of her bridesmaids. It was a combination of determination on her verger's part and softness on her own, she supposed. It was certainly true that when the older lady set her mind on something she made The Terminator look half-hearted. As soon as she'd known the vicar was getting married, Sheila had been dropping hints heavier than the mooring weights in the harbour. Jules could have ignored these if it hadn't been for a chance comment Alice had made after helping Sheila arrange flowers for the latest St Wenn's wedding.

"If I had a pound for each time Sheila mentioned weddings, dresses and how much she's always wanted to be a bridesmaid, St Wenn's would have a new roof by teatime," Jules had remarked as she and Danny's grandmother sat on a bench in the churchyard basking in the September sunshine. The village was drizzled in golden light and at its ripe end of season best with cottage window boxes spilling jaunty nasturtiums down whitewashed walls, the pub beer garden dotted with stripy umbrellas and chip stuffed seagulls snoozing on piled up fishing nets. All was as replete and content as any Keats' poem.

Alice gazed out to sea. Her faded forget-me-knot eyes were trained on a spot far beyond the horizon.

"I do feel for Sheila when there's a wedding. She gave up a lot when she stayed here to look after her parents."

Jules knew Sheila had been the sole carer for her mother and father. Although they had died some time ago, Sheila still lived in the family home, Lavender Cottage and never ventured much further than Polwenna Bay. Sheila wasn't alone in this; many locals didn't go 'up country' but to her shame Jules realised she'd never thought about why this might be the case. In fact she'd never thought much about Sheila at all really, beyond how bossy she could be or how difficult. Now she was intrigued.

"What happened?"

"It was a long time ago now and I'm a bit hazy because I had a lot on myself, but I seem to recall she was engaged to be married."

"Sheila was getting married? Seriously? To a man?" Jules was staggered.

"Yes, to a man! We're not that progressive here now, yet alone forty odd years ago!" laughed Alice. "Don't look so surprised, love, she wasn't always a spinster in her sixties. We were all young once, you know, even Sheila Keverne."

Jules let this sink in. It was hard to imagine Sheila being anything other than old and cranky. But she wasn't really old, was she? Early sixties at the most and Jules's mum Linda was always telling her how sixty was the new thirty. Or in Linda's case, the new fifteen…

"You might not believe me, but Sheila was very popular when she was a girl and a pretty little thing too," Alice continued, taking Jules's quiet shock for disbelief. "Just ask Roger Pollard and Eddie Penhalligan! They were both sweet on her, but Sheila only had eyes for her young man and their noses were well and truly out of joint because he wasn't even from Polwenna. I think she met him at a dance over Bodmin way. I think it broke her heart when things didn't work out."

Jules suddenly had an image of Sheila as a Polwenna's answer to Miss Havisham, wafting around in the ashes of a rich wedding dress and eating rotting wedding cake for breakfast. This didn't quite fit with her wearing tweed and cooking big stews for her lodger, Neil the handsome young curate, but what did Jules know? Not much, as it turned out.

"So what went wrong? Please don't tell me he jilted her?"

"Oh no, love. Quite the opposite. From what I remember the young man was batty about her. Love's young dream they were until Sheila's father fell ill. The family couldn't do without her wage or help and since Sheila was an only child, she had to choose between helping her parents or getting married and leaving home. You can probably guess what she decided to do."

Jules could and her heart twisted for Sheila. How would she feel if she were asked to make such a choice? Torn and heartbroken, she imagined. A sacrifice like that would change your life and was bound to scar you. It also explained an awful lot.

"But she had no choice at all."

Alice shook her head. "I'm afraid that's how it was back then, my love, and sometimes life doesn't give us any other options, but I've never once heard Sheila complain about her lot. She only lost her mum a few years before you arrived, and the church and the village are her family now. Even so, to spend most of your life arranging flowers for other people's weddings while knowing you gave up your own chance of happiness must be very painful."

Jules's throat tightened. She felt terrible for judging Sheila by appearances and busy body behaviour, although it was fair to say that Sheila had written the book on being bossy and interfering, but what would Jesus do? See beneath the surface and into hearts, that was what. Jules comforted herself with the knowledge Jesus had the advantage of being the son of God while she was only human. The next time Sheila fished for information about bridesmaids, Jules had taken a deep breath and asked whether Sheila might consider being her maid of honour. She needed somebody she could rely on, Jules explained, and who was used to organising church and village events so who better than her verger? With every word, Sheila swelled a little more with pride.

"I didn't like to say anything before because it was none of my business and you know me, Vicar, I'm not one to interfere," Sheila said, which was news to Jules who had plenty of experience of Sheila *not interfering* with everything from impromptu bell ringing to the infamous Polwenna Naked Calendar.

"But you do need somebody at the helm with experience of things," she continued, whipping a notebook from her bag and brandishing a pen. "Now. What we need is a list. That Morwenna's a flighty one, always has been, and I wouldn't trust her to organise your hen night! You'll end up with those Chipmunks dancing in their underpants, you mark my words, but leave it with me and you'll be in safe hands."

"Chippendales," Jules corrected automatically and then, and as Sheila's words sank into the part of her brain which wasn't screaming "*Sheila as your maid of honour? What are you thinking?*" she added, "What hen night, Sheila?"

"*Your* hen night, Vicar! Oh! Won't it be fun? You leave it all with me. It'll be wonderful!" She scribbled a few words into the notebook. "L plates are definitely on the list and hoodies with the names of all the hens will be fun. Yours can say *Bride* and be white. Do you want glitter? And how about angel wings? That would be lovely!"

"I don't think I need any of this," Jules said faintly, as visions of whipped cream and strippergrams drifted past her vision like a hen night themed circle of Hell. "Maybe a meal out at with a few friends?"

"A meal out?" Sheila echoed, shocked. "Absolutely not, Vicar. You deserve far more than a mere meal out. Leave it with me! In fact, leave it all with me!"

Jules hadn't had any choice but to give in and leave it all with Sheila. She only hoped her hen night wouldn't go the same way as Sheila's calendar themed fund raiser. She liked being a vicar and the bishop only had so much patience!

Chapter 2

Saturday 19th December

Joining Mo, who'd taken her *mmm* as agreement and was buying several yards of ribbon the exact hue of communion wine, Jules did her best to quell her rising sense of trepidation because the hen night was fast approaching and the exact activity was a closely guarded secret. Mo, equally horrified and mystified by Sheila's appointment to the top job of Maid of Honour, had said that there was absolutely nothing to be worried about.

"We'll be like nuns," was all she would say. "You put Sheila in charge, so what did you expect? If it was up to me, we'd have had some proper fun."

None of this made much sense but Jules was simply relieved the Chipmunks were well and truly out of the equation. Behaving like a nun was fine by her. Better than fine. God worked in mysterious ways indeed!

Ribbon purchases completed; Mo stuffed a brown paper package into her bag.

"If it doesn't match the buttonholes, don't blame me," she grumbled.

Jules shrugged. "There are worse problems to have."

Like the fact that tomorrow both her parents were due to be arriving at the vicarage. This really was a problem and one giving Jules sleepless nights. She'd look like a panda by the time she walked down the aisle.

Mo shot her a sideways look. "Tell that to your maid of honour. She'll have my guts for garters if I get this colour wrong. Oh! Look at those cute little wooden horses on that stall. Give us a second! I might get one for the nursery."

While Mo was preoccupied by a selection of expensive wooden toys, Jules chewed the skin around her thumb nail and eyed the mulled wine stand longingly. She'd need to mainline the stuff after just ten minutes with her parents. Surely a little cup wouldn't hurt. It was chilly now the sun had slipped behind the cathedral and stars were sprayed above. She could even see her breath rising in the air like Bishop Bill's incense. Christmas excitement was no longer quite enough to keep her warm. A glass of mulled wine would do the trick nicely, and a mince pie wouldn't go amiss either. It couldn't make that much difference to her waistline now, surely?

Jules joined the queue at the mulled wine stand, listening to the haunting notes of Silent Night drifting on the icy breath of the night breeze. Her eyes filled and she swallowed back tears. How was it possible just a few bars of a carol could whisk her back across the decades to become a child again, sitting at the top of the stairs listening to Alistair and Linda Mathieson hurling insults at one another? Carols had been playing on the radio that night and Jules had known instinctively this would be their last Christmas as a family. Although the atmosphere in the Mathieson family home had been strained for a long time Jules, like all children, wanted nothing more than happy parents who loved one another. She'd understood that evening her family was fracturing, and her heart had broken a little more with every note of the carol.

The warring couple finally divorced when Jules was fifteen, something which came as a relief to their daughter who was all but wearing a tin hat and bullet proof vest whenever her parents were in close proximity. For a few tricky years she shuttled between the two, spending miserable holidays listening to each complain bitterly about the other's shortcomings and the passing years had done little to soothe any animosity between them. Now she was an adult their paths rarely crossed and Jules couldn't really remember the last time they'd met. It wouldn't have been her ordination because her atheist father had been too disappointed to attend, and it wasn't when Granny Mathieson died either because only Jules and Alistair had attended her funeral. Jules realised their last face to face encounter must have been at her graduation when Linda turned up a few sheets to the wind and Alistair refused to sit next to her. They'd ended up hissing at each other across the auditorium, the warmup to a full-on screaming match outside witnessed by most of her friends while Jules clutched her degree certificate to her chest and longed for the earth to swallow her whole.

Oh Lord. What if they did this in the church? It would ruin everything. This was if Alistair even agreed to attend the wedding. Jules had tentatively asked her dad to give her away (knowing full well this would result in a lecture about patriarchy and marriage as an outdated bourgeois contract) but apparently he was ideologically opposed to being inside a church, religion being the opium of the people and all that. It was bad enough his only child was a Church of England vicar, worse again that she expected him to participate in an outdated ritual belonging to the very kind of organised religion he despised.

"I'm asking you to give me away, Dad, not join a religious order," Jules had pointed out, once Alistair eventually stopped lecturing her down the telephone line. She always felt as though she ought to be taking notes and preparing for an exam when her father went off on one. Her right ear hot and throbbing, she swapped the receiver over and took a deep breath. Time to play her trump card.

"Fine, I understand. If you can't do it on principle, I'll ask Mum instead."

"What?" Alistair spluttered.

"I said I'll ask Mum to give me away."

"You can't possibly be serious. Apart from the fact Linda will turn up dressed like one of those Towies and half cut, it's a father's job to give the bride away not a mother's."

So much for stepping away from patriarchy, Jules thought.

"Come on, Dad. We've all moved on a bit from those days. Aren't you lecturers all woke nowadays?"

"Really, Julia, it's too bad of you to put me in this position. All I asked was that you considered getting married somewhere secular - if you really insist on getting married at all."

Jules rolled her eyes at her reflection in the kitchen window and reflection Jules rolled her right back. She had heard all this before.

"I don't care what you want to call it! I do insist on getting married to Danny because I love him! I'm a vicar, Dad, and St Wenn's is *my* church and this is *my* wedding day. Of course I'm getting married there! If it's not you who walks me down the aisle, then it's going to be Mum. I want one of my parents present when I make my vows. It's going to be the most important day of my life."

There was a brief silence while Alistair debated the merits of standing firm versus not letting his ex-wife to get one over on him. They both knew Linda would gloat forever if she was the one to give Jules away.

"If it means so much to you, I can probably compromise," he said eventually. "Now then, when did you say this wedding is?"

There was the sound of flipping pages as he thumbed through his desk diary and Jules could picture him in his Oxford college study, a lanky figure dwarfed by looming bookshelves and veiled by plumes of cigarette smoke.

"Christmas Eve," Jules said patiently. "You do know what date that is, Dad?"

He laughed drily. "I do and I'll be there. I'll stay with you at the vicarage."

"Sure you won't combust when you step over the threshold?" she teased.

"I'll take the chance. All I ask is that you make sure your mother doesn't embarrass us all for once."

"Mum will be fine. She's calmed down a lot lately," Jules promised, thinking even as she spoke it was little short of a miracle she wasn't been struck down by holy lightning herself. *Linda Mathieson* and *calmed down* went together like oil and water. Hopefully she'd be on her best behaviour for her daughter's wedding and at least if her second husband David was present she wouldn't flirt with the best man or, worse again, Jules's new father-in-law. That had been rather awkward the last time Linda stayed in the village.

The conversation then turned to politics, fairly safe as Jules and her father were both left of centre and generally in agreement, before switching to the latest Booker Prize winner, a Victorian murder mystery which Jules hadn't heard of but promised to read when she had time. This was always a handy little caveat since time, like spare cash, was something vicars never had and Jules's taste in reading was more bodice ripper than Jack the Ripper. Once he'd rung off, she'd put the kettle on and worked her way through an entire packet of biscuits, which ruined her diet but felt like a reward for checkmating Professor Mathieson. Now all Jules had left to worry about was breaking the news to Linda that her ex-husband was attending after all and also staying at the vicarage, a job easily put off until the right moment arose.

Unfortunately, the right moment still had to materialise, and she sipped her mulled wine Jules knew she'd messed up. There was no way she dared to confess at this late hour to either parent that they would be staying under the same roof. Linda would throw the mother of all hissy fits and demand Alistair went elsewhere. He was bound to be only too happy to comply and might even see this as the perfect excuse to avoid the ceremony altogether. Having worked this hard to persuade him to give her away, Jules was not prepared to fall at the final hurdle. All she wanted was her parents to be present for her special day and preferably without throttling one another. Was that too much to ask?

"Help me out here, Lord," she said out loud. "Make me a channel of your peace. Oil on troubled waters and all that."

The problem was the only peaceful channel between Linda and Alistair would be the English Channel and Shell didn't produce enough oil to soothe their choppy waters. She'd have to sort them out when the situation arose, Jules concluded as she unwrapped the foil casing of her mince pie.

"What on earth are you doing? You've got a wedding dress to fit into!"

Mo swooped in like a gull and snatched the mince pie from Jules's fingers.

"Hey! That's mine!"

Jules lunged for it, but she wasn't fast enough. Mo crammed the whole lot into her mouth and chewed furiously.

"*I'm* the one meant to be eating for two not you!" she said through a mouthful of pastry.

Jules glanced down at the empty tin foil casing. Not for the first time wished she was getting married in jeans and a hoody. The white sparkly DM boots she'd bought would look perfect with her favourite Levis and she knew Danny would be happy to marry her no matter what she wore.

"I was looking forward to that!"

Mo brushed flakes of pastry from her chin.

"You'll thank me next weekend. You can eat as much as you like once the ring is on your finger. Stuff your face – I intend to! Symon's menu looks great. Tom Elliott tells me he's never seen so much food in the hotel's freezers and being the manager he ought to know. We could feed the whole village."

The plan was for a sit-down reception after the service for one hundred people (One hundred? Did they even know that many people?) followed by an even bigger evening do and buffet. They would then spill over into a marquee where Zak Tremaine and *The Tinners* would provide the entertainment and everyone could dance off the delicious food Symon Tremaine cooked up.

"Sy and Ella certainly have it all under control," Jules said.

"Shame Evil Ella comes as part of the package," Mo muttered.

Jules shot her a warning look.

"I know, I know! I shouldn't call her that but it's hard to break the habit of a lifetime."

"The season of good will is a good time to start."

"I can see I'm going to need to be on my best behaviour with a vicar as a sister-in-law. Fear not. I'll be as nice as pie to Ev— to Ella," grumbled Mo.

One less thing to worry about at the reception, Jules thought with relief. Mo and Ella had been feuding since their school days but now Ella was dating Mo's brother Symon, and Ella's grandfather had recently married Mo's grandmother, their childhood squabbles could make life a little awkward. Since Sy and Ella were in charge of the wedding reception the last thing Jules needed was any tension between family members and she was losing count of how many times she fired off prayers to this effect.

The problem was the closer she came to her big day the more worried Jules became that unless a miracle happened the people of Polwenna Bay would remember their vicar's wedding for a very long time indeed and maybe not for the best reasons.

Maybe prayers were like control knickers and best doubled? It was time to up the ante, Jules thought.

Chapter 3

Saturday 19th December

Toys and ribbons purchased, Mo threaded her arm through Jules's to tow her through the High Street. A snow machine was blowing foam into the darkening sky where the first shy stars were peeking out. The air was growing colder by the minute and the gathering night had frost in its breath. A Christmas cold snap was forecast for the entire country but it seemed to have arrived early and Jules burrowed deeper into her quilted jacket. There was already a hint of frost on the hills and her breathing clouded the air.

Would they all be warm enough in the church during the wedding service, she wondered? St Wenn's was beautiful but the Normans hadn't been big on central heating and the old asthmatic radiators wheezed out a few warm gasps. During the winter months Jules wore her thermals during services but there would be no room for these under her wedding dress and layers of control knickers. Oh dear. The last thing Danny needed was a hypothermic bride.

"You guys are still coming up to us for Christmas dinner, aren't you?" Mo was asking, interrupting Jules's worried reverie. "It's Ashley's first time hosting the family gathering and he's really keen to make sure it's a success."

"Of course. We're not going on our honeymoon until Boxing Day."

"I really hope you're going somewhere warm. A beach in the Caribbean would be good because it's meant to get below freezing here." Mo tugged her scarf tighter. "If Dan's booked a skiing holiday that's grounds for divorce."

Jules had no idea where they were heading for their honeymoon. This was Danny's department and he'd been highly secretive about it too. Being the kind of person who struggled to sit still for long, Jules couldn't imagine he would have chosen a beach holiday but on the other hand he knew she wouldn't want to be hiking through the jungle or whizzing down mountains. As much as she trusted Danny to have thought of something good, Jules would have been equally happy to hole up with him at the vicarage, snuggled under the duvet watching Netflix – and doing a few other things, of course!

"Your brother knows me well enough not to book a ski holiday," she said. At least Jules hoped so, but men could be strange sometimes. Look at how over the top Danny had become about this wedding when only a year ago she would have sworn he'd have been happier with a small affair.

"Christmas dinner at ours will be a good change from Seaspray," Mo said as they crossed the cobbled high street and veered left across the still crowded pavement. "Ash is cooking and promises me faithfully it's all under control. He's ordered two turkeys from the Pollards so there'll be lots of food. Apparently Little Rog never stops feeding those turkeys and they're huge. I just hope our oven's big enough."

"Maybe you should have a contingency plan?" Jules suggested nervously.

"Like commandeer your oven? We'll bear it in mind."

This hadn't quite been what Jules meant but she decided to keep any reservations about Pollards' Poultry to herself. Not content with ghost tours and (sometimes) doing building work, this yuletide the Pollards had decided to branch out by raising organic turkeys. For months scratching and gobbling could be heard from their garden shed and now Big Rog had a lengthy customer list - and a very healthy bank balance if his prices were anything to go by.

"Our birds are organic see, Vicar? Nothing but the best feed for *Pollards' Poultry*. Happy birds don't come cheap and you get what you pay for," he explained when Jules, costing up lunch for the pensioners' Christmas party, nearly fell down with shock at the extortionate price tag.

"But that's a fortune!"

"You are what you eat," he said piously.

"What are you feeding them, Roger? Gold bars?"

Jules's brain was doing some rapid mental arithmetic. She could provide a Christmas meal for every pensioner in Cornwall for the price of two Pollard birds!

"They have to eat special turkey food and there's no cost spared at Pollards' Poultry!" Big Rog declared proudly. "Beautiful birds they are, Vicar. Beautiful."

"They must be avian supermodels at those prices," Jules agreed.

Taking this as a compliment, Big Rog beamed and pulled a spiral pad from the back pocket of his jeans.

"Shall I put you down for a couple?"

There went the church roof fund. And the new minibus!

"I don't suppose you'd donate a couple? Since it's for charity and the Lord's work?" Jules asked hopefully. It was a low shot but worth a punt. St Wenn's was only just in the black and sometimes a vicar had to do what a vicar had to do.

For a few seconds Mammon and God had a wrestling match in the dark recesses of Big Rog's mind and Jules thought she had him - and a free turkey dinner for the old folk. They really ought to teach this stuff at ecclesiastical college. It was far more useful than all the Church history she'd had to study!

"I suppose I could since it's for the Church," Big Rog said eventually, looking pained. "Son, go home, pick a couple of smaller ones out and wring their—"

"They're not ready to go yet! They need at least another couple of weeks fattening up!" protested Little Rog. "These aren't any old turkeys, Pa!"

"That's right my boy, that's right," agreed his father. "They can't be rushed!"

"Really? But there's only two weeks until Christmas," Jules said, surprised.

Big Rog shook his head sadly. "We wouldn't want to compromise on the quality of our product."

"Each one is special," added his son. "They need extra care now."

"That's right, my boy. We wouldn't want to get a bad reputation," added Big Rog.

It was a little late in the day to worry about this, Jules thought. She'd toyed briefly with the notion of a little more emotional black mail, but Little Rog was extolling the virtues of each individual bird and there was no hope of anyone else getting a word in. It was actually the most Jules had heard him say in nearly five years.

"Leon has a toy swing. Noel likes tomatoes. Sparkles will do anything for cheese. Gobbles kicks a ball and Mr Wattles can count to ten already," he said, more animated than Jules had ever seen him. "They're actually very intelligent birds and they have great personalities, isn't that right Dad?"

"That's err ... right my boy, that's right," nodded Big Rog, although he wasn't looking wholly convinced. "They'll taste bleddy handsome too, won't they son?"

Little Rog's mouth snapped shut like a Venus fly trap. He looked a little queasy.

"Well we can't let the old age pensioners' Christmas party get in the way of Mr Wattle's education," Jules said wryly. "Will he be applying for University next year?"

Big Rog fixed her with a pitying look. "It's a *turkey*, vicar."

"But maybe Britain's Got Talent? I think he could win that! And there's big money!" said Little Rog, lighting up like the village Christmas tree. "And you could meet Amanda Holden, Pa. You like her!"

"I can't deny it, my boy, I can't. Fine looking woman," agreed Big Roger, his eyes a little misty.

Leaving them planning a show business career, Jules wasn't sure she could face eating Mr Wattles or any of his feathered friends anyway, especially after glimpsing the pride on Little Rog's face. Nut roast for Christmas dinner had never been more appealing. Maybe she ought to put an order in now with Ashley? Joking aside, Jules was actually becoming concerned how Little Rog would cope when the dark day dawned for his turkeys to make the transition from pets to plates.

"Has Ashley got the turkeys yet?" she asked Mo now.

"Not yet. Apparently, it's better to collect them on Christmas Eve because that way everything will be just right."

"What does that mean exactly?"

"No idea. I'm just telling you what Little Rog told us this morning. Like I said, Ashley's in charge of the Christmas dinner. I've quite enough on cooking our baby and I think it's already turkey sized!" She rubbed her belly and grinned. "I thought Ash would be all for getting caterers in, but he's determined to do it himself and you know my husband; once he puts his mind to something there's no stopping him."

Jules did indeed know Ashley Carstairs, and this did not bode well for Mr Wattles and his chums. Lost in thought, she was trailing after Mo into the next shop when a glimpse of the window display brought her up short.

Sexy Mrs Santa costumes, complete with red suspenders and white fake fur trimmed hand cuffs? Sparkly whips and glittery blindfolds?

Have yourselves a naughty little Christmas!

Jules tugged Mo back from the shop entrance. "I can't go in here!"

"What? Why on earth not?"

"Why do you think? I'm a Church of England vicar! I can't go in a … a…"

Mo put her gloved hands on her hips.

"In *what* exactly?"

Jules glanced around furtively. Bishop Bill lived in Truro.

"A sex shop," she whispered, feeling her face flame.

"*Sex shop?*" shrieked Mo, so loudly lost tribes in the Amazon covered their ears. Several shoppers shot them curious glances. "This is Truro, not Soho! *Anna Winters* is an adult themed store. They do parties and sell knickers. Chill out, Jane Austen! What century are you living in?"

"One where vicars don't frequent *adult themed stores*?"

"You're an adult and you're getting married in six days! Anyway, it's all perfectly respectable. Pretty boring actually post *Fifty Shades*, I'd have said. Vanilla even. Now stop making such a fuss and let's go in."

Jules, eyeballing an inflatable sheep wearing tinsel angel wings and a knowing lip-sticked pout, was unconvinced.

"I think you and I have different definitions of respectable and boring! I'm not going in there, Mo, and that's final."

Mo sighed. "Fine. Fine. So where do you suggest buying inflatable willies for the hen night?"

"I don't suggest buying them at all," said Jules. "Anyway, Sheila's in charge of the hen night so that's her department."

Mo pulled a face. "I can't exactly see Sheila shopping in here, can you?"

No, thank goodness, thought Jules, although one thing she had learned during her time in the ministry was that people constantly surprised you.

Sheila could have a whole double life as an *Anna Winters* party rep for all she knew.

"We'll simply have to manage as best we can," she told Mo. "Now, can we please go? Preferably before the Bishop comes past?"

"He'll probably pop in to buy a gift for his wife," said Mo who really didn't get it. "Look, one of us needs to go in to buy your blue garter."

"My what?"

"Your blue garter. You know! Something old, something new, something borrowed, something blue. Something old is granny's wedding ring, something new is your dress, you're borrowing my veil and now we need the blue."

"Can't I have a blue hanky?" said Jules hopefully.

"A hanky? That's not very sexy. No, absolutely not. Everyone knows it has to be a garter."

They did? This was news to Jules.

"What about stockings?" Mo added.

Since the vicarage central heating had last worked properly in about 1973, and St Wenn's was the kind of building where you went outside to warm up, Jules usually wore woolly tights. Some days even several pairs layered on top of one another. Not sexy, perhaps, but neither was hypothermia.

"I don't wear stockings," she confessed.

"So you don't even have a suspender belt?"

Jules had a utility belt for when she was doing DIY around the vicarage, and very handy it was too, but she didn't imagine this was quite what Mo had in mind and unless Danny had a thing about Bob the Builder she wasn't aware of, it was hardly sexy.

"I can see from your face the answer's no," Mo sighed. "Leave it with me. I'll sort this one out for you and before you start to squawk, no I'm not trekking all the way back to Marks and Sparks. This is your wedding and we want a bit of fun."

Jules knew Mo well enough to know when her soon-to-be-sister-in-law had the bit between her teeth. She'd be trussed up like one of the Pollards' ill-fated turkeys whether she liked it or not. If she'd known all this lay ahead when Danny proposed, would she have said 'yes'?

Of course she would. There was no doubt in her mind marrying Danny was the right thing to do. He was her soul mate and Jules loved him with all her heart. She couldn't wait to be his wife and to begin their new life together. It was just such a pity their wedding was feeling more and more like a feat of endurance rather than something to look forward to. Maybe all brides felt this way? Jules had taken enough wedding classes to know the big day always put couples under all kinds of pressure, but she had never imagined for a moment she and Danny would succumb to these. In her dream small wedding everything was simple and fun and, most of all, uncomplicated.

Leaving Mo to peruse lingerie and heaven only knew what else, Jules set off to meet the others at the bistro. Her laden carrier bags, twisting around her gloved fingers as they bashed again her calves, seemed to grow heavier with each step and her heart was heavy too. When shop doors opened and even merry snatches of *Wham* and *Slade* failed to lift her spirits, Jules knew she needed time out. Glimpsing the warm glow of light spilling from the cathedral's windows she knew exactly where to find solace.

Set in the heart of the city and surrounded by a basin of gently swelling Cornish hills, Truro Cathedral had watched over the city's comings and goings for decades. In the summer the building's cool pools of quiet were a welcome escape from heat and pressing of crowds, while on a busy

December Saturday it offered respite from the gathering frenzy of Christmas shopping. As she climbed the steps and pushed open the door, Jules felt the peace of centuries wrap itself around her like an embrace as years of prayer and faith drew her inside.

The Cathedral's Christmas tree was at the back by the entrance and lovingly decorated with twinkling white lights and little paper prayers tied onto the lower branches with red wool. With their requests for healing, peace or messages of love for a much-missed family member, each one was a little glimpse into someone's heart and Jules never failed to be moved when she read them.

Please let my mum be out of hospital for Christmas.
I pray for peace in this difficult time.
In memory of our wonderful daddy – he loved this place.
Thank you that my cancer is in remission!

It was humbling to read these petitions and they certainly put her concerns into context. I ought to have come here first, thought Jules popping a pound coin into a tin placed on a nearby table and picking up a card and a pen. As she pondered on what to write (*let me fit into my wedding dress* seemed dreadfully trivial all of a sudden) Jules glanced down at a little girl standing and scribbling away. With a triangle of pink tongue poking out in absolute concentration, was intent on drawing a horse.

Her mother caught Jules's eye and smiled.

"I think Amelie may have got this a little confused with Santa. I did tell her this isn't *quite* what's intended but she wants God to know she'd like a pony!"

Jules smiled back. "I'm sure He won't mind if she pops that on the tree. Who knows? Maybe he'll answer her prayer this Christmas."

The mother looked horrified. "I hope not! Maybe I should write one too asking that we can have the money to afford it!"

"Will God bring me a pony?" asked Amelie hopefully, looking from her mother to Jules.

Jules thought carefully.

"I'm sure He will one day, but it's important to know God doesn't do things the same way as Santa. He'll wait until the time is absolutely perfect for all of you so the pony might not arrive *quite* when you're expecting him."

Amelie seemed happy with this answer. "I'd like a pink bike too. With ribbons. I'll write that down as well. God can choose which one to get me for Christmas."

"Great idea," said Jules. Maybe she should do the same? *Please stop my parents rowing? Please can Danny and I have a quiet day? Please let everything run smoothly?* The problem was that she couldn't choose either! Could she have three cards?

"Thanks so much for that," the mother was saying now, giving Jules a grateful look. "Come on, Amelie. Let the nice lady write her prayer in peace."

Leaving Jules with her blank card, they tied theirs to the tree and headed to the cathedral shop. Jules sighed. If only everything in life could be solved so smoothly. Still, her problems no longer felt quite as insurmountable as they had when she'd walked into the building. Jotting down *Bring peace and love to all at my wedding,* Jules found an empty branch and left her card with all the others. She couldn't help thinking peace and joy between her parents was a tall order even for the Almighty, but maybe she ought to listen to her own advice? Her Boss's timing was on a different scale entirely.

Although it might be nice if it could coincide with hers just this once!

Deep in thought, Jules walked slowly through the cathedral. The soft lighting caught the stained glass of the beautiful rose window at the far end and the altar candles threw leaping light and burnished the candlesticks. Her heart rate slowed and by the time she took a seat Jules had found the sense of peace she was been longing for. Folding her hands she listened to her own thoughts as they mingled with the footfalls and hushed voices of other visitors. Time slipped by as she thanked God for Danny, her family and friends and her forthcoming wedding – even if it wasn't quite what she'd had in mind.

On her way out of the cathedral Jules always stopped to admire a painting of Cornwall which depicted every church in the county marked by a small Celtic cross. Titled *Cornubia: Land of the Saints* it depicted each cross as a little glimmer of light which lit up the sky and cast a golden glow across the entire peninsula. Jules never failed to be amazed by just how many parishes there were and loved picking out St Wenn's. Knowing she was playing a small part in something far, far bigger never failed to put her troubles into perspective and as she studied the image Jules knew blue garters and squabbling parents weren't really such a big deal.

She exhaled slowly because it would all work out. Somehow!

"That's a big sigh, my dear."

An elderly man at her elbow was contemplating the picture quietly and Jules flushed to realise how loudly she must have sighed. With a thick mop of snowy hair and skin folded like laundry, he was far from young and leaned heavily on an ornately carved stick yet the faded blue eyes which met hers sparkled with life and were somehow ageless.

"I'm so sorry," Jules said. "I didn't mean to disturb you. I was just thinking about how this picture makes me feel."

He laughed. "It takes more than a sigh to disturb me! Besides, I feel the same way myself because there's something very moving about this painting, isn't there? Something that makes you feel deep down there's is more?"

Jules nodded slowly. "Yes, there is."

"I think it's one of my favourite paintings," he continued thoughtfully. "And I've seen a lot of holy art in my time."

"Which church is yours?" Jules asked him.

"There isn't one in particular, my dear. The church is the people really, isn't it? Not a building."

"It is," Jules agreed. She'd preached on this topic enough times and tried to remind herself of it whenever Sheila and co were driving her round the bend. She pointed to the spot of coastline where Polwenna Bay dipped its toes into the sea.

"That's my church."

"Ah, St Wenn's. A very special place," he said warmly. "Although all are special and beacons of hope. Together they are a bright light in the darkness just like the people in them. It makes one feel that no matter how difficult life can be, all will be well in the end."

His words chimed so beautifully with her own thoughts that Jules was taken aback.

"That's exactly it! Or, at least, I hope so anyway."

"You don't seem wholly convinced?"

She shrugged. "Yes and no. I'm getting married you see, which is wonderful, but it's all become a bit much which isn't so great. I hope it will all turn out all right in the end."

The elderly gentleman said nothing to this, neither prompting Jules to elaborate or adding his own thoughts – which she had discovered most people were very keen to do as everyone had an opinion on weddings. She glanced at his left hand and noticed the ring finger was bare.

"I love my fiancé and I can't wait to marry him," she explained quickly in case she had given him the wrong impression. "I just wish we could have had the kind of wedding we wanted. It all seems to have been rather hijacked and now it doesn't really feel as though it's about us anymore."

He leaned heavily on his stick, still saying nothing. More visitors shuffled past, some pausing to glance briefly at the painting before moving on, and their low chatter mingled with the chink of plates being stacked as the cathedral café packed away for the day. There was something very restful about the elderly man and Jules had the oddest conviction that she could pour her heart out and he wouldn't mind. Maybe he was a retired vicar? He certainly had an air about him that invited confidences and spoke of understanding. Being a vicar herself, Jules was unaccustomed to having somebody to listen to *her*. Her Boss aside, Danny was far too close to the wedding to be impartial, Mo was off on a tangent half the time and Tess was always busy with school. Jules often felt unable to voice her worries and this put her in a lonely place.

"I guess all brides feel this way," she said.

"I've attended more weddings than I can count, and I think it must be easy to forget what it's all about in the first place," he said slowly. "There's a great deal to think about."

She nodded. "Exactly! But there are so many people who wanted to be included that there was no way either of us could bear to hurt them by leaving them out. And then there's my parents which is a whole different can of worms."

He raised a white eyebrow. "Sounds intriguing."

"That's one way of putting it. They were divorced years ago, but they still can't get on. They're both staying with me and I'm dreading it. Then, just to make it even more difficult, Dad doesn't want to attend the church ceremony because he doesn't believe in God so any excuse, like a fight with Mum, will be enough for him to make a scene. I am absolutely dreading them both being under the same roof."

"Maybe just trust in God to make your parents behave?" he suggested.

Jules sighed again. This was easy in theory but hard in practice.

"I do try but I'm running out of time. Besides, you don't know my parents!"

"But God does, and His timing is absolutely perfect."

Jules was struck by his answer because hadn't she just said something similar to little Amelie? Maybe she ought to listen to her own advice?

"That's true," she said. "Of course it is."

"And when you're standing at the altar it will be just you and your fiancé. Nothing else will matter. You've told me a great deal about everyone else and what they want but precious little about yourself," he said. "Tell me, how would *you* like your wedding to be?"

Unable to stop herself, Jules was soon pouring her heart out to the elderly stranger. As the cathedral settled and sighed around them and the choir set up for a rehearsal, Jules told him how she and Danny had originally planned a simple service on Christmas Eve with their closest family and friends in attendance. She explained how much it would mean to have Alistair and Linda make their peace and described how much more comfortable she would feel in her trusty jeans and hoody. While he listened, doing little more than inclining his white head, Jules explained how the reception was now at a smart hotel when in her heart she and Danny had hoped to have a simple fish and chip supper in the village hall where everyone could celebrate. The more she described what they had hoped for, the more Jules realised just how far out of hand the entire affair had become.

"So there it is. Our wedding has run away with us," she concluded. "It's not going to happen the way we'd hoped."

"Maybe not, but perhaps it will work out better than you could have ever dreamed?" he suggested kindly.

Jules wasn't pinning too much hope on this, not with Mo on a trolley dash round an adult store, but there were some things you couldn't share with an old man no matter how kind he was.

"Maybe," she said doubtfully.

"I think you just need to have faith and believe," the old man said firmly. "Things have a funny way of working out sometimes, especially when you have done your very best to put everyone else first. That never goes unnoticed and it is Christmas, after all. Perhaps you'll be pleasantly surprised, Reverend?"

In Jules's experience surprises tended to be called shocks but he was a kind old soul and she didn't want to sound ungrateful.

"I'm sure you're right. It's been lovely to chat to you," she agreed, picking up her shopping bags and glancing at her watch. "Anyway, I'm supposed to be meeting my friends for dinner. I'd better get a move on. Have a happy Christmas!"

"And you my dear," he said. "May it be everything you and your young man hope for."

What an absolute sweetheart, Jules thought as she hurried through the cathedral to the exit. He'd been so easy to talk to and she felt dreadful she had just rabbited on about herself. Why, she'd not found out a single thing about him, yet he knew almost everything about her woes. She'd never even asked his name. Thinking to apologise, Jules turned around to retrace her steps but to her disappointment he was no longer standing by the painting. She peered into the shadowy nave but there was no sign of him anywhere. The restaurant was in darkness and the cathedral shop had closed while they were talking. The choir were settling into the stalls for a final carol practice and the far end of the presbytery was cordoned off. How strange. Where on earth could he have gone?

She paused, perplexed, and expecting him to reappear at any moment. When he did, she'd thank him for his time and apologise for being so self-obsessed! Yet minutes passed and still there was no sign of him. How strange. He must have walked away down the aisle and been obscured by a pillar. Or he could also have left by another door, maybe the one which led to the Cloister Court? Wherever he had gone, he must walk swiftly for an old man with a stick because he'd totally vanished.

Disappointed, she turned for the exit. He'd been so easy to talk to, Jules reflected as she re-joined the tide of people still flowing between shops and restaurants and the pantomime. He understood what it meant to be part of somewhere like St Wenn's and his wise words had really lifted her spirits. Jules also liked his suggestion she left her parents' behaviour down to her Boss. She needed to trust a lot more.

I'll do my best, she prayed, *but in the meantime please could you keep an eye on Mo? Or even better, stop her credit card?*

Smiling at this, she wandered down a narrow side road where the delicious smell of garlic and herbs announced she was close to her destination. The windows of a small bistro spilled buttery light into the night, and she spotted Summer and Alice at a table deeply engrossed in menus. Her heart lifted at once because a wonderful evening lay ahead with dear friends who loved her. What was she worrying for? What had the old man said? *All will be well, Reverend.* Maybe he was right?

It was only as she hung up her coat and caught sight of her reflection against the darkness of the street outside, that Jules realised she wasn't wearing her standard clerical giveaway of white dog collar. How on earth had the old man known she was a vicar? That was strange.

There had to be a simple explanation. He knew of St Wenn's so maybe he'd seen her picture in the Cornish Times? Or perhaps he was a senior clergyman who recognised her from one of her visits to see Bishop Bill? Yes, that must be it, Jules decided as she draped her scarf over a peg. There could be no other explanation.

Still wishing she'd asked his name so she could have thanked him for his kindness, Jules joined her friends at the table where before long the contents of the bag containing Mo's final purchases and loud shrieks of mirth left little space for thinking of anything else. By the time the starters were ordered, the strange cathedral encounter was all but forgotten.

Chapter 4

Saturday 19th December

While his bride-to-be pounded the shopping streets of Truro, Danny Tremaine was in The Ship with the groom's party enjoying a rare evening away from wedding planning. It was just as well he'd given up alcohol, Danny reflected as he waited for Kelly to pour his round, because he didn't think his stress levels had been this high since he was on active service in Afghanistan. Ever-present danger aside, at least his men had been well-drilled and followed his command. Trying to pin the Pollards down was like trying to sieve jelly, the weather forecast was predicting a rare arctic blast and now his brother Symon was refusing to allow Danny to triple check the reception arrangements.

"Ella and I have everything sorted," Sy had insisted, shooing Danny away when he'd attempted another sweep of the ballroom. Could they shoehorn in a few more guests? Linda Mathieson was very keen Jules's second cousin could attend and had texted him twice in the space of an hour for a definitive answer and Granny Alice was wondering whether Great-Uncle Edward might attend the reception? It hardly seemed fair to exclude these two when the rest of the world and his granny was invited.

"I'd just like to check the seating. See if there's anywhere we're adrift or whether we can squeeze another couple of folks in," Dan had begun but Symon was not to be argued with.

"Are you micro-managing again?"

"I don't micro-manage," Danny protested.

"No, nothing that subtle. You bark orders like we're all on parade! I almost want to click my heels!"

Danny was about to protest when he was jolted by the realisation his ex-wife often said something similar. Tara Tremaine was always complaining that she felt like she should jump to attention and salute when he came over to collect their son. It was on the tip on Danny's tongue to say it might help if she could be on time for once, but he'd learned to smile and let Tara's haphazard timekeeping go. Danny knew being with Jules had taught him a great deal about himself and how he reacted to others. Since meeting and falling in love with her Danny knew he had changed. He was a better man for being with Jules. She had brought out the best in him and when nobody else could see beneath the anger and the toxic self-pity she waited and listened. As a consequence of loving her he was far more patient these days and Danny would often take a deep breath and remind himself that even though she drove him mad, Tara was a great mum to Morgan and a good friend to him too. The days of their squabbles were long past – another thing that was in no small part thanks to his fiancé.

He'd taken a deep breath. "Sorry, guys. I just want everything perfect for Jules."

"And it will be," Ella St Milton promised. "We've got every detail planned. The food will be all prepped and ready for the day. The guest suites are gorgeous. I promise it's all going to be just fine, isn't it, Tom?"

The Hotel Manager, busy tweaking decorations on an enormous Christmas tree, looked up and nodded.

"Sure. Relax, Danny. This is what we do. Nothing will go wrong."

Although he was engaged to a vicar, Danny felt a superstitious urge to lunge for the wooden reception desk and cling to it. This felt horribly like tempting Fate.

"So there you go. Natural disasters aside, we've got everything covered," said Ella airily.

Danny placed a finger against his lips.

"Don't let it hear you. The weather forecast is looking bitter. There'll be a snowstorm or something."

"So ask Jules to have word with the top man. That's surely got to be a perk of the marrying a vicar?" Ella suggested with a grin and, when he glowered at her, added hastily, "That's a joke! Chill out, Danny, for heaven's sake. It's all fine here, I promise. And even if we do have a full-on blizzard, we have salt and a snow plough on call so there's nothing to worry about. Nothing can possibly go wrong."

While watching Kelly pull another pint of Pol Brew, Danny reflected that as much as he wanted to relax, he also wanted the wedding to be absolutely perfect for Jules and this meant doing things himself. Nobody could organise their wedding the way he could or with such painstaking attention to detail. His fiancée asked for so little and did so much for everyone else; it was time she was spoiled rotten. Danny couldn't risk leaving things to chance because he was determined that for at least one day Jules Mathieson would be treated like a princess. This was going to be her dream wedding. She deserved nothing less and although Danny would have happily married Jules in her jeans and hoody and with a fish and chip supper at the pub rather than a big reception, this wasn't the point. All women dreamed about their wedding and, as much as she might insist otherwise, he wasn't going to let Jules down.

When they first began to plan their wedding Jules had suggested a simple ceremony held on Christmas Eve followed by a village hall reception. Danny had been more than happy with this idea. He didn't need a fuss because as far as he was concerned the wedding was about how he and Jules felt about one another. The part of the wedding which made him tingle with anticipation was the part where he would make his vows and finally being married to the person who made his heart leap and his soul sing. Danny had loved the idea of holding the wedding service in St Wenn's when it was dressed for Yuletide when Christmas wonder sparkled across the world like hoar frost and the whole village was lit up by twinkling fairy lights. He'd first kissed Jules on Christmas Eve so to be married on this date carried a wonderful sense of completion. Just as their relationship felt like coming home after a long and exhausting campaign, so taking their vows on Christmas Eve felt like the closing of one chapter before the page turned to begin a brand-new story.

Yes, he'd been more than happy to go along with Jules's plans for a modest wedding. Delighted and relieved even. But this was before his ex-wife, of all the unlikely people, had made him think twice. Tara worked at Polwenna Manor and on discovering Danny and Jules were planning a small family meal there as a wedding reception, she had been horrified.

"A meal for fifteen isn't a wedding reception. What about speeches? And dancing? And all of your family and friends? People will be left out and hurt and it looks as though you can't be bothered to celebrate your marriage," she scolded just when Danny, lured inside her house on the pretext of a cup of tea after dropping off their son, was about to bite into a biscuit. "What on earth are you thinking?"

He swallowed the biscuit and with it the sharp retort that his thoughts were none of her business these days, but he knew Tara wouldn't take any notice. With Morgan upstairs and her doctor partner on call, she'd chosen the perfect time to ambush him.

"What about all your friends?" she added, "they'll want to celebrate with you. You can't leave them out."

Ah. Now Danny understood. Tara probably wanted invitations for Richard's receptionist, their mother and the dog next door. Having a wedding in Polwenna Bay made you even more popular than being a war hero. Saying 'no', however, did not. At this rate he and Jules would have no friends left - which would be one way of solving the who to invite problem!

"We want a small gathering," he said calmly.

"Who wants that? Jules? Or *you*?"

Danny thought about this. It was true he didn't particularly want a big do, shy by nature he liked the idea of sitting down with Jules and their nearest and dearest for dinner and some informal speeches. It would be good to be able to focus on his new wife too. He'd attended enough weddings, his own to Tara included, to know the bride and groom were usually lucky to be able to snatch five minutes of time together. This marriage was about his love for Jules. It was a celebration of how they felt about one another, and Danny was looking forward to being able to share every moment with the new Mrs Tremaine rather than making small talk with distant relatives and people he hadn't seen for decades.

"Well, yes, it's true I'm more than happy with something intimate," he began, ready to try and explain this to Tara who was staring at him as though he'd grown two heads. "Don't look at me like that! Jules totally agrees. She says she wants a small wedding too."

"Well, duh. Of course she does. She's bonkers about you and wants to make you happy."

"What's that meant to mean?"

"That she'll do what she thinks you want! She also knows how anti-social you can be."

"I'm not anti-social!" said Danny, stung.

"Yes, you are. You make Heathcliff look sociable." Tara had never been the kind to hold back. "Jules is also conscious you've been through all this before with me and that it's second time around. She'll think you want the wedding to be low key because you're a divorcee."

This idea hadn't even occurred to Danny. He and Tara had married when they were very young and for all the wrong reasons too. Their short union had been a disaster and although they were friends now, and co-parents to their amazing son, the notion they had ever been together felt like a strange memory of a life that had belonged to someone else. For Danny Tremaine there was only Jules.

She was his *everything*.

"Would Jules worry about something like that?" he asked.

"I worry Richard might if we ever get married," said Tara.

"But you and I…"

Danny wasn't sure what to say. The words shrivelled and died on his lips. Danny didn't want to hurt Tara by explaining that what he felt for Jules was light years away from what he'd felt for her and a mere shadow in comparison. It seemed…tactless.

But Tara waved a dismissive hand as though swatting any awkwardness away.

"Yes, yes. *I* know all that, but I've had a big day in the past, and I can't imagine Richard will be sorry if we run off to a sunny island and tie the knot, but this isn't about you or me. This is Jules's wedding, hopefully the only one she'll ever have if she can put up with you, and she'll secretly be longing for a huge fuss. I'm a woman and I know these things. Trust me!"

"I'm not so sure, T," said Danny doubtfully. "She's never said anything along those lines to me."

"Of course she hasn't! You know Jules. She'll always put everyone else's feelings first."

This rang true for Danny. Tara was right; his fiancée was the most unselfish person on the surface of the planet. Her vocation as a vicar aside, Jules was always doing things for other people and often to the detriment of herself. Just look at how she'd asked Sheila Keverne to be maid of honour even though the older woman had often gone out of her way to be difficult. Or how she'd gone along with his plans to relocate to London when her heart had been well and truly in Polwenna Bay? Or how she even gave the Pollards the benefit of the doubt each time they bodged yet another repair on the vicarage? He felt a twinge of unease and put his mug down with a thump, sloshing tea onto the coffee table,

"Has she said something to you?"

"Of course not. Jules won't say anything at all – that's my point! She'd never admit she'd really like the full works if she thought it wasn't something you wanted. Jules would far rather go along with a quiet wedding just to make sure you're happy."

Danny's head was beginning to ache. He often felt like this when he was talking to Tara. Conversations with her were like trying to cross a minefield; you thought you were in the clear and going in one direction and then boom! Everything blew up in your face. While Tara fetched a cloth from the kitchen and mopped up the spilt tea he looked out of the window and across the harbour. It was a bright day and the water was sparkling, just like the ring he'd so proudly slipped on Jules's finger after an Easter egg hunt. She'd loved that romantic gesture and he also knew she was a sucker for slushy romance novels – there were a stack of them piled next to her Biblical concordances.

Was Tara right? Had he got this totally and utterly upside down?

"She's never mentioned she wants a big wedding," he said again while Tara mopped the table.

"That's because she knows you don't want one so why even bring it up?"

"So how do you know it's what she wants?" Danny asked. He pinched the bridge of his nose with his thumb and forefinger and inhaled deeply. He could already feel his blood pressure rising just at the thought of massive guest lists, big receptions and taster menus. The quiet heartfelt ceremony, simple meal and the honeymoon he'd planned in a country hotel near Fowey, a blissful interlude of long lazy lie ins followed by day trips to local beauty spots, suddenly seemed woefully inadequate if Tara was to be believed.

Tara laughed. "I know because I'm a woman! Trust me, Danny, from the day she watches Cinderella for the first time every little girl's planning her wedding. Net curtains made into veils! Barbie dolls dressed up in loo roll. Sobbing when Harry married Meghan. It's what we all dream of no matter how un-PC it sounds these days. Jules might tell you she's happy to get married in jeans and DM boots and with fish and chips on the quay for her reception, but deep down inside she's always imagined the dress she'd wear and how her big day will be - and small it ain't!"

This hadn't sounded much like Jules at all to Danny. She hated dressing up and often said the weddings she conducted seemed more about elevating stress levels than having fun, but on the other hand he knew she would always do her very best to put him first and her own ideas aside.

"All women want that stuff?" he asked. "Are you sure?"

"I'm one hundred percent certain of it. *Fact*, as our son might say! Lord, Danny, you lot really are from Mars, aren't you?" said Tara. "Of course we want what you describe as *that stuff!* Look at Mo when she married Ashley. I bet you never thought she'd turn into Bridezilla? We'd have all put money on her getting married in jodhpurs and with straw in her hair." Tara returned to the kitchen and slam dunked the cloth into the sink, calling over her shoulder. "And what about Alice when she married Jonny in the summer? It was a massive do and she's eighty!"

Tara was right. Even Danny's horse mad tomboy of a sister had gone the full meringue. As had his grandmother. Come to think of it, most of the girls he'd grown up with had all plumped for the full works even though their partners had thought they were having small weddings. It was a revelation. There was no way Dan would let Jules go without. No way in the world. She deserved nothing but the best.

"So how can I give Jules her dream wedding if she won't admit what she really wants?" He said out loud. Like understanding the finer workings of the female mind, this problem felt as though it was up there with figuring out Relativity. No Einstein himself, he felt his blood pressure start to rise - something he'd never thought would happen while planning this wedding.

"Don't look so worried. It's simple!" Tara said.

"It is?"

She grinned at him.

"Of course it is, silly! You tell her it's what *you* want. That way Jules won't argue!"

Danny had taken this advice to heart and, rather against his better judgement, had run with it. Although Jules protested when he extended the guest list and accepted Jonny and Alice's offer of hosting the reception at the Polwenna Bay Hotel, he'd seen the huge pile of bridal magazines on the vestry desk and heard her pleading with Alistair Mathieson to give her away. Before long the whole occasion had quadrupled in size and was now shaping up to be the biggest wedding Polwenna Bay had seen for a long time. It wasn't at all what he'd wanted, and Danny still secretly wished they'd continued with a small affair, but at least Jules would be spoilt rotten.

"Four pints of Pol Brew, one G and T, Scrumpy and a Diet Coke. I've put them on your tab, Dan."

The rattle of glasses jolted Danny from his thoughts as Kelly pushed a tray of drinks across the bar.

"Thanks," he said. "Pop a couple of packets of crisps on too, would you?"

"Sure, it's not as though you're the one having to watch your figure for the big day," Kelly teased. "Thanks for the invite, by the way! Joel and I can't wait. We're really looking forward to it."

Danny couldn't remember writing an invite for Kelly, let alone her latest boyfriend but he'd handed out so many he was losing track.

"My Rose has spent a fortune on a new outfit!" boomed Adam Harper, the landlord, looking up through a cloud of steam from where he was unloading the dishwasher. He wiped his shiny brow with the back of his hand. "Maybe I ought to be charging you, Dan? Ha! Ha!"

He'd invited the Harpers too? Exactly how many people were coming to this wedding now? Danny felt a little faint, although this could also be down to the heat from the roaring log fire in the crowded pub as much as pre-wedding nerves. Christmas always saw an influx of holiday makers arrive for the festive period and now the big day was just over a week away cottage windows filled with jaunty fairy lights chased away the darkness and the narrow streets were August busy. Although it was only early evening *The Ship* was packed to the gunnels and outside visitors strolled along the quay eating fish and chips wrapped in paper. It would have been fun to have a fish and chip reception, Danny thought wistfully. Oh well.

"Marriage driving you to drink already, son?" Eddie Penhalligan asked, peering over Dan's shoulder and raising a bushy eyebrow at the drinks lined up on the bar.

"It only gets worse," warned Caspar James, perched on a bar stool and sipping a violent pink cocktail.

"What would you know? You've never been married, you harris!" pointed out Big Roger Pollard.

"Love from marriage, like vinegar from wine. A sad, sour sober beverage," Caspar quoted theatrically, swirling his drink before raising his glass.

"Lucky I don't drink," said Danny.

"What would you know about being sober anyhow, Cas?" scoffed Eddie.

"Or about wine when you drink those big girls' drinks?" added Big Rog.

"I make my living writing about love," Caspar huffed. "Besides, one doesn't need to be a car to know how to drive."

"Eh?" said Big Rog. "What's cars got to do with it?"

"It's a metaphor, you utter heathen," said Caspar.

Big Rog scratched his balding head. "Like in *Armageddon?* Wasn't that an asteroid? Not a meteor?"

"Metaphor!" screeched Caspar.

Big Rog shrugged. "I don't know much about astronomy, but I do know you still owe me for a turkey." He held out his hand. "Fifty quid should do it."

Caspar spluttered pink drink all over the bar. "Fifty quid?"

"Pollard Poultry is a quality operation. Organic feed and only the best care," piped up Little Rog from his usual bar stool shoved under the stairs. Peeking out from between dangling strands of tinsel and ivy, he added, "and they cost twice that in Fortnum's, don't they Pa?"

"That's right, my boy, that's right," nodded Big Rog. He crossed his arms over his rotund belly. "So pay up."

"I'll pay when I see it," said Caspar, crossing his arms too. "And not a penny beforehand. These turkeys do exist, I take it, since nobody's had a delivery yet?"

"Course they bleddy exist. They're in our shed," huffed Big Rog. "Ask Silver Starr. She's always complaining about the noise they make. Says it interferes with her aura. And don't get me started on *Meat is Murder*. If she tells me that one more time it will be! No, the reason nobody's had a turkey delivery yet is because they're still…still…"

He paused.

"Still?" Danny prompted. Two of these birds were destined to be the Tremaine Christmas dinner. He glanced across the bar to where Ashley, his brother-in-law and Christmas dinner chef, was deep in conversation with Zak and Tess. He didn't fancy the Pollards' chances if they let Ashley down at the eleventh hour.

"Still err…still with us as it were," admitted Big Rog rather awkwardly.

"Alive, you mean?" Eddie Penhalligan was shocked. "Shouldn't they have been dispatched by now and plucked? Feeling squeamish, Rog? Do you need me to help? I don't want to miss out on my Christmas dinner because you're too soft to do it."

Eddie had gutted fish for decades. Wringing turkeys' necks wouldn't worry him.

"I've got repetitive strain injuries in my hands from building, I'll have you know!" huffed Big Rog, flexing sausagey fingers and wincing in a very exaggerated fashion. Nobody was convinced. Big Rog hadn't done any serious building for years. "Anyway, my boy's going to do deal with the birds, but if you're happy to help I don't see why not—"

"You can't rush these things! The meat won't taste as nice if the birds are stressed!" cried Little Rog, bursting through the tinsel in the manner of a seventies game show host.

"*Stressed?* They're going to the table with some cranberry sauce, not attending counselling!" exclaimed Eddie. He mimed a twisting gesture. "Kindest to be quick, son."

Little Rog, frantically trying to untangle himself from tinsel, shook his head.

"They're not ready yet, Ed."

"It's Christmas in a week's time!" Caspar pointed out. "If you don't get a move on it'll be too late! And then what will people eat on Christmas day?"

"Fish?" suggested Eddie hopefully.

Little Rog gulped. He didn't have an answer, Danny realised. Thank goodness Symon hadn't relied on the Pollards to supply the food for their reception! Everything was already sourced and much of it already prepared and frozen. All the same, Danny made a mental note to text his brother and check. You couldn't be too sure.

"I think it's horrible! How can you kill innocent turkeys! They haven't done you any harm! Why can't you leave them in peace to be happy?"

This outburst was from Penny Kussell who was standing behind Danny waiting patiently for her turn to be served. A quiet girl who worked at Mo's stable yard, animal loving Penny wouldn't usually say boo to a goose, let alone shout about turkeys, but she was glaring at Big Rog. Her brown eyes were bright with anger, her face was flushed and even her ginger plaits swung backwards and forward with indignation.

"They're for Christmas dinner, maid," said Big Rog, confused. "Your folks are on the list to have one! Your grandad was one of the first to put his order in, wasn't he son?"

But Little Rog didn't answer. He was too busy staring at Penny as though he'd never seen her before, and Danny knew just how he felt. He'd hardly heard Penny speak, let alone shout.

"It's barbaric," she choked.

"You'll not think that when you eat one with a big dollop of cranberry sauce," promised Big Rog, who'd clearly been bunking off on the day God handed out emotional intelligence. "You'll never taste anything better than a turkey from Pollard Poultry. Just ask my boy!"

But Little Rog was still unable to utter a word especially when Penny shot him a look that should have laid him out by his bar stool.

"I'm a vegan!" she spat. "But you, Roger Pollard? You're a murderer!"

"Me?" spluttered Big Rog, his mouth swinging open.

"I'm not!" squeaked Little Rog.

"Both of you are!" Penny cried. She spun on her heel and elbowed her way out of the pub, almost colliding with Ashley Carstairs who was on his way to help Danny carry the drinks.

"What's upset Pen?" Ashley asked, surprised.

"Your choice of Christmas dinner apparently. She's rather upset about *Pollard's Poultry,*" Danny said.

"Ah, yes. She wouldn't like that at all."

Ashley picked up the laden tray while Danny tucked crisp packets under his arm. Once they were seated and the drinks distributed, he added, "Pen wouldn't speak to us for days when she though Mo was going fox hunting. Mo tried to explain it was a drag hunt, which apparently isn't actually men dressed in wigs and makeup galloping about, but for once my wife couldn't get a word in."

"Goodness," said Danny, impressed. His sister was usually hard to keep quiet.

"Yep. I thought about asking her to show me how it's done! Penny might be quiet most of the time but not when it comes to animal rights, trust me on that one. She's always on at us to go vegetarian."

Normally Danny would have found this fascinating since all he knew about Penny was that she mucked out for Mo, once fostered a painful crush on their brother Nick, and was the subject of Little Roger Pollard's unrequited affections, but all he could think about now was another potential wedding disaster.

"I hope we've got some vegetarian options at the reception," he said frowning. Danny was sure Symon had mentioned this at some point but what about vegans? Were they catered for? And other special diets? Did they have any guests with allergies or who had religious rules to obey? He whipped out his phone.

"What are you doing?" Ashley asked.

"Checking with Sy we have a vegan option."

Ashley raised his eyes to the tinselled beams. "I thought we were having an evening off from the wedding?"

Danny laughed but the noise sounded strangled.

"I'm not sure that's possible. I'm even dreaming about it now."

"You," said Ashley sternly, "need to relax. Get that Diet Coke down you and have a look at the menu. This is the groom's night off. There's nothing to stress about."

Danny slid the phone back into his jacket pocket.

"I just want it to be perfect for Jules."

His brother-in-law smiled. "As long as you're the man waiting for her at the altar Jules will think it's perfect, no matter what else happens."

"I hope so," said Danny.

"Trust me. Mo could have turned up in her mucking out gear and I wouldn't have cared. At the end of the day it's all about you and Jules saying your vows. The rest doesn't matter much at all, except for Isla's pink dress, of course. Your niece would never forgive you if she hadn't got to wear one of those!"

Danny appreciated Ashley's attempt to raise his spirits but remained unconvinced.

"There's a lot that could go wrong before we even get as far as our vows."

"Not when you've organised the whole thing like a military campaign! We're all expecting Ant Middleton to parachute in and bark at us any minute now." Ashley held up his hand and started ticking off items on his fingers. "The hotel's sorted, the guests are organised, the venue's taken care of, Neil will be back from Mull to marry you both, Tess has trained the primary school choir, your son's taking the pictures, Zak's arranged the band, and the honeymoon's booked. Even the weather's going to be dry. I could go on, but I think you get the point! It's going to be the perfect Christmas wedding and your fiancée has the top man on side too!"

Ashley was right. He was worrying about nothing.

"Vegas is booked for the stag do. We should have you back in time for the wedding," interrupted Nick Tremaine, peeling himself away from texting his girlfriend for long enough to tease his brother. "I've watched all *The Hangover* movies as part of my stag night training. You do like tigers, right?"

"Very funny," said Danny, refusing to rise.

He'd made it clear he was in no way, shape or form up for a stag night. Nothing appealed less. Fortunately for Danny's nerves Jake, his eldest brother was the best man and had organised a civilised meal for the stags. Since Danny didn't drink there was little point having a pub crawl, no matter how much the Penhalligan brothers tried to persuade him otherwise, and luckily Nick had calmed down a lot recently and no longer wanted to party long and hard, but even so Danny felt his blood pressure rise. Although doing his best to get into the spirit of the evening, his heart wasn't in it.

While the others teased him about all the pranks they intended to play Danny did his best to join in but his gaze kept sliding to the window. With the lights of the harbourside Christmas tree scattering dancing rainbows across the inky water and the night sky sprinkled with stars, the scene reminded him of the magical night he'd first kissed Jules. How he wanted their wedding day to echo that sense of wonder and magic! It was what he'd hoped for when he'd suggested they were married on Christmas Eve. Yet if the twinkling stars could grant wishes, Dan would have asked for a quiet wedding in St Wenn's rather than a big affair. Unassuming yet heartfelt, this kind of wedding was more in keeping with the way their love had blossomed.

He pushed this idea aside. It was far more important Jules would have the kind of wedding which would make her happy. He wanted this above anything he might hope for himself. Before he dragged his attention back to Nick's tall tales of trips to Amsterdam, Danny gazed over the chimney pots and up to the bright December stars and wished with all his heart Jules's wedding day would be everything she had always hoped for.

Chapter 5

Sunday 20th December

Sundays might be viewed as a day of rest for most people but for vicars they were always the busiest of the week. Throw Christmas into the mix, thirty primary school children waving candles about a little too near to tinsel for comfort, and a wedding that was only four days away and there you had it: a recipe for absolute exhaustion.

A sleepless night spent tossing and turning while she fretted about the imminent arrival of her warring parents, followed by an early start for the communion service meant that several times during the Christingle Service Jules found herself swaying. She would have shared the work load with her curate but because Neil was filling in while she was away on her honeymoon, he'd driven up to Scotland to visit his family. This left Jules juggling everything from last week's pensioners' party to this evening's harbourside Carol Concert. She still had to squeeze in her hen night, a trip to the hairdresser and the wedding rehearsal and the closer the big day drew the more overwhelmed she was feeling.

Jules hung her advent robes in the vestry cupboard, extinguished all the candles and checked for the umpteenth time she'd switched off the thousands of fairy lights Big Roger Pollard, in a fit of competitive enthusiasm with the famous Mousehole Christmas lights, had strung up everywhere he could reach. Since this was St Wenn's not Las Vegas Jules had been forced to put her foot down when she'd caught him winding a string of flashing red ones around the pulpit. Blazing above the village, the church could have doubled for Blackpool illuminations. It seemed that Big Rog's ambitions knew no bounds since attacking the harbour and the marina. Jules only hoped St Wenn's wiring could cope. She was also getting a rather nervous about the next quarter's electricity bill.

The church was already decorated for Christmas with a tree set up by the porch, the nativity scene on the table by the vestry and red ribbons woven through the greenery festooned from the ends of the pews, strewn across the window sills and wound around the font and lectern. Tomorrow Sheila and Alice would add the wedding flowers to this display and then the church would be ready. Her vicar's hat firmly in place, Jules had chosen arrangements that easily doubled for Christmas decorations and would save St Wenn's coffers a few pennies. Potted poinsettias would be placed on the windowsills and tables, arrangements of white and burgundy roses coiled up the pillars and ribbons threaded with pine cones slices of dried oranges strung from the pews. It would be beautiful, and Jules felt a little tingle of excitement because she always loved seeing St Wenn's dressed up for Christmas. The ancient building must have witnessed hundreds of couples marry and as she walked through the nave and switched off the last of the lights Jules felt a sense of peace. No matter what happened outside these walls beforehand the service taking place within them, and the vows she and Danny exchanged, would be exactly what she had wanted. That was the important part, and all would be well.

Once the lights were turned off only the winter sunshine lit the old church, spilling coloured splashes of light onto the worn stone floor and catching twirling dust motes in a sunlit ballet. The weather was brittle and bright and once outside Jules's breath rose like smoke and her nose tingled. The forecast cold snap had arrived, and the iced world sparkled. Too cold to fly about or even squabble, the seagulls puffed themselves up to double the size and huddled together on the rooftops where chimneys coughed clouds of smoke that drifted over the village and filled the air with the heavy tang of woodsmoke.

The long-range forecast was giving exceptionally cold weather with unusually high winds, but snowfall had not been mentioned and Jules was relieved about this. Romantic as the idea was, having to rescue stranded guests and clear paths would have added a whole new level of stress to the wedding. Pulling her coat around her, she scurried along the path which linked St Wenn's to the vicarage. The wind sliced through the fabric and by the time she let herself inside Jules's eyes were running and her nose could have doubled for Rudolph's.

Jules switched on a fan heater in the kitchen and ventured into the sitting room to do battle with the temperamental wood burner. She needed to get it going and make the house warm before Danny returned from Newquay airport with his soon-to-be mother in law. Used to the warmth of Tenerife, poor Linda would freeze. Jules consoled herself with the knowledge even if she'd commandeered the Eden Project's heating system the atmosphere in the vicarage would still be arctic when Linda Mathieson discovered her ex-husband was also staying there.

"What did your mum say when you told her your dad's staying at the vicarage too?" Tess Hamilton had asked earlier on when they sat in the vestry, wrapped in scarves and hats, while turning oranges, candles and assorted sticky sweets into Christingles.

Jules hesitated because the answer to Tess's question was *absolutely nothing*, mainly because she still hadn't managed to pluck up the courage required to break the news.

"Um..." she said. "Err..."

Tess shot her a stern teacher look.

"You haven't told her, have you?"

"I was waiting for the right moment," Jules confessed which sounded feeble even to her own ears. There was never going to be a right moment and if Linda chose to go to def con nine it might have been better she did it while she was several thousand miles away rather than in Jules's living room.

"You mean you chickened out," said Tess, shaking her head. "Jules! What are you like?"

The poor kids in Tess's class didn't stand a chance. They must get away with nothing.

"Like a chicken," Jules said sadly. "Stick me in a bargain bucket and send me to KFC."

Tess laughed. "I'll call Colonel Sanders as soon as I'm home! I don't blame you, though. That wouldn't be an easy conversation to have. Parents, eh?"

Yes, parents, thought Jules despairingly trying to wrestle ribbon around an orange. Unlike Tess's neat affairs, her own Christingles looked more like land mines than symbols of light in a dark world. Jules really hoped this wasn't metaphorical.

"Here, give that to me." Tess reached across and relieved Jules of her task. "Stick some Dolly Mixtures onto cocktail sticks instead. Three on each should work and different colours, please."

"Yes, miss," said Jules, stabbing a few and helping herself to several more. Yummy. And Dolly Mixtures were tiny. There couldn't be many calories in those?

"Don't eat them all," Tess warned.

"I know, I know, I've got my wedding dress to fit into."

"I wasn't going to say that. I was going to say I've only got one more packet so we mustn't run out," said Tess. "Anyway, back to the subject - you've seriously not told your mum that your dad's staying with you?"

"There never seemed to be a right time," Jules confessed, spearing sweets onto her cocktail stick. Stab. Stab. Stab. It was rather cathartic. "What if she refused to come?"

"Then it would be her choice. I wouldn't want to stay anywhere near my ex," shuddered Tess. "So what does your dad say? Is he OK with it?"

Jules stabbed another sweet. And another.

"I haven't told him either."

Tess looked up from unknotting Jules's attempts at ribbon tying.

"And they both arrive this afternoon? Seriously?"

Jules nodded miserably. She felt thirteen again, sitting at the top of the stairs with her knees hugged against her chest as she listened to her parents rowing and tried to think of a way to stop them. Over twenty years later she was still struggling for a solution. She'd had good intentions of telling Alistair and Linda they'd need to be civil for just a few days and had scripted several wonderful conversations where she spoke to them as though they were parishioners in need of guidance, but as with most fantasies none of these were really suited to the cold light of day. It was also a sad fact that although Jules might be a respected pillar of the community in Polwenna Bay, she was still little Ju Ju to her parents and they were as likely to take her advice as they were to retake their wedding vows. In the end, she'd put off telling them and decided to ride it out, which was a great idea when their meeting was weeks away but not nearly quite as attractive when there were only hours to go. Danny had warned her this might not be the best tactic but, up to her eyeballs in Christmas events and wedding preparations, Jules hadn't listened to him. Now she really wished she had. Linda and Alistair *hated* each other. What had she been thinking to imagine they could put their animosity aside for the sake of her wedding? All of a sudden she was spinning down the years and back being that nervous child sitting in her bedroom with a chocolate bar for comfort while she listened to their spats.

Her stomach clenched.

"Do you think you ought to call your mum and warn her before it's too late? Give her time to come around to the idea?" said Tess gently.

Jules's gaze flicked up to the vestry clock. Linda was already in the air and drawing closer by the second. It was too late now. Besides, Linda could have a thousand years and she still wouldn't 'come around' to the idea of being in close proximity to Alistair Mathieson.

"She's landing in under an hour, Tess. It's far too late."

Tess's eyes widened. "And when does your dad arrive?"

"This afternoon, I think?"

Actually, Jules wasn't quite sure. Alistair had sent a text to say he'd been feeling under the weather for a few days so would travel by train rather than drive. Alarmed because her father was never ill and it was unlike him to even mention his health (unlike Linda who loved ailments and procedures) Jules offered to collect him from the station, but he'd insisted on making his own way. Alistair could be in a taxi at this very moment and on a direct collision course with Linda. It didn't bear thinking about.

She stabbed another sweet and another.

"Don't take it out on the Dolly Mixtures," Tess scolded, scooping them over to her side of the table. "Look, the way I see it this wedding is a happy occasion and it's about you and Danny, not your parents. They're supposed to be the adults here and you are the child. They should be supporting you."

This was all true – in theory. The reality was Jules would be refereeing from the moment they stepped over the threshold until the moment they departed. Her breath shortened at the mere thought of the days which lay ahead. If a week was a long time on politics it was an eternity in the proximity of feuding parents.

"What can I do?" Jules asked.

"My advice is you lay down the law with them straight away just like I do when I get a new class," said Tess. "If you visualise it you can have it, or so they say!"

Jules, who was always trying to visualise herself as a size ten or being in the black, wasn't convinced but Tess sounded certain. Then again, Tess always sounded like this. It was how she would soon successfully direct thirty primary school children armed with Christingle candles to sing carols around the crib scene without setting the church alight.

"So do what I do every September," concluded Tess, finishing the final Christingle. "Set the rules, enforce them without fail so everyone knows where they stand, and don't smile until Christmas!"

Jules had been certain she could manage the last instruction. As she cajoled kindling onto piles and rolled up newspapers, she recalled her friend's advice and was resolved to act on it. Not only was Tess a great teacher but she'd managed to bring the wild Zak Tremaine to heel too, something which a long line of broken-hearted women had failed to achieve, so she must be onto something! Yes, Tess was right; all Jules needed to do was be firm and clear. She would sit her parents down together, read them the riot act and tell them this wedding was about her and Danny not their ancient grudges. They would be surprised, and they were bound to protest a little, but she was sure they would understand. From then on everything would go beautifully. Besides, she was in her thirties, not thirteen, and they were staying in her house and in her village and attending her wedding! She was in charge! She'd got this! She was ready!

Hell, yeah!

As if sensing her determination even the fire behaved for once and burst into flames. Logs caught, twigs crackled and before long a merry blaze was warming the sitting room. That had to be a good omen, thought Jules sitting back on her heels and feeling proud. Tess should be a motivational speaker!

Feeling buoyed by her fire lighting prowess, Jules flew around plumping cushions, switching on Christmas tree lights and putting one of Alice's casseroles in the oven to warm through. Maybe her parents could even sit down together for a civilised lunch followed by a wintry walk on the beach before heading to the quayside carol concert? An image drifted through her imagination of her holding Danny's hand and singing carols by lamplight alongside her parents. Everyone was dressed in hats and scarves, neither parent was trying to drown the other in a rock pool or glowering like a misplaced Brontë hero while making snide comments about religion, and there was even a festive sound track playing in the background. Quite when her hopes for peace on earth and goodwill between her parents had turned in to a John Lewis Christmas advert Jules wasn't sure, but hadn't Tess said visualising things was the key to having them? This was definitely more pleasant than her usual visions of rows and slamming doors.

The vicarage warmed up and soon smelled delicious too as Alice's concoction of rich gravy, onions and herbs simmered in the oven. Feeling cheered, Jules checked the bedrooms and made sure the bathroom was clean and sparkling. Since the vicarage was a small 1920s house, the original Georgian heap at the top of the village being sold as a second home long ago, there was only one bathroom and the rooms weren't huge. Alistair would sleep in the spare room and Linda would have Jules' bedroom. Jules had decamped to the sofa bed in her box room office. Even so, there wasn't a great deal of space and it would be very hard for her parents to avoid one another. If Linda still had a habit of wallowing in the bath for hours and Alistair needed the loo the World War Three could break out.

No. Stop. This wasn't positive visualisation. Try again. Peace on earth, goodwill to men and think John Lewis vibes. Everyone would get on just fine.

Jules was sitting on the top stair taking a moment, when a hammering on the door heralded the arrival of Alistair Mathieson. She didn't need to venture outside to know a tall figure with wild grey hair, bushy brows and an impatient expression would be waiting on the doorstep; Jules would have known that impatient thud of knuckles anywhere and had grown up listening to it - usually when Linda had locked Alistair out following a row. All trepidation forgotten, she flew down the stairs and flung the door open, thrilled to see him.

It didn't matter how old you were; a girl always needed her dad!

"You're here!" she cried hugging him and inhaling the familiar scent of coal tar soap, cigarettes and washing powder.

"I wouldn't miss your wedding day. I'm not a complete ogre," Alistair said, hugging her back.

Jules was glad to hear it because she did sometimes wonder. Linda, of course, would have totally disagreed. As far as she was concerned Alistair Mathieson could teach Shrek a thing or two.

"Final arrangements in place?" he asked, once Jules had taken his holdall upstairs and they were drinking tea in the kitchen.

"I think they're almost there. It's a bit stressful though."

This was an understatement. Every time she thought she heard Danny's key in the door Jules nearly leapt through the ceiling. Her blood pressure must be off the chart.

"I thought you looked a bit peaky," her father said. "Is there anything I can do to help?"

This was her moment; she'd tell him yes, there was something he could do. He could be civil to his ex-wife for the next few days.

But unfortunately this was a rhetorical question for just as Jules was about to launch into her *laying down the rules* speech (hastily composed while cleaning the bathroom sink) Alistair added darkly. "Apart from saying think hard about what you're signing up to, that is! I remember when I was marrying your mother how events have a habit of running away with you and before you know it, it's too late to reconsider."

"Dad! I don't want to reconsider anything! I love Danny and I can't wait to marry him!" Jules couldn't believe her father. He'd only been in the vicarage for five minutes and already he was lecturing her. "If you can't be nice about my wedding maybe you shouldn't have come!"

Alistair pinched the bridge of his beaky nose and inhaled sharply.

"Yes, yes. Sorry, Ju Ju. I just don't want you making the same mistakes I did. Linda couldn't think about anything else but wedding dresses and flowers for almost a year and I couldn't get any sensible conversation out of her. I ought to have known then, I suppose, but when you're young you don't think things through. You make mistakes and you won't listen to advice."

Jules couldn't believe what she was hearing.

"Thanks for telling me you shouldn't have married my mother just days before my own wedding and that I'm making a mistake."

"Don't be so over sensitive. I'm just trying to be helpful. That wasn't what I meant at all," he said.

But it was *exactly* what he'd meant and they both knew it. Jules bit down hard on her lip and looked out of the window. The sun was still shining but the day seemed a little less bright and shiny and her dreams of Sunday lunch and beach walks had vanished. Jules gulped down the lump of disappointment in her throat and took a steadying breath. Time to take control. Time to be a grown up. Time to tell Alistair he would be sharing this stay with his ex-wife.

"Look, Dad, I need to tell you something—"

"Oh!" Alistair doubled over clutching at his chest. "Ouch!"

"Dad? Is everything all right?"

Jules was at his side in moments, all upsets forgotten.

"Just a touch of heartburn."

As a lover of midnight snacks, Jules was no stranger to Rennies herself, but she never sweated or grew ashen faced like this and she was worried. Unlike Linda who loved ailments and had an expensive Nurofen habit, Alistair scorned illness and shunned painkillers. More evidence, as if she needed it, of opposites attracting.

He hauled himself to his feet with a grimace. "I've got some Gaviscon in my bag. I'll go and take some. It's an age thing."

That her father even knew what Gaviscon was, let alone had come armed with a bottle, suggested this had been going on a while.

"Shall I call a doctor? Richard Penwarren's only a few minutes down the lane."

He flapped a hand at her. "Don't be such a drama queen - I'm not your mother!"

"But Dad, you look awful," Jules said. She knew she should have renewed her first aid training! He wasn't about to keel over on her, was he?

"It's a touch of indigestion. I'm not about to fly up into the sky or whatever it is you think is going to happen to me when I snuff it," he said scathingly. "If that happens you can say, 'I told you so' all day long! I'll be down in a moment for lunch."

He headed upstairs, still with the heel of his hand pressed hard against his chest. Jules slumped at the table. So much for positive visualisation. Her father couldn't have been in the village for more than five minutes but already he'd told her she was making a mistake getting married, been scathing of her beliefs and sniped about Linda. So much for setting out the rules and being firm.

She'd be an utter failure as a teacher, thought Jules, although there was one piece of Tess's advice she wouldn't struggle to follow: at this rate not smiling until Christmas was going to be very easy indeed.

And her mother hadn't even arrived!

Chapter 6

Sunday 20th December

"David feels terrible he can't make the wedding, love, but he'd promised to spend Lily's first Christmas with the family. She's his first grandchild and he's besotted, bless him."

Linda Mathieson must be powered by Duracell, thought Danny Tremaine. He didn't think she'd paused her monologue since he'd kissed her hello in the arrivals' lounge. While they'd waited for her four bags of luggage to loop around the carousel she'd filled him in on the new pool she and David had installed at their villa, the romantic weekend they'd enjoyed in Madrid (including far more details than any son-in-law ever wanted or needed to hear) and described how excited David was to have become a grandfather. All Danny really needed to do was nod now and then or make agreeing noises for Linda to be thrilled. Yes, when it came to greeting his in-laws, he had got off lightly because Jules's father was much harder work than Linda.

Danny was under no illusions that Alistair approved of the wedding. Unlike Linda who could scarcely wait to don her mother-of-the-bride outfit (she'd packed three and could hardly wait to stage a fashion show so he and Jules could pick their favourite and had startlingly white veneers fitted especially) Professor Mathieson was attending under sufferance and couldn't understand why anyone might feel the need to have anything other than a legal contract drawn up. If they *had* to get married, of course.

It was an old-fashioned thing to do but Danny liked to do things properly so after he'd proposed to Jules it had seemed only right that he call Alistair and asked his permission for his daughter's hand in marriage. As

Jules had warned, this gesture had gone down like the proverbial lead balloon.

"She's not a parcel! She's got a mind of her own!" Alistair had snapped, his clipped vowels fired down the phone like pistol shots. "Whatever next? A dowry? You don't need my permission, young man. If Julia insists on getting married it's her choice, not mine. She knows my thoughts on the matter."

Danny had been lost for words, but Jules wasn't surprised in the slightest. Marriage to Linda, she'd said sadly, hadn't endeared her father to the institution. Danny was no psychologist but after his life changing injuries in Afghanistan he'd seen several and had also done enough work on himself to recognise when somebody was hurting. If he'd had to hazard a guess, then Danny would have said Alistair Mathieson was still wounded by the end of his marriage. After all, didn't the old adage say love and hate were two sides of the same coin?

In any case, romantic Alistair was not and as Danny drove Linda away from the airport, listening to her chat excitedly about the flowers and the dress and helping her daughter get ready on the big day, he wasn't at all surprised that she and Alistair hadn't gone the distance. How they'd ever got together in the first place was the mystery, although as Linda flirted mildly with him, flashing her tanned thighs getting into the car and fluttering her eyelash extensions, Danny had a fair idea! Alistair might be a funny old stick, and far too intellectual for Danny to keep up with, but he was still a man and even he'd been young once.

And young men, as Danny knew only too well, often made daft choices.

Not for the first time, he thanked his lucky stars for Jules. Whatever had he done right to have met her? Not only was she funny and sexy and kind but she was also his best friend and his North Star. He couldn't wait to marry her on Christmas Eve, big wedding or not. Alistair could be as miserable about it as he liked but the sooner Danny slipped the ring on Jules's finger the happier he would be. A new chapter was about to start, and he could hardly wait to begin writing it.

"Ooo! Doesn't the village look pretty! It's like a Christmas card with all the trees in the windows!" cried Linda as the car swung around a bend in the road and began the descent into the village. "And look at the tree on the harbour! It's huge! Not that size matters, of course, it's what you do with it, as I always say to David! Ha! Ha! Don't tell him I said that, will you?"

As if, thought Danny. Embarrassed, he fixed his gaze on the road, slowing the car as they passed the school and the road began to narrow. Although it was winter the bright and cold weather had drawn visitors like a magnet and Fore Street was as busy as any summer. Christmas lights were strung all the way along in cheery yuletide welcome and shop windows sparkling with tinsel and crammed with wonders drew people towards them just as skilfully as Cornish wreckers once lured ships onto rocks. Linda, keen to wreck whatever was left of David's bank balance, *ooed* and *aahed* as they drove by and wound the window down for a better view. Ice sharp air, heavy with woodsmoke, billowed inside and Danny shivered but Linda, even fresh from Tenerife, was oblivious to the cold and having a lovely time waving to all the locals she recognised.

"Goodness! Look at all the fairy lights! It must look like Oxford Street at night!" she cried.

Danny made a face because in his opinion Big Rog had gone rogue. Every day Ivy Lawrence complained to Jules that her lights were flickering – as if Jules had any control over what the Pollards got up to.

"Yes. It does a bit."

"It's lovely! I can't wait to see it at night. Maybe we can go out for a little drinkie poo at The Ship?"

When she discovered her ex-husband was staying at the vicarage she might need one, thought Danny. Jules certainly would and even he was tempted. He really hoped the pair wouldn't cause too much of a scene. It really wasn't fair on their daughter and it meant the world to Jules to have them both close for her big day. It would have been impossible for her to choose between them, but he did wish she'd broken the news before they bumped into each other at the dinner table.

He pulled himself out of his thoughts and turned his attention back to Linda who was asking him about how her luggage would be carried up to the vicarage. She was hugely disappointed the Pollards were no longer in business and, whipping out her mobile, was organising Chris the Cod with the harbour fork lift instead.

"I'm the mother-of-the bride, you know!" she trilled. "Drinks are on me at the reception!"

This was good enough for Chris and soon Linda's cases and bags were deposited outside the *Codfather*. Although Danny was relieved not to have to carry them because the cold weather made his old injuries ache, he was alarmed by the idea of offering free drinks.

"They'll bankrupt us," he warned her as they began the climb up Church Lane, but she just laughed.

"David's paying for the first hour of the bar, not me!"

Linda had Jules's big brown eyes, Danny realised as she beamed up at him, and her heart-shaped face was Jules's too. Would those same features be passed on again, someday? The possibility made his heart squeeze with hope. Life was full to the brim with possibilities Danny hadn't dared dream might be his again one day. He was the luckiest man alive and if a huge monster of a wedding was the price he had to pay for it, there was really very little to moan about.

"That's more than generous but he doesn't need to."

"He wants to. Besides, it's the least he can do to make up for not coming to your wedding! Maybe he should pay for two hours?"

"You may have to sell your villa to settle the tab if Big Rog and the others hear about that!" Danny pointed out. "Anyway, David doesn't need to make up for anything. Jules and I totally understand why he wants to be with his granddaughter for her first Christmas. It's fine by us."

Linda elbowed him in the ribs. "Maybe it'll be my turn to do the same next Christmas? Hmm?"

Danny laughed. "Subtly isn't your strongest point, is it?"

"If you don't ask you don't get in my book. I'll be a wonderful granny - if I don't die of old age first!" she sighed.

In high heeled knee boots which made her wobble on the cobbles like Bambi, a huge white faux fur coat and tossing a head of new extensions, Linda couldn't have looked further from old age if she'd tried. Chris the Cod's eyes had almost fallen out of his head and rolled into the harbour when she'd delivered her luggage to the *Codfather*.

"Is this sudden desire for grandchildren so you can compete with David?" Danny knew his fiancée's mother well by now.

Caught out, Linda blushed. "I am getting a little bit tired of his boasting and if I look at any more baby photos I'll scream, but it's not just that. I know my daughter will be a wonderful mum. She's nothing like me."

That was certainly true, thank heavens. Danny knew he was going to find it hard enough having Linda to stay for a week – he couldn't imagine being married to her. High maintenance was an understatement. He wasn't the biggest fan of Alistair Mathieson, but Linda was very glamorous, and it was easy to be swept away by that kind of thing. Once upon a time Danny had done exactly the same but he was older now and hopefully wiser too. Jules wasn't glittery or glitzy, but her heart was made of pure gold and she was secure in her faith and in the direction of her life. She was his rock and his safe harbour as well as his best friend and Danny knew just what a rare find she was.

He couldn't wait to slip the ring onto her finger on Christmas Eve.

The air seemed to grow colder and by the time Jules opened the vicarage door and flung her arms around Linda, Danny's feet were numb and his nose was tingling. The fairy lights in the windows twinkled a welcome and, following Linda inside, casserole scented warmth wrapped itself around him like a hug. All seemed suspiciously quiet.

Danny glanced around. There was no sign of Alistair Mathieson. He caught Jules's petrified gaze over Linda's peroxided head and raised his brows questioningly, but Jules flicked her eyes up at the ceiling and pulled a face. *Does he know she's coming?* Danny mouthed and Jules shook her head. Oh. No wonder she looked terrified. Danny didn't need the powers of Silver Starr, Polwenna's resident psychic, to know things were about to go badly wrong.

"Would you like a cup of tea, Mum?" Jules asked.

"I'd rather have champagne!" trilled Linda. She glanced around the living room and clapped her hands. "Oh! Isn't this lovely? So cosy and Christmassy! I'm so happy to be here."

Jules cleared her throat. "We're really glad about that, Mum. I've been looking forward to you staying with me."

"Where else would I stay, you silly billy?"

"A hotel maybe?" Jules offered, a note of rising hysteria in her voice. "It's not too late if you'd rather. I know the vicarage is poky and walking up the hill is a pain. The central heating's not great either and the forecast's Baltic. I know how you hate the cold—"

"This is your wedding and you're my only daughter; of course I want to be here with you," Linda interrupted. "I'll be getting your breakfast, doing your nails and helping you get your dress on."

"I'm not doing my nails and I can make toast," Jules said.

"I know you can, love, but I *want* to help! It's your wedding day and this what every mother dreams of doing with her daughter. I can't wait! Hill or not, wild horses couldn't drag me away. Nothing could!"

Danny wasn't so sure. Wild horses were one thing. Grumpy ex-husbands quite another entirely.

"Great," said Jules faintly and Linda folded her in another bear hug.

"Darling, I can't tell you how happy I am to be here. I wouldn't be anywhere else! You pop the kettle on while I powder my nose and put my bag in the spare room. Won't be a jiffy!"

She swung an enormous LV holdall up onto her shoulder, nearly taking out the Christmas tree, and had bounded halfway up the stairs before either Jules or Danny could draw breath. From the bathroom overhead they heard the loo flush and the tread of footfalls.

Alistair Mathieson was on the move.

"Please tell me he knows she's coming?" Danny said, giving his fiancé a searching look.

Jules gulped. "I couldn't find the right moment."

"That's because there was never going to be one!" he groaned. "Sweetheart, this isn't going to end well."

They stared at each other as the horror of the situation dawned.

"I've been a huge coward, but I didn't know how to tell either without upsetting one of them," said Jules miserably. "They'd want me to choose and I can't do that. They drive me mad, but I love them both. I want them both here. Is that too much to ask?"

She sounded heart-broken and Danny couldn't bear it. Not for the first time he could have merrily knocked the Mathieson parents' heads together for being so selfish and causing their wonderful daughter such unnecessary worry. He pulled her close and pressed a kiss into the top of her curly head.

"Of course it isn't. They're adults and I'm sure it'll be fine."

Jules tilted her head and looked up at him.

"Really? You actually think that?"

Danny couldn't fib to her. "No, not really. I was being optimistic!"

"This is my parents we're talking about. There's no room for optimism," she said.

"Good point. So your Dad's got absolutely no idea that he's about to walk out of the loo and come face to face with the woman he's been avoiding since you were twenty-one?"

Jules buried her face in his shoulder. "None whatsoever."

The bathroom door clicked open, footsteps passed over their heads and Jules and Danny looked at one another with trepidation. Any minute now…

"Ju Ju! Why is there a suitcase on my bed, darling?" Linda carolled from the landing. "Is there somebody else stay— Alistair? What are you doing here?"

"I could ask you the same thing, Linda."

"Me! I'm staying here!" There was a scuffle of footfalls followed by a shriek. "Get out of my room!"

"I'm afraid you're mistaken of the facts, although admittedly not for the first time. This is *my* room." Alistair's voice was so icy Danny half expected a glacier to creep down the stairs.

"This bloody well isn't your room. Move that case! Now!"

"I most certainly will not. I'm staying here for our daughter's wedding."

"Says who?"

"Our daughter," said Alistair calmly. "She's invited me to stay."

"No she hasn't. She's invited *me*!" Linda shrieked. "Now get out of my room!"

Alistair sighed gustily. "Why do I always have to repeat myself? Have you been drinking? I said, I'm staying here for our daughter's wedding. This is my room."

"We'll see about that!" snarled Linda. Moments later there was a thud on the ceiling followed by a dragging sound.

"What are you doing, woman? Are you mad? Put it down!"

There was the sound of a scuffle and several curses.

"Do you think you ought to go up and pour some oil on troubled waters?" Danny said to Jules.

"I'd need a super tanker of the stuff," she said. "Danny, I'm so sorry. You were right. I should have said something sooner. They were never going to just say hello and have lunch, were they?"

Danny kissed her. "It was pretty unlikely. Should we call in the UN Peace Negotiation Team?"

There was another thump and crash. The entire vicarage shook.

"Don't you lay a finger on me or I'll have you for assault you…you…subjugator!" Linda yelled.

"Subjugator? Me? Do you even know what that means? Or spell it?"

"Subjugate this, asshole!" Linda screeched.

This outburst was followed by a series of almighty thumps as something cumbersome and heavy tumbled headlong down the stairs. Alarmed, Danny and Jules tore into the hall, both gripped by the unspoken fear that years of simmering anger had finally reached boiling point and Alistair had hurled his ex-wife over the bannisters. His heart ricocheting against his ribs, Danny was beyond relieved to discover Alistair's case lying on the tiled floor rather than Linda. Underpants, Rennies, bottles of Gaviscon, socks and books were strewn across the stair treads, several ties spewed out like innards and there was a gash in the wallpaper but there was no blood and no body which was a relief.

White-faced, Alistair hung over the landing bannister with his glasses slipping from his beaky nose.

"You're an utter lunatic, woman! I can see you haven't changed."

"I told you to move it, but would you listen? Oh no. Of course not. You never did listen. You've only got yourself to blame," Linda panted.

"Mea culpa," he agreed, "since I married you in the first place. That was the biggest mistake of my life. Second is coming to this wedding."

"Mum! Dad! Stop it right now!"

Jules strode forward, tipping back her head to see both of her parents who were still teetering at the top of the stairs. She was close to tears and Danny was a heartbeat away from throwing both selfish parents out and dragging their daughter up to Gretna Green and far away from this whole bun fight.

"Tell me what *he* is doing here?" Linda hissed, glaring at her ex-husband.

"Julia! Why wasn't I told *she* was coming?"

"Why do you think, you stupid man? Because she knew you'd behave like this, that's why!" said Linda.

"You're the one throwing people's bags down the stairs!"

"I wouldn't need to if you hadn't put your bloody bag on my bed!"

"It's my bed!"

"Says who? Typical of you to claim it for yourself!"

And they were off again, hurling insults and trading years of pent up resentments. They made Punch and Judy look like pacifists, Danny thought as he fought the urge to give them an army style bellow that would make both parents leap to attention, no wonder Jules had been so worried about having them both under the same roof. At this rate the vicarage would be a pile of rubble by teatime.

"Stop it! Both of you! Right now!"

Jules didn't often raise her voice but when she did there was such authority in her tone that people always stopped in their tracks and listened. Danny had seen her bring difficult parishioners to heel at meetings and it took a core of steel to keep the Pollards on the straight and fairly narrow. Anyone who underestimated Jules as a meek and gentle soul were usually in for a big shock and her parents were no exception. Their daughter's raised voice had stopped their row in its tracks and they stared at her, slack mouthed.

"This is why I couldn't face telling either of you that the other one was coming," Jules said, her face flushed and her eyes bright with tears. "Don't you think I knew you'd fight or make excuses not to come because you'd rather carry on your stupid feud than put it aside for my wedding?"

"It's not a stupid feud," huffed Alistair.

"No, it isn't," agreed Linda.

"Shut! Up!" Jules roared so loudly even Danny's feet left the ground. "I've had enough! Do you hear me? Enough! I love you, both of you, and I didn't dare tell you I'd invited you both because I knew this was just how you'd react! I don't love one of you more than the other. I don't want to take sides or choose between you. I never have and I never will. This isn't about you for once – it's about me! I'm your daughter and all I wanted was to have my mum *and* my dad with me for the few days before my wedding and for both of you to be there on the most important day of my life. Is that really so much to ask? Well, is it?"

There was an awkward silence. Then Alistair cleared his throat.

"No, Ju Ju. Of course not. Right, Linda?"

Linda, who was halfway through shrugging back into her white coat, looked abashed. Faux fur dangled from her shoulders. Although loathe to agree with Alistair, she knew she was in the wrong.

"No," she admitted. "I suppose not."

Jules glanced at Danny who gave her an encouraging smile. He didn't think he'd ever been so proud of her. It didn't matter how old you were or how important you became as an adult, being with family always catapulted you right back to the child you'd once been. His own family had all but fallen apart when Granny Alice remarried and moved out because it had felt like losing their mother all over again. His father had gone on a bender with the local drinking posse, Nick had sunk into a decline for weeks and Issie was still sulking. Danny understood better than most that for Jules to speak to her parents like this had taken a huge amount of courage.

But Jules, being Jules, was prepared to offer them an olive branch.

"Look, I'm really sorry I didn't warn you both. That was wrong of me, but I so wanted both of you here and I was afraid you wouldn't come if you'd known," she admitted.

"I suspect you may have been right," said Alistair, glaring at Linda.

"I know she is," snapped his ex-wife. "I wouldn't have come near the place if I thought you were here. I'd have stayed in Spain."

"Mars would be too near for me," parried Alistair.

Jules pressed the heels of her hands to her temples.

"This is *exactly* my point! But now you are here can't you at least call a truce? For my sake? It's my wedding and neither of you wants to be the one to ruin that, surely? Do I mean so little to you that you'd rather fight with each other than be supportive?"

Neither parent wanted to appear the villain in the piece. Linda and Alistair were checkmated and exchanged horrified glances.

"I don't expect you to both stay," Jules told them. "There's room at the hotel."

"But not at this inn? How Biblical," said Alistair.

Jules ignored him. "Mum, you might like a suite at the hotel. I can give Tom a call and see if there's one free."

"But you wanted us here with you," protested Linda.

"Of course I did. I'd made up the sofa bed for me, Mum, and you were meant to be in my room which is why I'd put Dad in the spare one. But I can see that won't work."

"I can drive you to the hotel right now," Danny offered, pulling his keys out of his jacket pocket and jingling them. "It's not a problem."

Linda raised her chin. "Why should I go? I'm not leaving my daughter, not when she wants me to stay. Alistair can stay at the hotel."

But her father folded his arms. "I'm not going to a hotel."

"Against your Marxist principles?" Linda asked scathingly. "Are hotels the opiate of the people now?"

"Don't be flippant, Linda, it doesn't suit you," he snapped. "I want to be here with my daughter and I'm staying put. If it's what Jules wants I'm going to make sure it happens."

So now neither parent was prepared to leave. How typical, thought Danny. It was time to intervene.

"You can't both stay here if you're going to fight. It's not fair on Jules," he warned them. "And the vicarage can't take it either. We need somewhere to live once we're married!"

"I know you haven't seen one another much since the divorce but surely you can manage a few days?" Jules said.

"It was a long time ago. All water under the bridge, surely?" Danny added.

Alistair nodded. "True, unless you're not over me, Linda?"

Linda snorted. "In your dreams. I've hardly given you a second thought. Our marriage is like a bad dream."

Alistair pressed his hand against his chest. "I'm wounded. Still, there we have it. We can manage to be civil for a few days. Don't you agree, Linda?".

"I *know* we can be," countered his ex-wife, not to be outdone. "I'm not going to let our daughter down."

"And neither will I. So it's settled. We'll both stay."

"I said it's settled first," Linda said quickly. "I'll take the sofa bed. Your back won't cope with it."

"Nonsense. I'll be fine. You need to be nearer Jules."

"You needed the toilet at least three times in the night, fifteen years ago. You need to be near the bathroom. I'll have the sofa bed."

"Why do you never listen to me? I said *I'll* take it."

They were off again, squabbling now over who could be the most selfless and the most helpful. Jules looked at Danny and grimaced.

"Shall I add 'therapy sessions' to our wedding present list?"

"For them or for us?"

"For us of course," Jules replied, and Danny laughed despairingly as the voices from above grew louder.

"Better book them now, Jules. A week is going to feel like a long time with this pair under same roof. Please be careful what you pray for in the future!"

Chapter 7

Sunday 20th December

Although she'd lived at Seaspray for most of her adult life, raising her son and latterly a tribe of grandchildren within its whitewashed and ivy clad walls, Alice St Milton was surprised just how quickly she had adjusted to living at Harbour Watch. She did sometimes miss the breath-taking panoramas from her old home but in recent years these had come at a breath-snatching price and Alice thought there was a lot to be said for being able to walk back from the village shop without feeling the need for climbing gear and an oxygen cylinder! The sadness she'd felt at saying farewell to the home she'd loved for over half a century had also been eased by her new home's beautiful views across the bay. Alice knew the constantly shifting tides with their kaleidoscope waters and coyly revealed stretches of beach were a living picture she would never tire of admiring.

This would be her first Christmas as Mrs St Milton as well as her first back living in the heart of the village. Alice was loving spending the evenings gazing out across the harbour and watching the jewelled reflections of festive lights from the tree spill colour into the dark water. During the day she often overheard snatches of excited conversation as winter visitors, fatly swaddled in coats and scarves, strolled past her house on their way to the beach and she and Jonny had been entertained for days watching the Pollards string up the Christmas lights.

December had begun with a modest strand of primary coloured bucket lights threaded along the edge of the quay and through Fore Street while a substantial Norwegian spruce was erected at the marina entrance. This was usually as far as the Polwenna Christmas Lights' fundraising efforts would stretch to, so Alice had been taken aback to open her curtains one morning to discover a giant illuminated Santa lashed on top of the fish market roof. Alongside this were several jaunty reindeer and a heavily laden sleigh and Big Rog stood on the fish quay directing operations while his son clung to the roof doing his best not to plummet into the harbour.

"What in God's name is that?" her husband Jonny spluttered over his toast and marmalade when he spotted this display.

"I think it's Father Christmas, love," Alice replied. Goodness, shouldn't Little Rog have some sort of harness? Health and safety was still a thing, surely?

Jonny rolled his eyes. "I've worked that out, Ally. I'm not senile quite yet! I was wondering why it's up there? And what the hell are those? They look like they should be on the entrance to a strip club. Not that I'd know about such things, of course!"

He was pointing to the giant flashing angels Big Rog had attached on scaffold poles to the far end of the building. Alice, an early riser, had watched the Pollards struggling to manhandle their celestial illuminations for at least half an hour while she drank her tea and had tried hard not to laugh as the angels swung around the poles in a manner that was far removed from angelic. As gold and crimson strobed the early morning gloom she'd watched in disbelief as snowmen, a giant star and finally Santa and the reindeer joined the throng. Big Rog was taking the Polwenna lights seriously and she really shouldn't tease, Alice had decided. He must be putting hours of work into them and between this and providing turkeys, was fast becoming Polwenna's Mr Christmas.

"Don't be such a grinch," she'd scolded her husband. "It's a bit of fun for Christmas. Jules did say Big Rog wants to give Mousehole some stiff competition."

"This lot gives Vegas a run for its money," Jonny remarked. "They'll be able to see Polwenna from the International Space Station at this rate!"

But Alice and Jonny hadn't seen anything yet and over the next few days several hundred more lights and many decorations joined the heavenly host. As they lay in bed at night their room was lit up like a disco and the flashing made Alice feel as though she'd had far more to drink than just a cup of cocoa. Amusing as it was to be transported to Stringfellows in your eighties, Jonny and Alice were growing more tired with each passing day of advent and just the thought of a big family wedding followed by Christmas was exhausting. Not wanting to complain and be party poopers they invested in a blackout blinds and decamped to the back bedroom while Big Rog, channelling Oxford Street, added more lights with each passing day. It was all in aid of the highlight of Polwenna Bay's run up to Christmas, the harbourside carol service.

"Will you be warm enough?" Alice asked Jonny for the umpteenth time as they prepared to head out into the night for the service.

"Just digging out the final touches to my outfit," he replied from the under stairs cupboard.

The weather was as cold as any Alice could remember and the air brittle with ice. They would be standing outside on the quayside for over thirty minutes and she worried about her husband's chest in the bitter night air. Alice knew there would be stalls selling mulled wine and hot spiced cider to keep the chill away and they could warm up on chestnuts and pork rolls too. Adam Harper from the pub always loaned out his patio heaters for the elderly folk to cluster beneath but Jonny would rather risk frost bite than stand with Ivy Lawrence and the others.

"That's for old people," he'd said, horrified when Alice had gently suggested this was where they should head.

"We are old people, you silly old idiot! We're eighty!"

"Speak for yourself," he huffed. "I'm sixteen and I'm not sitting with the old duffers!"

Her husband really was a teenager in his head, Alice thought with fond exasperation as she checked her bag for the bobble hat she knew he'd refuse to wear but would need later on, but weren't all men boys at heart? Look at Big Rog with his Christmas lights obsession or her grandson Zak who'd been practising carols in the marina workshop with his friends all week which had made her think back to when he'd been fifteen and setting up his first band.

Alice sighed. Where did the years go? It seemed only yesterday she'd been wrapping up her grandchildren in their coats and hats before holding mittened hands and walking them down the cliff path to see the lights. Now they were all grown up and some even had children of their own which made her a great-granny. If this wasn't enough of a reason to claim her spot under the patio heater she wasn't sure what was!

"That's a big sigh, Ally. Is everything all right?" asked Jonny from the depths of the cupboard.

"I was just thinking about how fast time flies as you get older."

"Ah yes, youth is wasted on the young and all that," he agreed, pulling out a big duffle coat and held it up. "Aha! Warm enough?"

"Should be with a scarf and gloves," she replied. "It's bitter out there."

Jonny was shrugging it on. "Will you still fancy me when I look like Paddington Bear?"

"What makes you think I fancy you in the first place?" Alice deadpanned.

"Well, if you didn't before you will now! Trad da! What do you think?"

He reached into his pocket and with a flourish pulled out a deerstalker hat which he rammed onto his grey curly head.

"Very Elmer Fudd. Should we be expecting Buggs Bunny any time soon?"

"Elmer Fudd? How dare you! I'll have you know this is pure Sherlock Holmes! Anyway, it doesn't matter how daft I look; it's brass monkeys out there."

"I can't remember it being this cold since '63," Alice said. That had been a cold winter. She had scraped ice off the inside of the windows up at Seaspray, the water in the outside toilet had frozen and she'd given herself chilblains by warming her socked feet on the Aga.

"*The Beast from the East Returns*' was how the weatherman described it on the telly earlier. It's going to be icy this weekend, so I've asked Little Roger Pollard to salt the path for us. No point taking chances."

"Good thinking, love. We don't want broken bones at our age," agreed Alice.

Jonny pulled an outraged face. "As if we'd fall! I was thinking more about Pete the Post slipping, but it's a fair point. We can't risk doing anything daft. Not when there's the wedding coming up."

Alice couldn't wait for the wedding and to welcome Jules officially to the family. Guests were heading to Cornwall from far and wide and it would be wonderful to catch up with so many folk too. Alice was rather surprised the wedding had become such a big affair, but Danny had explained that Jules secretly wanted the full works and it did make sense to Alice that Jules would never dream of breathing a word about what she wanted. Yet as she and Johnny left the house arm in arm to join the other Polwenna residents by the Christmas tree, Alice reflected she would have never imagined Jules Mathieson to be the sort of girl who longed for big white dresses, a bevy of bridesmaids and a four-course reception. In fact, if she was a betting woman Alice would have wagered everything on Jules preferring a small do with a buffet and disco in the village hall. Still, Danny knew her best and Alice was touched by how keen he was to make sure his fiancée had everything she longed for. They deserved to be as happy; second chance love was doubly precious.

The quayside was packed and the anticipation filled atmosphere sparkled as brightly as Big Rog's lights. People stood sipping from steaming cups of mulled wine and queued for chestnuts before muscling their way through the crowd to find a good spot for the singing.

Sheila Keverne was setting up her electric piano, a complicated process which involved all manner of flexes and wires Big Rog was laying out across the quay like spaghetti. It looked lethal and not for the first time Alice hoped he knew what he was doing. Every now and then speakers screeched feedback which made everyone jump and, worrying, the lights flickered at the same time. Alice looked around nervously, hoping to spot her grandson Jake who knew about electrics, but he was nowhere to be seen. She really hoped they weren't all about to be sizzled.

"Have you seen my boy?" Big Rog asked Alice as he staggered past with arms full of leads. "I can't find him anywhere and I needed somebody to check the mic."

"I'm afraid not, Roger. Could he be helping the Penhalligan brothers? Nick said they want to put lights on their trawler."

Big Rog's forehead corrugated like the side of his poultry shed.

"I helped with that earlier. No, 'tis a mystery. He's not answering his mobile either. Where is the boy?"

"I'm sure he won't be far. Maybe he's having a glass of mulled wine and warming up? It's freezing out here," said Alice, burrowing into her scarf. Could she abandon Jonny for the patio heater? There was no point both of them getting hypothermic.

"He's probably checking on those bleddy turkeys. Boy's obsessed with them, Mrs St M! I keep telling him you don't fatten the pig by weighing it!"

This reminded Alice. "Talking of turkeys, when are you delivering ours? Ashley ordered two, remember?"

"I wouldn't forget Cashley — err I mean Ashley's birds. At Pollard Poultry we pride ourselves on customer service," boasted Big Rog. "The turkeys are going to the big shed in the sky tomorrow and they'll be delivered on Thursday. You won't get fresher or better in the south-west!"

"Super," said Alice. "I'll let him know."

That was Christmas dinner sorted. It would be strange not to be cooking it herself and up at Seaspray but also a pleasant change to be waited on for once. Maybe getting older wasn't all bad?

"You hoo! Alice!" Sheila Keverne was waving at them. "All set for Tuesday? I've organised the mini bus and booked the tickets. Oh! I can hardly wait. It's going to be wonderful. I can't tell you how much I'm looking forward to it!"

Alice had known Sheila all her life, but she couldn't ever recall seeing her look so excited. Being appointed Jules's Maid of Honour had put a spring her step, that was for sure.

"You've worked so hard," Alice said, joining Sheila as Jonny queued for mulled wine. "Is there anything I can do to help?"

Sheila shook her bobble hatted head. "It's all in hand. All you need to do is show up in your costume and make sure you have a spare for Jules. She's going to love it, don't you think?"

"Absolutely," Alice agreed, although she wasn't convinced. Still, Sheila's plan was far safer than Mo's suggestions of willy hats, strippers and cheeky games. Maybe putting the verger in charge wasn't quite as much of a daft idea as it had seemed? Alice had followed her instructions to the letter, and everything was in place. Nothing could possibly go wrong with Sheila at the helm. The hen night was go!

"Would you mind handing out some carol sheets?" Sheila asked. "I've printed fifty but even so people will have to share. It's a good turnout, isn't it?"

Alice nodded. The quayside was easily as busy as it would be in the summer and it made her feel all glowy inside to see how many happy and excited people had made the effort to brave the chilly weather. This was such a lovely time of the year and it was wonderful to be out and her about with her new husband and all their family and friends.

Everywhere Alice looked she spotted a Tremaine or member of their extended family. This was what Christmas was really about, Alice decided, being with your family and friends. There was Jules, dog collar on and looking very official as she carefully mounted the makeshift stage Little Rog had cobbled out of bright yellow fish boxes. Festooned with tinsel and yet more fairy lights it looked festive, if a little unsteady, when Jules attempted to walk across it. Danny was calling instructions while his son Morgan clutched his drone to his chest, no doubt waiting for the best moment to launch it into the air to film proceedings. Linda Mathieson, looking as though she'd stepped straight from the set of one of those reality shows Issie was addicted to, was standing beside a stern-faced man and even though they were on the far side of the quay Alice could sense the animosity between them. This had to be Jules's father because he looked as though the smell from the boxes had got right up his nose. From what she knew of Alistair Mathieson, Alice suspected this had less to do with the stench of rotting haddock and more to do with finding himself attending a carol concert. How on earth had such an old misery produced a lovely girl like Jules?

"Get this down you, girl. Adam added an extra tot of brandy to warm the cockles." Jonny handed Alice a paper cup of mulled wine and judging by the ruddy colour of his cheeks he'd already had a couple! She inhaled the delicious aroma of spices and cloves and her senses reeled.

"Are you trying to get me drunk, Jonny St Milton?"

He winked and raised his cup. "I did tell you I was still sixteen in my head!"

They linked arms and made their way to the seats set up in front of the tree. Alice cast a hopeful look at the patio heaters but Jonny, fuelled by mulled wine and Christmas spirit, was determined to buy some chestnuts.

With less than ten minutes to go until the start of the carol service, the quay was filling up fast. The local TV people had backed their outside broadcast van as far as the marina and were busy interviewing Silver Starr and Ivy Lawrence, which Alice thought would make for interesting viewing! Across the fish market her grandson Nick and girlfriend Meg were doing a roaring trade in prawn rolls and frites from their seafood shack while his brother Zak and Tess were chatting to their friend Alex Evans who was proudly showing off new baby Noah who, wrapped up like a little Eskimo in his snowsuit, was gazing at the tree with wide eyes. As Tess reached out to hold him in her arms, Alice smiled because so it went on and would always continue. From the start of time to now and into infinity they were all part of an invisible chain of which she was just a small and one day long forgotten link. Alice wondered what her first husband, dear Henry Tremaine, would say if he could see the wonderful family they had created? She really hoped wherever it was it he'd gone after he closed his eyes for that last time, he could see them felt every bit as proud and as happy as she was.

Chestnuts purchased, and as burnt, sweet and crumbly as anyone could ever wish, Alice and Jonny threaded their way through the press of people. Ashley Carstairs, standing near the stage with Isla riding high on his shoulders beckoned them over to join Mo in the seating area.

"Keep her sitting still!" he begged Alice. "Your granddaughter's like a Jack in the Box. I'm going to ask Eddie Penhalligan for some rope in a minute so I can tie her down."

"That's the kind of behaviour which got me in this mess in the first place," giggled Mo, raising her eyebrows at him. "Oh dear. My hormones are all over the place! Let's go home right now, Ash! Granny will look after Isla."

"Great offer, Red, but the doctor said we have to keep your blood pressure down, remember?" Ashley said sternly, although his mouth lifted at the corners.

Mo pulled a face at Alice. "See how bossy he is? I thought Danny was the Sergeant-Major in the family!"

Alice took the seat beside Mo and tugged one of the folded blankets over their legs. Her breath was rising in clouds and her feet were going numb.

"He's right, my love. Your blood pressure's been a little high after shopping and you need to take it easy."

"Don't tell him he's right, Granny, he'll be unbearable. Anyway, it's all right for Ash. He's not the one with ankles like balloons and heartburn, is he?"

"Red, if I could give birth for you I would," said Ashley, "but, as impossible as it sounds, there are some things even I can't do."

"Mummy's got a baby in her tummy," Isla told Alice, her blue eyes serious. "But I wanted a puppy."

"That would have been much easier," said Mo, resting her hands on her belly and grimacing. "At least you only went through this once, Granny Alice."

Alice thought about telling Mo this wasn't strictly true but the hurts and tears and bitter disappointments of a lifetime ago were only remembered by her now and although they hadn't so much lessened over time they had become bearable in the inexplicable manner that these things did. Over the years there had been many moments of pain and regret, and white-hot anger too, but these memories were locked deep in Alice's heart. If the opening bars of Silent Night always reduced her to tears and made her arms ache for the ones who hadn't been able to stay, then she could pretend this was down to being sentimental and old. Dear Henry had shared her grief, but he was long gone and although Jonny knew a little of it these weren't his heartaches to carry. Instead, Alice had put them away and if even fifty years on the sadness still crept up on her to tighten her throat and suck away her breath, Alice had learned how to acknowledge this and live with it.

But she said none of this to Mo but just patted her granddaughter's gloved hand.

"I know, love, but bear in mind I did end up with your father! That's more than enough for any mother."

"I should say so," agreed Mo with feeling. Jimmy Tremaine was notorious for getting into scrapes and even in his sixties still caused Alice more worry than all her grandchildren put together. Leaning forward and, dropping her voice so Isla couldn't hear, Mo added, "Dad's dressing up as Santa tonight and wearing the tightest red leather trousers ever. Patsy Penhalligan and Silver have gone all twittery because he's asking every woman he meets if she's been a naughty girl and does she want to sit on his lap?"

Alice raised her eyes to the star sprayed sky. Her handsome son had always been one for the ladies and while he was growing up a procession of lovesick Polwenna girls, Sheila Keverne among them now she came to think of it, had trailed up to Seaspray hoping to catch a glimpse of him. Jimmy had caused havoc and broken countless hearts until he'd fallen head over heels for his wife and settled down. If only life had been kinder, Alice thought sadly. He'd been so happy when he was married but cancer paid no heed to things like that. Life could be so cruel.

Mo was still grumbling. "Can you believe Ash has even banned me from going to the stables? He says I have to stay at home and put my feet up."

"Sounds marvellous. Maybe I should have a baby?" said Jonny.

"It's bloody boring," snapped Mo, who was having a sense of humour failure at the thought of not going near her beloved horses. "I've got seven eventers to see to. I can't sit around all day. I need to be at the yard."

"You don't, my angel. That's what we pay Penny for and I've already told her you'll be nowhere near the stables until you blood pressure is lower," Ashley pointed out with a weary patience which suggested they'd already had this conversation several times. "You're always telling me how good Penny is and we certainly pay her enough! You just need to look after yourself and little Tarquin."

"We're not calling our baby Tarquin!" flared Mo, side-tracked by this notion just as her husband had known she would be.

"There's the wedding coming up too. It's going to be a busy week and you need to rest," soothed Alice.

"Oh great. I can't wait to waddle around and ruin the wedding photos," grumbled Mo.

"You'll look as beautiful as ever, Red," Ashley said kindly. "Unless the wind changes and you're stuck with that expression, of course!"

"I hate him," said Mo to Alice. "How much is a divorce?"

"More than you can afford with all those horses to feed, Red, so you're stuck with me. Put your feet up, drink your mulled apple juice and relax. It's about to start," her husband said.

"How on earth can you tell that?" Jonny asked, impressed

Ashley tapped the side of his nose. "My amazing psychic powers. How else do you think I keep one step ahead of Mo?"

"Ignore him," said Mo. "He's seen Morgan's drone take off."

Sure enough, Alice saw her great-grandson's flying camera hovering high above the harbour and moments later Jules climbed onto the fish box stage and stepped up to the microphone.

"Good evening everyone and welcome!" she said, her breath misting in the cold air. "This is one of the most special evenings of the year and thank you all for turning out when it's so cold! Let's warm up by singing our first carol, *Deck the Halls*!"

Sheila brought her hands down onto the keys and the first bars of the cheerful carol echoed merrily around the harbour. Carol sheets rustled, throats were cleared as villagers and visitors alike prepared to launch into song. Alice felt a surge of Christmas spirit as potent as any mulled wine. She slipped her gloved hand into Jonny's and squeezed his fingers just as every light went out, the music stopped, and the entire scene was plunged into darkness.

Chapter 8

Monday 21st December

"Apart from the incident with the electricity, I thought the service was lovely," Jules's mother said over brunch at the Harbour Café the following morning. She stirred some sweetener into her black coffee and smiled at her ex-husband. "Didn't you think so, Alistair?"

Alistair Mathieson looked up from his copy of The Guardian.

"I suppose so, if you like that sort of thing."

"Which we do," Linda snapped, "because we're here to support Jules. Or at least *I* am."

"And so am I, even though you clearly wish I wasn't. Give up, Linda. It won't work. For once I'm not going to rise to your baiting."

He pushed his half-eaten full English away and fished a packet of Rennies out of his jacket pocket, popping several into his mouth and gnashing his teeth down on them. Jules winced, knowing he was wishing he was grinding his ex into dust instead.

"Baiting? Moi?" Linda widened her brown eyes in surprise as faux as her coat. "I just know how you feel about religion. I was surprised you didn't combust or something."

"I'm an atheist not Voldemort," Alistair said wearily. "And before you ask, the answer is 'no'."

"No?" Linda echoed.

"No, I wasn't the one who flipped the shut off switch on the harbour's electricity supply. Apart from the fact I was standing beside you when it happened, I wouldn't know where the distribution panel is, would I?"

"I wouldn't put it past you," muttered Linda, plunging her knife into her avocado toast. "Nothing would surprise me."

"Not even glimpsing those teeth when you look in the mirror?" Alistair raised his eyebrows. "Don't Armitage Shanks own the copyright of toilet bowl white?"

"Some of us take care of our looks," Linda said. "You should try it. Maybe get a haircut? If you care about Ju Ju's wedding so much you won't let her walk up the aisle beside Worzel Gummidge."

"That's giving your age away. I suppose even Botox can't erase cultural references."

"I don't have Botox!" Lied Linda, trying to glare at him and only managing to look faintly surprised. "I just happen to have good genes!"

"Rubbish woman! You look younger now than when I married you!"

"That's because I got rid of you! You're worse for wrinkles than smoking!"

"Better move away then because here comes some more," he replied, pulling out a packet of cigarettes and tapping one out.

Linda wrinkled her nose. "How disgusting. I'm glad I gave that vile habit up when I threw you out."

Alistair flipped his lighter. "I think you'll find *I* left *you*, Linda. False memory syndrome is such a curious thing, isn't it?"

Jules placed her head in her hands. It had seemed such a lovely idea to take her parents out to the Harbour Café to enjoy a leisurely brunch before another busy day finalising wedding arrangements but, as usual, she'd forgotten to factor Alistair and Linda into the equation. Both were now either so intent on proving they were the most helpful parent that it was exhausting, or they would forget their truce and spar like gladiators in the Colosseum. Jules was even too stressed to eat her bacon sandwich - a very bad sign indeed. As if last night hadn't been difficult enough…

Jules had been cheerfully leading the first carol when the electricity had cut out. Ripples of surprise and a surge of conversation had echoed around the harbour while Sheila valiantly continued singing for a few more bars. Luckily it was a clear night with bright stars and a fat moon spilling light across the harbour and the chestnut stall had a blazing fire. Within seconds mobile phone torches were switched on, floating in the sea of people spread below the stage. For a brief and heady moment Jules felt like Madonna about to play Wembley stadium.

"Sorry everyone. It's just a minor glitch!" she'd called into the darkness. "Give us five minutes and we'll be back in business!"

At least she hoped they would be. What on earth was going on?

"What's happened?" she asked Danny as he helped her clamber down from the stage.

"The electric's gone off."

"I worked that much out! How?"

"No idea but I suspect it's got something to do with a Pollard. Did anyone check Big Rog's wiring?"

"He's a builder, Danny! Did we need to? Half the cottages in this village are in big trouble if this is down to him. And St Wenn's will probably be condemned!"

Danny nodded. "I'm no expert but they've been overloading the circuits on the harbour for weeks with all these lights. Maybe Sheila's electric keyboard was the last straw? Her singing definitely was for me! Perhaps we should be grateful?"

"Don't be naughty," scolded Jules and then, as the thought occurred, she asked, "Where are the Pollards?"

Danny was scanning the press of bodies. It was hard to see in the darkness where anyone was.

"Hiding? At the mulled wine stand? Syphoning our power off to illuminate the church? Who knows with them?"

Jules stared at him. "Is that even possible?"

"With the Pollards all things are possible," said Danny solemnly. "And they certainly work in mysterious ways – when they actually do some work, that is!"

Jules looked across the water to the quayside. Luckily for the crowd the crab shack had its own generator and was doing a roaring trade, as was the mulled wine stand and everyone seemed more than happy to carry on chatting and drinking and playing hoopla. The atmosphere was, if anything, even more festive in the darkness and beneath the star sprayed sky and as long as Adam Harper didn't run out of mulled wine Jules figured things would be fine for a fair while yet.

"I'll call Jake. He knows exactly how the harbour's wired because it was done at the same time as the marina," said Danny, pulling his phone out of his pocket.

Jake did know but when he met them by the harbour office he seemed puzzled, as did Big Rog who was already there wrestling with the padlock and insisting over and over again none of this was his fault.

"I checked everything," he said, lifting off his woollen hat and scratching his balding head. "There's nothing wrong with my wiring or my boy's – he trained as a sparky, see, and knows exactly how all this works because he planned it out and wired most of it. Oh! That's bleddy annoying! There's a bit of something stuck in here and my key won't fit. Here, Jake you have a go. Your eyes are younger than mine."

They weren't crossing with drink either, but Jules bit her tongue and let Jake do his best to let them in. Squabbling wouldn't help now.

"The harbour's lighting runs on a totally different mains circuit from the rest of the village and we have our own substation too, that's why the cottages aren't in darkness," Jake explained as he attempted to turn the key before blowing into the lock. Some fragments flew out and he tutted. "Looks like someone's put a bit of chestnut shell in it for a laugh. You get some idiots, don't you?"

He pushed the harbour office door wide open and illuminated the shadowy room with his powerful marine torch as Jules, Danny and Big Rog filed inside. The building smelled of salt and fish and diesel. Jules's nose wrinkled and she felt out of place among oil skins and boots and copies of The Sun. This was the domain of Eddie and the fishermen and the Pollards and Jules had never stepped inside. She felt as though she was intruding.

"Great. The ice machine's off and the walk-in fridge," groaned Jake, fiddling with the bolt on a large cupboard.

"The Penhalligan brothers won't be pleased if their catch spoils," said Big Rog gloomily. "They'll blame me and try to make me pay for the lot, I shouldn't wonder."

"Don't worry, Rog. The profits on your turkeys will more than cover the fish," Danny reminded him.

"What's in the cupboard?" Jules asked Jake.

"The master switchboard. It was placed in here for easy access when the harbour and marina were rewired. Basically it's a giant fuse box so it should be clear what's tripped the electrics, although I'd be amazed if it was anything to do with the Christmas lights because this is an industrial set up designed to run ice machines, landing flood lights, the walk-in fridge and derrick cranes. There's shore power too for visiting yachts. The circuitry should be able to handle twice the capacity."

"That's right, my — err Jake," nodded Big Rog, looking more cheerful. "When we put the Christmas lights up, the boy hooked into the shore power."

"It might be handy if he was here right now," said Danny.

"He's mooning over that Penny, I wouldn't wonder." Big Rog sounded perplexed. "He's probably buying her a bean burger or some of the rabbit food she's into."

"Vegetables?" Danny said.

"That's right. He's got it bad. Do you know, he even told his Ma he's going vegan? Karenza said she'd brought him up C of E and he was changing religion over her dead body!" Big Rog slapped his knees and his chins wobbled with mirth. "She was even less impressed when he explained what it meant! She said he could blooming well eat his Christmas dinner first!"

Not for the first time Jules felt rather sorry for Little Roger Pollard.

"That's odd. The main breaker's down." Jake stepped back from the master circuit, puzzled. "I wouldn't have expected to see that. It's never happened before. Usually I'd expect to see a circuit or two off but not the main breaker."

"What does this mean?" Jules asked, feeling distinctly low wattage herself. Less time reading romance novels and more time studying electrics would be on her agenda from now on, she decided. St Wenn's was always shorting out too. Maybe she could moonlight as a sparky and supplement her vicar's wage? Or combine the two? She could call her company *Let there be Light* and have a van and a halo logo…

"It means somebody has to physically flip the switch to close the whole lot off," Jake said slowly.

"We do that each time we add new lights," Big Rog told them proudly.

Jake sighed. "I know. Each time you do it I have to check every single boat on shore power to make sure the bilge pump batteries aren't switched off too. Six times in one day is the current record, I think?"

"Safety first, Jake, safety first," Big Rog said piously.

"So are you saying somebody has turned the lights off deliberately?" Danny asked.

"It's possible," Jake said, "but I can't imagine why."

"So it's also possible the lights did trip it?" Jules needed to be clear on this because the thought of anyone being spiteful enough to sabotage the carol service was too horrible to bear.

"Theoretically," Jake agreed.

"Absolutely not!" Big Rog protested.

"Can we flip it back on and get back to the carol singing?" Jules asked hopefully.

But Jake shook his blonde head. "I'm afraid not. Because we don't know why it's tripped we'll need to run through the circuits first to make sure they're safe and reset the ice machine. It's going to take at least half an hour."

Jules's heart sank. Everyone would have grown very cold by then and it wasn't fair to expect them to hang about. She'd have to cancel the service.

"Don't look so sad," Danny said as, hand in hand, they walked back into the cold night. "It's not over yet. The show will go on, you'll see. We'll get to sing carols."

"How?"

He kissed her softly. "Trust me. You'll see. Polwenna folk don't give up that easily."

Jules did trust Danny so she shouldn't have been surprised that by the time she was back beside the stage Zak and Tess were already on it, armed with a guitar and a violin and ready to take over where Sheila had left off. A crowd of Tess's primary school pupils joined them while Sheila had rounded up the WI choir and just about anyone else who wanted to sing on the stage. Even Silver Starr was there with her ocarina and didgeridoo. Polwenna was bursting at the gunnels with wannabe pop stars all happy to help their vicar out and as Jules hopped up onto the stage she didn't think she'd ever loved the village or its crazy occupants more.

"Deck the Halls! From the top! One! Two! One, two, three, four!" cried Zak and they were up and running with everyone else singing along at the top of their voices and waving their mobile phone torches in time with the music or holding candles gleaned from gift shops and harbourside homes. By the time they were belting their way through *Oh Come all Ye Faithful* Jules had all but forgotten none of this had been planned and felt disappointed when the lights blazed back into life. There was something special about singing carols by candlelight underneath the stars and in the frost bright air. By the time the final notes faded away and Jules closed proceedings with a Christmas blessing, everyone was in agreement this had been one of the best carol services Polwenna Bay had ever seen. Even the TV crew was raving about community spirit and festive atmosphere.

A disaster had been averted and all had gone well. Jules could only hope this boded well for the fast-approaching wedding.

"What if it happens again?" she'd fretted as she and Danny had packed away. "Or the Pollards put up even more lights and short the church out on the day?"

Danny placed his stack of carol sheets on the edge of the fish box stage and pulled her into a hug.

"Stop worrying, sweetheart. You heard Jake, there was nothing he could find that could cause the switch to trip. For once we can't blame Big Rog.

Besides, the Pollards must know something about wiring and electrical safety or half the village would have burned down by now."

"Is that the half they haven't flooded?" Jules asked wearily. "There's something almost Biblical about their exploits. Should we be expecting the locusts any time soon?"

Danny laughed but Jules hadn't been joking. No matter how many times her fiancé reassured her, she just couldn't shake off a sense of unease. The cause of the tripped circuit might be a mystery with Jake and Big Rog finding nothing wrong anywhere, but there was just something about which she couldn't quite put her finger on. Something was off and this made Jules uneasy.

"Little Rog is going to check it all through again first thing tomorrow," Danny reassured her. "He said he'll be here at sunrise and look through everything again just to be on the safe side."

Jules nodded. Little Rog had come to find her as soon as the carol service ended, very upset in case his father was blamed and Jules was touched – mostly because generally speaking this kind of thing *was* Big Rog's fault.

Danny kissed her again. "Please try not to worry, sweetheart. Nothing's going to spoil your special day. You're going to have to your dream wedding, I promise."

This was her moment, Jules thought. This was the perfect opening where she could say her dream wedding was nothing like the bunfight about to take place on Christmas Eve, but Danny looked so determined she hadn't got the heart to disillusion him. What would this achieve anyway? It was too late now. It was better she followed the advice of the elderly stranger in the cathedral and just trusted that all would work out and their wedding would be wonderful. Danny had worked so hard on the arrangements and it was important to him; she couldn't ruin that. All she cared about was that it would be Danny standing at her side when she made her vows. Nothing else mattered.

Luckily Linda and Alistair had arrived at this point, both keen to help Jules pack away and desperate to outdo the other for sheer helpfulness and sniping at one another non-stop - rather like they were doing right now. Spending time with her parents together as an adult had given Jules a fresh perspective on the past and she was starting to think they deserved one another. Alistair could be stubborn and an intellectual snob but Linda was relentless in her nit-picking and fault finding. As they bickered over the remains of brunch, Linda was telling Alistair off for eating a fry up and smoking, reeling off all the facts she'd learned on a recent first aid course.

"I'm the designated first aider for our apartamentos," she concluded proudly, her chin raised in the determined expression Jules recognised from her own mirror. "So I know about these things. Cholesterol and nicotine will kill you. And stress. Stress is fatal and you, Alistair, have always been far too tense."

"I can't imagine why," he said.

If stress was a killer she was doomed, Jules thought wearily. Was it too early in the morning for a drink? The sun was over the yardarm somewhere, surely?

It was Monday December the 21st, another cold and bright day with glacial blue skies and an unusual frost crackling underfoot. The sugared rooftops sparkled in the glare from the low sun as Jules and her parents walked down to the café, their feet slithered on the un-gritted lane. Even the beach was stippled white as though an artist had already been at work and the lattice of ice on rocks and piled nets a match for the filigree lacy webs spun across the sand as the tide sighed and shivered. The sea gulls were too cold to scavenge for left overs and huddled together on top of net bins or sulked next to warm chimney pots. Without their usual cries the village seemed quiet as though deep frozen.

Although they were sitting in the sunshine Jules was cold even zipped into a thick coat and with a knitted scarf wound several times around her neck. The forecasters were giving even colder weather over Christmas and as pretty as the glittery world was she feared St Wenn's would be arctic. Could she even fit thermals underneath her dress? And what about the bridesmaids? They'd have frostbite by the time the first 'I do' was exchanged. What had she and Danny been thinking, planning a wedding in the middle of winter?

While Alistair paid the bill and Linda sashayed to the railings to admire the view, Jules tried to breathe slowly. Exhale stress. Inhale calm, Exhale stress. Inhale—

"There you are, Jules! I've been calling you non-stop! Luckily Kathy Polmartin saw you heading this way or I might have missed you!"

Sheila Keverne, pink cheeked from a cold walk across the village, scuttled through the clusters of tables and chairs scarcely noticing in her haste that she was jogging people and slopping latte in saucers. Jules's heart sank; she recognised the look of Sheila on a mission. Was it any surprise she always left her phone at home on her days off?

"I don't work on Mondays," she began but Sheila rolled her eyes.

"I'm not here about *church*!"

"Good," said Jules. Then another thought occurred. "Didn't we say no wedding stuff today since it's the hen night tomorrow?"

In her capacity as Maid of Honour Sheila had compiled a list as long as Mr Tickle's arms and each day saw her finding something more to add to it. Jules had put her foot down at a hair style rehearsal or visit to a Spa – unless it was the kind that sold chocolate and pink wine – but Sheila on a mission was like the Terminator and nothing would stop her.

"Wedding?" Sheila echoed looking mystified and as though she hadn't talked of little else since Jules had announced she was engaged. "Oh, no. It's not that. Ooo! You'll never guess what, Vicar?"

"No, I probably won't," Jules agreed. "But try me."

Sheila puffed herself up with importance at being the one to impart information.

"You haven't heard? You don't know?"

Jules struggled to think about what she might not know. Quite a great deal actually, some of it theological in nature, some of it trivial (where did the second sock vanish to when a pair always went into the washing machine?) and some questions even Einstein and Hawking would have struggled to answer - such as why were her parents such a trial? But these trivial matters were not Sheila's concern.

"It's a terrible shock in a village like Polwenna to know there are thieves among us!"

Jules was surprised. Polwenna Bay did have a low crime rate, everyone knew everyone else's business here and it was hard to get away with much at all let alone a crime, but there were still petty thefts from time to time. Chris the Cod often had his sign pinched and last spring somebody had picked all the daffodils from the *Polwenna in Bloom* boat. Still, it was hardly Gotham City and, as yet, Batman was surplus to requirements.

"What's happened?" she asked. Not the Church candlesticks surely? Jules never locked St Wenn's in the daytime because she believed her Boss's house should always be open. Had she been naïve?

Sheila's eyes were wide. "We've got cattle rustlers! I've just seen Karenza Pollard and she said Big Roger's in a dreadful state. Every single one has vanished!"

Not for the first time Jules wondered if she was in some parallel universe, one where the Pollards raised steers and wore Stetsons and cowboy boots.

"Since when did the Pollards have cattle?"

"Well, not cattle exactly," Sheila admitted, deflating a little. "I'm not sure what the word for turkey stealing is but that's what's happened! They've gone. Every single one. Vanished! Overnight too! It's like space aliens beamed them up!"

Jules's first thought was that Sheila had been on the mulled wine a little early in the day because there was no way fifteen huge turkeys could disappear. Apart from the fact these were massive birds that would need shoehorning into most Polwenna ovens, they were noisy too. Silver Starr had been moaning for weeks about the din from the Pollards' garden shed. Her second thought was that Ashley Carstairs would flip. The success of his Christmas dinner depended on those turkeys.

"The turkeys have gone? All of them? Even Mr Wattles? Gobbles? Sparkles?"

"Even the one that can count," Sheila confirmed.

Jules took a moment to digest this news. Little Rog must be in pieces. No wonder he was yet to appear on the fish market roof to check the lights. He was probably at the police station filing a missing turkeys report and describing their individual talents.

"Every single one has vanished," Sheila said. She dropped her voice. "And there was no sign of a break in or a disturbance either. Only some tyre marks leading to the door. Karenza says Little Rog keeps the shed locked so that can only mean one thing!"

Mr Wattles could pick locks as well as count to ten?

Jules wracked her brains. "Aliens have taken them?"

Sheila looked at her as though she was exceptionally dim. It was a look Jules had seen a lot when she'd first arrived in the village.

"Don't be daft, Vicar, aliens don't celebrate Christmas. No, it's obvious what's happened. It's like on *Midsomer Murders*."

Jules really hoped it wasn't. Didn't the village vicar usually get bumped off on that show in a really gruesome and unusual fashion? It would be just her luck to be crushed by a giant pasty or electrocuted by Christmas tree lights just before her wedding. On second thoughts she would prefer aliens.

A big fan of cosy middle-class murder shows, Sheila was into her stride and running.

"The villain is always known to the victim so it must be an inside job, mustn't it? It's obvious. Somebody in the village Big Rog let use his shed has kept a key and stolen the turkeys. Find the key and you'll find the turkeys!"

Since Big Rog often moonlighted by renting out his shed this could be half the village. Even Jules had borrowed it a few times to store trestle tables for the St Wenn's jumble sale. Did this put her in the frame?

"I've already made a list of all the people I can think off who've used it. I have a good view of their garden shed from my bathroom window and I think I've got everyone. Caspar was last with that ridiculous motorbike of his. Or was it Silver? Didn't she store her yurts in there? Or did Adam store beer kegs there when the cellar had work done? Oh! It could be any of them. I wonder what Big Roger will think?"

"Maybe keep these theories to yourself in case the Pollards decide to investigate themselves?" Jules suggested quickly but the eager expression on Sheila's face said it was already far too late for caution. Big Rog was probably already hammering on doors up and down the village accusing his friends and neighbours of turkey rustling. *Midsomer Murders* would have nothing on *Cornish Killings*! Vigilante groups would be springing up all across the village.

"Roger's very upset and so am I," Sheila huffed. "Christmas is ruined without those turkeys. I was cooking one for Neil. He deserves a special dinner since he'll be doing all the Church services on his own, poor boy."

Like I have for years, Jules thought, feeling amused. Sheila, like most of the women in the village, had a thumping crush on the handsome curate. He lodged with her, which gave her great kudos at the WI, and nothing was too much trouble for Neil!

"Big Roger will soon find the turkeys. They're really noisy," Jules said but Sheila shook her head and drew her finger across her throat *Godfather* style.

"It's Christmas in five days. Nobody's keeping those turkeys as pets, are they? No, they're worth a fortune to go with a nice dollop of cranberry sauce. I'll be wanting a refund, that's for sure. The Pollards know how to charge."

They certainly did. Big Rog had been in the pub for days enjoying his profits. No wonder he was upset if everyone wanted their money back. Most of it was in Adam Harper's till.

"Little Rog must be distraught," Jules said.

"Between you and I, I think he's relieved," Sheila confided, sotto voce. "They were due to be dispatched this morning and Karenza said only yesterday how he's gone right soft over them - although if you ask me that boy's been soft in the head for years! Anyway, I can't stand here all day yarning with you, Vicar. There's investigating to do! I'll see you tomorrow for the hen night. My house at half three for some drinks before we leave. Don't be late!"

She spun on her heel and marched away intent on her new task. Jules shook her head. Sheila really wasn't a great detective but Jules already had a theory of her own, one she would be keeping well and truly to herself.

After all, pets were for life, weren't they? Not just for Christmas.

Parents were also not just for Christmas, Jules reflected as she pulled on her gloves and hoisted her bag onto her shoulder, and she had a busy day ahead refereeing hers. Catching sight of Linda and Alistair deep in a heated discussion, Jules knew she had far more important things to worry about than vanishing poultry.

If she didn't break these two up it would be less cosy crime and more a case for CSI Polwenna!

Chapter 9

Tuesday 22nd December

Jules was so busy with wedding rehearsals and listening to her parents attempt to outdo one another with passive aggressive helpfulness, that she almost forgot to be nervous about her impending hen night. Besides, how bad could things really be with Sheila at the helm? She might have a worrying penchant for gruesome murders in pretty English locations, and she was undoubtedly a busy body, but Sheila's idea of stripping was taking her cardigan off and a glass of wine was her version of heavy drinking. It would all be fine and perfectly respectable, something highly unlikely if Mo had been in charge. Then Jules would have been totally on edge, her feet leaving the floor each time there was a knock on the door in case a policeman/fireman/superhero stood on the vicarage doorstep poised to gyrate and strip down to just a posing pouch and a smile.

Although Sheila had been very secretive about what this evening's activities involved, Jules wasn't unduly worried because there were only so many choices open to them. She'd narrowed the possibilities down to a meal somewhere. A show in Plymouth. Or (and she really hoped not) a pampering evening at a local health club. The dress code was casual, which meant they wouldn't be out night clubbing, and as she brushed her hair and treated her mouth to a rare coat of lip stick Jules realised she was actually looking forward to the evening. She would be with her mother and her closest friends celebrating her upcoming wedding. What could be nicer and more relaxing?

Mo, confined to bed rest on doctor's orders, had sent Ashley to the vicarage earlier on, armed with a bag stuffed with L plates, fluffy pink willy boppers and T shirts with *Jules's Last Night of Freedom!* scrawled across them in glittery pink lettering.

"Apparently there were penis shaped chocolate lollies but Mo had an attack of the munchies and ate most of them," Ashley apologised while Jules rummaged through the bag, her face growing hotter by the minute when she pulled out a candy g string and nipple tassels. What the heck?

Danny peered over Jules's shoulder. "What on earth are they for?"

Ashley grinned. "The honeymoon, I hope! I'm afraid your stag do is looking very sedate in comparison, Dan."

"I couldn't be happier to hear it," said Danny.

The stags were having a meal at a new restaurant in the next town and Jules was quite envious of this civilised gathering. She didn't think Sheila would have planned anything inappropriate, but you never could be certain.

"I confess I stole the chocolate body paint," Ashley told Jules. "Isla and I were ravenous last night, and it was nice on toast which made me think I must stock up!"

"Nutella's just as good," Jules said and flushed scarlet when Ashley raised his eyebrows and grinned at her wolfishly.

"To eat on toast, I mean! Oh! Ashley! You know what I meant."

Danny put his arm around her.

"Stop teasing my fiancée, you! Now, is there anything else we need to know?"

"No, it appears Jules is quite the expert when it comes chocolate body paint!" Ashley laughed. "But in terms of hen night prep there's just this one bag here for Linda to take care of with strict instructions Jules is not to look inside until told."

"I'll take that!" Linda grabbed the bag, clutching it tightly to her chest as though Jules might snatch it away. "Perfect! Tell Mo, thanks!"

"And my work here is done," Ashley said. "The taxis are booked for six, mate, from outside the bakery so I'll see you then."

"I'm really sorry Mo can't make it," Jules said. "Is she doing OK?"

"She's fine. It's my blood pressure that's soaring having to keep her on the sofa," Ashley sighed. "She's driving me mad because she wants to go up and check the horses, which is exactly what Richard told her not to do, but you know Mo. Richard may have done years at medical school, but my wife knows better!"

"Can I do anything to help?" Danny asked. "Mucking out?"

"No thanks, mate, Penny's got it all sorted. She said we don't need to go near the place."

"She's dedicated," said Jules.

He shrugged. "You know these horsey types. Anyway, better shoot. Mo will be trying to rearrange the furniture or something if I'm not there to keep an eye on her. Have a great evening, Jules. Enjoy the Chippendales – oh! That was meant to be a secret!"

Recalling this conversation, Jules smiled at her reflection and was pleased to see the freckled face in the mirror beam back at her. She looked sparkly eyed and happy and her outfit of frilled ditsy print smock, dark blue jeans and knee boots was smart enough for a restaurant yet also casual too. Even her hair was playing ball for once and, grown especially for the wedding, hung to her shoulders in soft curls. If only she could dress like this for the wedding, Jules thought wistfully as she glanced at the bag hanging on the back of the bedroom door where her dress waited. She would feel so much more comfortable and like herself – and not a pair of control knickers in sight either!

It was late afternoon when Jules and Linda left the vicarage to walk down the lane to Sheila's cottage. The egg yolk sun was sinking fast, tugging the daylight behind it and basting the village in gold. As the waves ran in from the west, the light turned them silver as they gilded the wet sand. Although it was almost the end of the day, patches of white frost still remained where walls and hedges had shaded it from the pure light. Jules's boots stamped footprints into the ice and cold air curled into her nose. This was winter as it was supposed to be, sugary and glittery and magical, tinselling the village with ice. It was a winter which called for hats and mittens and thick socks, as they walked and chatted Jules watched their breath rise.

By the time they reached Lavender Cottage tobacco blue dusk was smoking in from the hills as though the night was enjoying a pipe and the windows of Sheila's small house glowed a welcome into the darkening afternoon. The village Christmas lights, all totally fine and safe according to Jake, cheered the gathering darkness while on the quay the fishermen were unloading the day's catch. The air was thick with wood smoke and seemed to grow cooler by the second and it was with relief that Jules and Linda stepped into Sheila's hall where there were instantly wrapped up in warmth and chatter.

"Come in!" Sheila beamed, shutting the door and ushering them through the hall. "Let me take your coats and fetch you a glass of mulled wine! The girls are waiting so come and join them!"

The hens were gathered in Sheila's sitting room, a feat in itself because the cottage was tiny and one which necessitated much squashing onto sofas, balancing on the arms of chairs and wedging into window seats. Jules's heart swelled when she saw just how many people had made the effort to turn out on such a cold evening at the busiest time of the year. Babysitters had been booked and all card writing and present wrapping put aside so they could celebrate this evening. As soon as Jules stepped into the room everyone cheered and a volley of party poppers were fired. A mug of mulled wine was thrust into her hand and before she could even draw breath, Jules found herself wearing L plates, willy boppers and a sash which read *Bride*. She pushed streamers out of her eyes and smiled at her friends.

"Thank you all so much for coming!" Jules was moved to see so many people gathered just for her. Age seemed no barrier to the party either for even Alice St Milton was present, boppers on and sporting a sash. Always thrilled to see Danny's grandmother, Jules was doubly pleased to have Alice here this afternoon. They couldn't get up to anything too cheeky with an octogenarian present!

"Try keeping us away. I flew back early to be here. I'm risking frostbite for you, Jules!" said Issie Tremaine, perched on the arm of her grandmother's chair and as close to the wood burner as it was possible to be without climbing inside. Her tanned bare legs swung back and forwards from beneath short hot pants. Jules had goose pimples just looking at her.

"If you put some more clothes on it might help, love," said Alice tartly. "You'll catch your death. You're not in Florida now."

Issie grinned. "This would be considered overdressed in Miami, Granny! Most girls wear tiny bikinis just to visit the supermarket."

"In that case I am never, ever letting my David go food shopping out there! I dread to imagine what he'd put in his trolley!" Linda declared and everyone laughed.

Jules settled down onto the sofa flanked by Kat Evans, enjoying a rare night away from her baby, and Tess who was overjoyed to have broken up for the holidays. It was so wonderful to have all her favourite people around her. Even Silver Starr and Karenza Pollard were present and very excited at the prospect of whatever mysterious adventures lay ahead. As Sheila made sure everyone had a drink, put willy boppers on their heads and wore sashes which read *Jules's Hen Night!* Conversations flowed as easily as the mulled wine.

"Here, love, have some crisps. I think you'll need to line your stomach," advised Karenza Pollard, passing Jules a bowl.

Taking her advice, Jules scooped up a handful. She didn't actually need asking twice. She'd been doubling her diet efforts over the past few days and her mouth was watering just at the mere sight of snacks. Besides, Sheila's mulled wine was potent and it wouldn't do to flag early on!

"Any news on the missing turkeys?" Alice was asking Karenza. Her lined face worried. "Ashley was hoping to cook Christmas dinner but that looks as though it may be on hold now."

There was a ripple of agreement because many Christmas dinner tables across the village were in danger of looking a little bare this year.

"I've got Alex's parents coming for the first time. Our Christmas dinner is ruined without a turkey!" fretted Kat.

"And mine," chipped in Sheila, not to be outdone. "I promised Reverend Cavendish a lovely turkey dinner."

But Karenza shook her head. "There's no sign of them, I'm afraid. My Roger's very upset because he's convinced it must be somebody we know. How else could they have been taken? Nobody saw anything and the door was locked."

"Maybe we're in a time slip vortex?" Silver Starr suggested, her violet contact-lensed eyes wide at this notion.

"You what?" said Karenza.

"A time slip vortex? You know, like a hiccup in the fabric of the universe? Or when you walk through standing stones and go back in time!"

"Standing stones?" Karenza Pollard stared at Silver.

"You know. Like Stonehenge," Jules offered but as soon as she spoke the words she knew she wasn't helping because poor Karenza Pollard was even more confused.

"You think our turkeys went to Stonehenge? How would they do that? It's not like they can catch a bus. How much have you had to drink, Silver?"

"That was just one example of a portal," Silver explained, leaning forward and looking a little unhinged as she waved her hands around. "Standing stones can be gates to other times. People can go through by mistake."

"Like in the show with the handsome Scottish man," said Kat.

"Outlander!" cried Sheila before adding hastily, "I've heard about it."

"Isn't the actor a dish? He's gorgeous in his kilt!" Linda fanned her face. "I think he looks just like Reverend Neil! Don't you, Ju Ju?"

Jules hardly had time to breathe these days never mind watch telly. And even if she did know what they were talking about this was a highly inappropriate conversation! Neil Cavendish was her curate!

"I think Neil's much fitter," giggled Kat. "I've never been to church so often although I only have eyes for Alex, obviously!"

"And Neil would look hot in a kilt!" agreed Issie. "Maybe I could get religion?"

"Me too! You know what they say about Scotsmen and their kilts," giggled Linda.

Enough, thought Jules. It was far too early for all this!

"These crisps are nice, Sheila," she said loudly. "Where did you get them from?"

"They're Pringles from the village shop. I think you've been dieting too long," Sheila told her, looking bemused as she shook some more into the bowl. "Fill your boots, Jules. It won't make any difference now."

"Unlike not having a turkey for Christmas dinner," Kat sighed as she helped herself to a fistful. "That's going to make a massive difference on the table!"

"Time slips aside, the turkeys can't be far away, surely?" Jules asked, relieved that Neil's kilt wearing had been forgotten.

"It depends whether Nature spirits took them. They could be in the spirit world now." Silver folded her hands in her lap and closed her eyes. "I can ask my guides, if you like?"

"Please don't," said Jules. Discussing how sexy her curate was and now contacting spirits? This hen night was already straying into inappropriate territory and they were only twenty minutes in. Something told her this was going to be a long night.

Silver looked hurt. "Fine. I wouldn't have told you what they said anyway. Good for the turkeys, I say. It's cruel to eat meat."

"It's also cruel I can't cook Richard a nice Christmas dinner when he works so hard at the surgery," pointed out Tara Tremaine, perched on the arm of the sofa. She reached for the crisps and chewed thoughtfully. "We'll all be refunded, I take it? I'll have to nip to the supermarket tomorrow before they sell out."

Karenza paled. "You'll have to ask my Roger about that."

"I fully intend to," said Ella St Milton who was passing to top up their glasses. "Symon's ordered one for the Manor's *Bird within a Bird* and it's going to be a little compromised without a turkey."

"Ashley will flip," said Issie. "He's meant to have two."

Silver shuddered. "I'm glad they've gone, poor things. Why can't little turkeys be left alone to live in peace?"

"You just sound like our boy. He even says he's changing religion now," Karenza Pollard sighed. "And he's been confirmed and everything."

"I don't think that's quite what he meant," Jules began but nobody was listening. They were all too busy demanding to know where their turkeys were. It seemed the season of goodwill could only stretch so far when

Christmas dinner was at stake and soon even Mrs Pollard was ready to throttle her husband. Next year, she said, he'd be going to Sainsbury's like everybody else and the shed would be turned into a gym. She'd always wanted an exercise bike and maybe a sauna?

Saunas aside, the whereabouts of the Pollards' missing turkeys was a mystery. Nobody had seen or heard a thing and there was no clue where they could be. How fifteen enormous birds could vanish into thin air was an enigma right up there with Loch Ness Monsters and the Marie Celeste - although the *Vanishing Turkeys of Polwenna Bay* didn't have quite the same ring to it! Jules had a few growing suspicions of her own, but she was waiting to talk these through with Danny. Voicing them now would cause a riot.

"Attention everyone!" Sheila was on her feet and clapping her hands, just as she did every time she organised the PCC or the WI, and as if by magic the chatter faded away. "It's nearly time for us to hop into the minibus and go to *you know where* so we need to get ready. Has everyone got their things?"

There was a chorus of affirmation accompanied by a Mexican Wave of boinging boppers.

"Linda, do you have the bag from Morwenna?" Sheila asked.

"I do! I do!" Linda cried, shooting her hand into the air in her haste to please.

"Wonderful! Now, Jules, if you'd just wait outside a minute." Sheila pulled Jules from the sofa and frog-marched her into the hall before shutting the door and calling, "We'll call you when you can come back in! No peeking!"

I could always do a runner right now, Jules thought nervously as she perched on the bottom stair listening to giggles and shrieks of laughter behind the closed sitting room door. What was going on in there? Should she be alarmed? It was certainly with some trepidation that Jules re-joined the hens when she was eventually summoned. Quite what she'd expected she wasn't sure, but it certainly wasn't a room filled with nuns.

"Surprise!" the hens chorused while Jules stared at them, lost for words. Yes. It certainly was a surprise. Had Silver doctored the mulled wine with one of her magical tea bags or were her friends and neighbours really dressed as nuns for a hen night? Had she been a little too insistent they were well behaved this evening?

"There's a habit for you too. Your mum has it," Mother Superior aka Sheila was saying proudly. "It's in the bag Mo sent. Are you pleased?"

"Pleased?" Jules echoed faintly.

Sheila gestured at the nuns. "I knew people always dress up on hen night."

"Normally as brides and hens," said Jules, still confused. "Why nuns? Or am I missing something? I'm Church of England!"

Sheila rolled her eyes. "Hurry up and put your costume on. We need to get going if we're to fit in having fish and chips first."

"We all know a fish and chip supper is one of your *favourite things*!" added Alice. "Get it?"

Jules was flummoxed. She knew she'd made it clear there were to be no strippers or suggestive outfits, but they were really going to eat fish and chips while dressed as nuns? No wonder Mo's blood pressure was through the roof. She must have been fuming at the loss of a wild hen night.

"Come on, Ju Ju, let's get you dressed," Linda said manhandling her daughter into a habit.

"Ouch! Mum! I'm not double jointed!" Jules yelped. "And I'm old enough to dress myself!"

"Because you're not *Sixteen Going On Seventeen*," said Linda, winking. "It's a clue, love! What could we be doing tonight?"

"We won't be *climbing every mountain,* but we will be driving across Bodmin," giggled Sheila.

"Come on, you must get it!" said Issie, who still somehow managed to make a nun's outfit look wildly inappropriate. (Jules was sure the sisters at the nearby abbey didn't wear their habits off shoulder and weren't wimples meant to cover the hair?) "We're nuns. We're singing." She took a breath and belted out, *"Polwenna is alive, with the sound of music!"*

Jules smiled as the penny dropped. "We're watching the *Sound of Music!*"

"Why would you think that? I always go out like this," deadpanned Sheila before she started to laugh. "Yes, tonight's activity is Sing along *Sound of Music* at St Crella's Cinema! Won't that be fun? An activity we can all enjoy and totally suitable for a lady of the cloth. I won't tell you what Morwenna was suggesting, Jules, but suffice to say you're lucky I'm in charge!"

"I don't doubt it for a moment," Jules said. "It's a brilliant idea, Sheila. I love musicals!"

She had to admit this really was a great idea. St Crella was a pretty town on the north coast, about an hour's drive across Bodmin Moor from Polwenna Bay and famed for its arts scene. The small 1920s cinema, once the jewel in the crown of the High Street had been renovated by a local group and turned into an arts centre which regularly held theme nights screening popular films. Jules and Danny had gone there to watch Grease a few months ago.

"I think I'm lucky to have you organise this for me," Jules told Sheila, kissing her cheek. "And I love *The Sound of Music.* Thank you!"

Sheila turned pink. "My pleasure, Jules. Thank you for trusting me."

"I didn't know you were a fan of *The Sound of Music* until Sheila organised this," Tess said to Jules a little later on as the mini bus rolled through the dark, headlights sweeping over the road ahead and slicing into the night. As Sheila drove them across Bodmin Moor a heavy frost fell and the road ahead sparkled in the headlamps as though it was made of magic. Ponies shivered against hedges, tors loomed dark and ominous against the starry sky and every now and then they rattled over a cattle grid with such ferocity that the whole bus shook. The intensity of the darkness was something else this far away from civilisation and the lights of distant villages became twinkling constellations in a faraway galaxy.

"I'm not really but it's a nice idea and best of all it can't get us into any trouble. I'll only say this to you, but I'm actually relieved Mo isn't in charge." Jules confessed.

"She was determined we were going clubbing. This is far too tame for her," Tess said.

"Heaven help me if Jake and I ever tie the knot," sighed Summer who was sitting behind them. "Mo and I promised we'd be each other's bridesmaids when we were about six so there's no escape for me."

"Nope," agreed Issie. "Strippers and rude word bingo for you! Seriously, Jules, you are missing out. This is so tame!"

"Well, I couldn't be happier," said Jules firmly. "The tamer the better as far as I'm concerned. This hen night is exactly what I want. No drama. No scandal. And absolutely nothing inappropriate. I can't wait!"

As far as hen nights went this might be low key but it was great fun. The hens sang and chatted all the way to St Crella and piled into the *Happy Plaice* for mounds of golden chips and crispy battered slabs of cod. They attracted a few odd looks from the other customers, which was fair enough since they were dressed as nuns, and when the man serving attempted to waive their bill Jules realised they must look very convincing.

Sheila pressed a fifty into his hand. "If you do that for everyone who's here for the show you won't make any money."

"Show?"

"At the cinema," Issie explained. "We're not real nuns."

"There must be loads of us dressed up tonight," added Tess.

The chip shop man frowned

"You're the first I've seen. Lots of others though and I can't say I approve. I didn't even know there were nuns in it but it's not really my thing, you see. Lots of people here were a bit funny about them showing it but you can't tell the arty crowd." He rang through the money and handed Sheila the change. "Each to their own, I say."

"I wonder why that man didn't approve of *The Sound of Music?*" mused Alice as she and Jules strolled along the promenade listening to metronomic Atlantic rollers pounding the sand with relentless determination. It was bitterly cold away from the fryers and a samurai wind was blowing in from the Atlantic but good company, full tummies and more mulled wine courtesy of thermos flasks, was keeping the chill away long enough to enjoy the festive lights.

"No idea. Maybe the Nazis in it?" Jules suggested, equally bemused. He'd seemed almost offended.

Alice shook her head. "Everyone knows they're the bad guys. I've always thought it's a very moral tale."

"I shouldn't worry too much, Alice. Maybe he was getting confused with something else? They have all kinds of shows here."

"Maybe," said Alice doubtfully. "I still think it's odd though."

By seven o'clock the hens threaded their way through St Crella towards the elegant old cinema. At first Jules didn't really pay too much attention the other cinema goers who began to fill the streets. The queue snaked around the corner of the building and away from the sea front. As they joined it, Jules was surprised not to see any other nuns. She was even more surprised to see lots of people dressed up in all kinds of bright costumes including several men in suspenders, stockings and sky-high stilettos. Which character was this meant to be? And who were the couple in front dressed as? Did anyone in *The Sound of Music* wear a lab coat or a French maid's outfit? Other people were swaddled in winter coats but sported rubber gloves or brandished water pistols, none of which Jules ever recalled featuring in the original movie. Lonely goatherds, Edelweiss and raindrops on roses maybe. Corsets, red lipstick and fishnet tights? Not so much.

"Look!" She hissed to her mother as a buff young man sporting not much more than a pair of Speedos and a blonde wig joined the queue. "See him?"

"Oh yes! Yummy! You are enjoying your last few days of freedom!" giggled Linda.

"He's almost naked. The boy will freeze." Alice, wearing a duffle coat and a gilet over her nun's habit, was instantly worried. "He needs to wrap up!"

"Never mind that!" Jules said, alarmed. "His costume's got nothing to do with the *Sound of Music*."

"Who cares?" said Issie.

Jules cared. She glanced about her frantically. "Do you see any other nuns? Do you?"

Alice and Linda looked up and down the street. Apart from their own party, straggled out in black and white and looking rather dull, everyone was else was lip-sticked, glammed up and not looking like they were off to see the *Sound of Music* at all. This bunch looked much more suited to watch something like the —

Oh no. Please no.

Surely not?

She turned to the young man in the tight pants. Look at his face. Look at his face. Not his – oh drat!

Cheeks flaming, Jules dragged her eyes back up.

"Great costume," she squeaked.

"Thanks! I like yours too. I've seen a nun costume at this before but there's loads here tonight. Anything goes though, eh?" He waved a goose bumpy arm in the direction of the hens. "Or have you recycled your costumes from last week?"

"Last week?" Jules felt a flutter of nerves in the pit of her tummy.

"Yep, for *The Sound of Music*."

"So that's not tonight?" But Jules already knew the answer.

Of course it wasn't. Mo, if she was here, would be laughing her curly red head off.

The young man was certainly laughing.

"Can you recall any men dressed in stilettos and fishnets in *The Sound of Music?*" he laughed, shaking his head at the notion. "My nan would pop! But, then again, she wouldn't dream of coming to watch *The Rocky Horror Show!*"

Chapter 10

Tuesday 22nd December

Several hours later, everyone spilled out of the theatre door into the cold night, laughing and breathlessly chatting and some singing snatches of songs. The streets, usually empty at this late hour, filled with people dressed in costumes which had appeared odd at the start of the evening but were now familiar and no more shocking than nuns' habits or lederhosen. As the hens walked back to the mini bus, Jules hummed *The Time Warp* and smiled. Who would ever have thought what had seemed to be such a disaster would end up being such good fun? She hadn't seen the Rocky Horror Show since she was a teenager and although it wouldn't have been her first choice of activity Jules really had enjoyed herself. It was cheeky and silly which was what hen nights were all about.

Sheila had been mortified when she realised her mistake and when the box office staff confirmed she had indeed ordered fourteen tickets for collection for this evening's feature – which most definitely was not *The Sound of Music* – she was nearly in tears.

"I'm so sorry. I was listening to *The Archers* while I was on hold and when the theatre answered I was so engrossed in what Eddie Grundy was saying to Shula I didn't pay close enough attention," she admitted, close to tears. "I've ruined your hen night."

"Of course you haven't," said Jules, giving her a hug. "This is a night I'll never, ever forget!"

Two men tottered past in basques and fishnets and Sheila wailed.

"For all the wrong reasons!"

"For all the right ones, I'd have said," Issie grinned as the young man in his underpants sauntered by, deep in conversation with a girl wearing a lab coat and suspenders.

"Come on, Sheila! Where's your sense of adventure? We've got tickets so let's go and enjoy the film!" urged Karenza Pollard.

"It's just a bit of fun," said Kat. "In fact it's pretty tame these days. You see far worse outfits on Towie!"

But Sheila pressed her hand against her chest and was hyperventilating.

"Jules is a *vicar*!"

"I'm also a girl out on her hen night," Jules told her. "And anyway, I've seen this show before. Twice, actually."

Sheila was stunned. "Really?"

"Yes, really. I wasn't always a vicar!" said Jules. Sometimes people acted as though she'd been born wearing a dog collar.

"We need to make a decision," Tess said, slipping seamlessly into teacher mode. "Shall we divide up? I'll go in with those who want to watch the film and you head to the pub with the others?"

Some of the hens were edging towards the auditorium and others were excited, if a little confused. Jules supposed she could go for a quiet drink with Sheila and Alice and meet the rest afterwards. The thought of sitting by the fire in one of the low beamed pubs in the back streets, sipping a large Baileys and chatting quietly was very appealing. It was just the kind of evening she'd had in mind.

"I think we should go on in," announced Alice St Milton to Jules's great surprise.

"Are you sure?" Tess said.

"It might not be your thing, Granny," warned Issie.

"I'm not so old that I don't appreciate a bit of daft fun," Alice told her sharply. "And I want to let my hair down!"

"But what if someone complains about us to the PCC?" worried Sheila.

"Who's going to complain? You're here!" said Karenza Pollard, which was a fair point since Sheila was usually the first to moan.

"Since you're the one who booked the show technically it's your fault and you they would complain about," Ella St Milton pointed out coolly. "So who's going to complain? Anyone here?"

There was much head shaking. Silver Starr and Karenza Pollard were already edging to the auditorium door.

"What happens on the hen night stays on the hen night," said Ella and everyone nodded.

"It also gives you a great hold over Sheila!" Issie whispered to Jules.

Jules had to admit this was a tempting notion. Sheila often caused trouble for her by complaining to the bishop if she felt things weren't done quite by the book. Organising a trip to see *The Rocky Horror Show*, and commandeering the Church minibus to do so, would certainly take some explaining!

"So that's agreed," said Alice. She linked arms with Jules and raised her chin. "Let's take our seats and see this show. It's time to have some fun."

And so they had and before long even Sheila relaxed and had a whale of a time, dancing and calling out the responses and behaving like the carefree teenager Jules suspected she had never been. All in all the show was a lot of fun and Jules now wondered why she'd ever had misgivings about the evening. Talk about worrying over nothing! The mix up was already a funny tale to look back on and she felt quite sad the night was almost over.

As the hens settled into their seats and Sheila started the mini-bus, Jules thanked her Boss that everyone was safely back on board in one piece. Nobody was horribly drunk or crying or had done anything daft. All in all it had been a great success. In an hour's time they'd be back in Polwenna Bay and calling goodnight to one another before walking home through the sleeping village.

The mini-bus wiggled its way through the town and before long was climbing away from the sea and gobbling up the miles of road which stretched between the lights of St Crella and the thick darkness of Bodmin Moor. Issie, making the most of the smooth B road before they rattled over the cattle grid and onto the moor, was busy sloshing champagne into plastic cups and passing them around to the hens.

"Let's play a game!" she cried once everyone except Sheila was holding a drink. "It's called *If you had to!*"

Tess, squashed next to Jules in the front seat, pulled a face. "Here we go. I thought it was too good to be true!"

"I don't think I know that game," said Karenza Pollard with a frown. "Is it hard?"

"Only if you haven't had enough to drink," Issie replied. "It goes like this: *if you had to and your life depended on it, out of every man you know - who would you choose?*"

"Who would you choose for what?" asked Alice.

Issie rolled her blue eyes. "Granny! Come on! You know. Who would you choose if you *had to?*"

"I heard you the first time, dear. I might be old, but my ears still work. Who would I choose to do what exactly?"

"You know. *That!*" Issie nudged her grandmother and winked. "If you *had to* and your life depended on it? Who would you choose?"

"Do you mean sex, love?" Alice said kindly. "Goodness, you are coy, Issie. You wouldn't be if you'd lived through the sixties. Well that's easy to answer. Jonny of course."

"You can't choose your own partner! That's cheating! It has to be somebody else."

"Why? And also, why does my life depend on it? What's happened? Is it the apocalypse? At my age it's not as though I can repopulate the planet, is it? What's the urgency?"

"I don't know, Granny! It's just the rules!" Issie said. "You're ruining it!"

"If I have to sleep with a man who isn't my husband, and my life depends upon it I think I need to know the reasons why," Alice said sternly. "That's a terribly serious thing to ask."

"It's hypothetical!" Issie was in despair. "It's a game!"

"And a very silly one," Alice tutted. "But all right, if you insist. I chose George Clooney!"

"You can't choose him! You don't know him!"

"I might if it's hypothetical," Alice said. "We could have met in a hypothetical situation? Or maybe Harrison Ford? He's nearer my age. Can I choose more than one? I know, since it's about saving the planet, what about David Attenborough?"

Jules caught Tess's eye and they both burst into gales of laughter. Alice knew how to stop Issie in her tracks, that was for sure, and the daft hen night game was neatly shelved.

"I need Mo," wailed Issie. "She knows how to play this."

"Can I choose your Luke, Issie?" Karenza Pollard wondered, sounding wistful. "He's a right hunk! Not that my Rog isn't, of course, but a change is as good as a rest, isn't that what they say?"

"We can't choose men linked to any of us," Issie said quickly. "That's against the rules."

"Well, that limits us. It's not as though we have a huge choice in Polwenna. I'm out," said Ella.

"Count me out too," said Summer.

"If you need inspiration, girls, my ex-husband has it all going on! I put up with a lot because of *that*!" cried Linda, fanning her face.

Jules clapped her hands over her ears. "Mum! No! Gross!"

"It's all true only don't tell him I said so! He'll be even more big-headed," giggled Linda who had clearly drunk more than her fair share of the bubbles. "And my David would not be happy!"

"What happens on the hen night stays on the hen night," declared Sheila, clinging to this mantra just as tightly as she was clinging to the steering wheel now the mini-bus had rumbled over the cattle grid and was bumping along the single-track moorland road.

"I'll have Chris Packham," said Silver dreamily. "He could move here, and we could set up a tree planting community."

"Brad Pitt for me!"

"Tatum Channing!"

"I give up," Issie said, knocking back her drink. "You lot are hopeless!"

As the champagne flowed and the conversation turned to celebrities the hens may or may not choose to favour if the fate of humanity depended upon it, Jules focused her attention on the dark road peeling away in front of them. The headlights threw white swords into the blackness, illuminating pot holes and piles of dung. Ahead was a sharp right-hand bend, just past an outcrop of rocks and where the ice glinted in the beam of the headlamps. Sheila slowed for the bend and the rocks flared with light for a few seconds before something moved across them and straight into the path of the minibus.

"Watch out!" Jules cried.

Sheila yanked on the steering wheel, but the vehicle lurched to the left-hand side of the road, hitting the ice and sliding. She braked hard but it was no use; the tyres simply slithered over the ice as the tussocks and boulders on the far side of the narrow road jumped towards the minibus. For an awful moment Jules thought the vehicle was going to slam straight into them but fortunately the road was raised above the moor and as the mini-bus's front wheel spun from the iced tarmac it slipped into a grassy dip.

Jules's drink sloshed all over her lap. Her hands gripped the dashboard so hard the knuckles glowed white through the skin. The hens shrieked, a thermos flask tumbled from a seat and clattered to the front of the mini-bus as the engine stalled. The headlights still poked skinny white fingers into the night and from her vantage point in the front seat Jules saw a sheep loom out of the darkness, its eyes blank discs as they caught the light and its wool a ghostly cloud.

"Is everyone one all right?" Sheila asked, her voice shaky.

"We're fine at the back," Summer called.

"And here," Alice said. As everyone reassured each other they were unhurt, Jules undid her seat belt and turned to Sheila.

"Was it the ice?" she asked.

"Yes, but something ran out in front of the bus," Sheila explained, her voice trembling. "I couldn't help braking. I'm so sorry."

"It's not your fault, Sheila, I saw it too. I'd have done exactly the same thing," Jules said.

"Anyone would brake. It's instinctive," agreed Tess.

"Was it the beast of Bodmin Moor?" Silver joined them; eyes wide as she stared into the night. "It roams these parts. A dread beast with eyes like burning coals and sharp fangs."

"Ooo!" gasped Linda, excited because this would make a great tale with which to regale her friends at the golf club. "Was it the Beast of Bodmin Moor?"

"In a way," Jules said. "It was a sheep."

"Just a sheep? Are you sure?" Silver was unconvinced.

"The thing I saw was white and woolly," Jules told her. "I'm fairly sure that doesn't meet the description of the Beast of Bodmin Moor."

Silver looked disappointed for a moment before remembering she was for animals of all kinds.

"Sheep deserve to live too," she said staunchly. "Well done for missing it, I say."

"No one's hurt either," Alice pointed out. "That's down to you, Sheila."

"Yes, well done for keeping us all safe," Summer said. "It's lethal out here. Good driving."

The others echoed these sentiments and Sheila brightened under their praise.

"I used to come out this way a lot when I was younger," she said. "I know the roads well."

"Can we get going again?" Kat Evans was asking, her pretty face scrunched up with worry. "Only I promised Alex I'd be home by midnight, and I can't call him because there's no signal."

The mobile coverage in Cornwall was notoriously patchy and on the moors often non-existent. Slipping her own phone from her pocket, Jules's heart sank when she saw no network was showing. She really hoped they wouldn't need recovery.

"It's really cold," said Karenza Pollard, blowing on her hands.

"Can we start the engine and get the heater going?" Ella suggested.

There were murmurs of agreement. The temperature in the minibus was dropping by the minute and their breath was starting to cloud the air.

"Let's just check for damage first and make sure it's safe," Tess said, taking charge of the situation. "Jules, could you bring your phone and use the torch?"

Horribly aware that the temperature outside was plummeting, Jules followed her friend into the night to inspect the mini-bus. The sharp air smelt of ice and the stars sprayed across the sky burned with a brightness which made the darkness seem more intense. The ungritted moorland road was like a skating rink and Jules shivered, pulling her coat closer. If anything the forecasters had underestimated how extreme the plunging temperatures would reach. This was not a good night to be stranded in the middle of nowhere.

The mini bus was only just off the road. The front righthand side wheel rested a little lower down in a marshy drainage ditch and when Jules shone her torch down onto the tyre she was pleased to see it wasn't flat and nor was the rim damaged. If Sheila could manage to reverse a little so the wheel was back on the road they should be able to be underway in minutes.

It was a good plan and it was certainly a relief to have the engine started and the heater blowing warm air once again. Unfortunately no matter how many times Sheila tried to reverse, the wheel simply span in the soft earth and was unable to get enough traction to pull the minibus back onto the road. After many fruitless attempts, Sheila slammed her hands onto the steering wheel in frustration.

"It's no good. The ground's too soft."

"Can we push it out?" Jules asked although she already knew the answer; the minibus was far too big and heavy for the hens to move and the earth was too wet. They were well and truly stuck.

"We need pulling out with a four by four," Summer said. "I'd call Dad to bring his Land Rover, but there's no signal."

"Maybe somebody will drive past and fetch help," Jules said hopefully but Sheila shook her head.

"I took a back route. It's quicker but not used often. I think we'll have to go for help. There's a village a couple of miles away, just over that tor. I'll show you the way."

"OK, let's get going," said Tess, already out of her seat. "Are you coming too, Jules?"

Jules nodded feeling glad she hadn't had drunk more than a few glasses of mulled wine. Stomping over the moors on wobbly legs would be hard work.

Leaving the rest of their party in the minibus with the engine running and the lights still on, Jules set off with Sheila and Tess. The further they walked away, the thicker the darkness seemed to become and air so brutally cold that it hurt to inhale. The sky was a heavy swathe of purple black velvet and the Milky Way a curve of glitter as thick and brilliant as any child's Christmas card. Somewhere a fox barked and an owl screeched but otherwise all was silent except their rasping breath and the scrunch of their boots on the road. The dark bulks of dozing moorland ponies loomed out of the night, breath smoking the cold air and their loud snorts of surprise making Jules jump. From the city originally, and latterly Polwenna Bay, she wasn't used to the intensity of a darkness devoid of street lamps. Out here on the moor with the limbs of twisted, leafless trees dark skeletons against the night all was still, the stars blazed like diamonds and she could almost feel the world turning. St Crella, the hen night and civilisation felt as though they were a thousand miles away.

"I think I may have seen this film," Jules remarked as they trudged along the deserted road.

"If we find a manor house belonging to an alien transvestite disguised as a mad scientist, let's not go in," Tess was saying, her long legs powering her ahead while Jules and Sheila scuttled behind like ladies in waiting. Nuns costumes flapped and several times Jules, who wasn't the tallest, caught her foot and almost went flying.

"I'd even welcome that right now," Jules sighed, rubbing her hands together and wondering if she would ever feel warm again.

"I seem to remember there's a hamlet not too far from here," Sheila said, squinting into the night. "I think it's just over the brow of that hill."

Jules ground to a halt, horrified. Hill? That wasn't a hill! It was a mountain!

"You're right." Tess backed this hunch up. "My year six class hiked up here in activities week last summer. There should be some mobile signal too in a bit. It's only a mile if we take the footpath over rather than the road. That's much longer."

"That's steep," Jules gulped.

"It's not so bad." Tess dismissed her fears in the way that only a skinny sporty type could.

"If I can do it, you can. I'm sixty-three you know," Sheila reminded her proudly.

Jules did know and this made her pride prickle – something she'd have to pray about later. If she didn't make it up this hill she'd never be able to live it down.

"We ought to go the long way around. It's best not to leave the road. What if one of us slips and hurts ourselves?" Tess was thinking out loud.

To Jules's great relief Sheila agreed this was a good point and they continued to trudge along the level road, checking their phones every now and then just in case there was a signal. The air crackled with frost and even the gorse seemed to shiver. Jules was just starting to wonder if she was becoming hypothermic when headlights swept over the crest of the hill they were climbing slowly.

"Stop! Stop!"

Arms flailing, Jules stood in the road waving down the approaching car. Moments later a sporty little mini pulled up alongside them. A young man with a bushy black beard, shock of dark hair and warm brown eyes wound down the window.

"Can I help?" he asked as two collies jostled one another to stick their heads out as well. He pushed them away good-humouredly. "Get down, you nosey dogs!"

"Our minibus has broken down about a mile away. It skidded onto some marshy ground and the wheels are spinning too much to get it out," Tess explained. "There's no signal so we couldn't call for help."

She held up her phone to show him and the driver nodded sympathetically.

"No, there wouldn't be out here. You must be frozen, sisters. Hop in. I'll take you back to the convent. I can get the landy and tow your bus back tomorrow."

Convent? Sisters? Jules was baffled for a moment before she remembered that although swaddled in coats and scarves they were wearing fancy dress and Sheila, a little too keen on it for comfort, was still sporting her wimple.

"We're not really nuns! We're on our way back from my hen night," she explained, and the young man laughed.

"I did wonder why you had L plates pinned to the back of your coat!"

"She is a vicar though," Sheila said patting Jules's shoulder proudly. "We thought we were seeing the *Sound of Music*, you see, but it was really *The Rocky Horror Show* but we stayed anyway and then a sheep ran out and we skidded."

He whistled. "Sounds like some evening!"

Sheila beamed at him. "I haven't had so much fun in years."

"I'll probably need therapy for years," sighed Jules. "Anyway, we'd really appreciate it if you could drive us to a place where we can make a call for help."

"I'll do better than that. I'm afraid it's a bit doggy in this car but hop in. My dad's farm is just up the road. The old man's pretty handy with a Land Rover winch and will have you up and running in no time."

Jules didn't need asking twice. Every time she spoke the words tumbled from her cold lips like ice cubes and the car, doggy or not, was nice and warm. Soon Sheila was in the front bucket seat while she and Tess squeezed into the back with a canine hot water bottle on each lap to help thaw them out.

Just up the road turned out to be several more miles over the moor and another along a sunken lane which twisted and turned along the course of a fast-flowing river. As he drove the young man chatted easily, telling them he was called Tim and ran the family farm with his widowed father, while Sheila talked nonstop about their evening's adventures.

"It's not an easy life," he admitted when Sheila paused to draw breath and Tess swiftly asked if he enjoyed his work, "but I think farming's in your blood and there's nothing else I've ever wanted to do. Our farm's been in the family for generations – although maybe if you ask me again when it's blowing a gale and I'm soaked through? I might wish I was in an office then! I hope my little lad will take over one day when I'm too old to carry on."

"Like you have for your dad?" Jules asked but Tim laughed.

"You haven't met my dad! He's not one to give up easily. He's still running the place and I'm not sure what it's going to take to persuade him to let me take charge!"

Finally, and when Jules had lost all bearings, the mini swung between two weather stone pillars, clanged over a cattle grid and bounced up a rutted drive. A large farmhouse wearing a hipster beard of bushy ivy waited at the far end and. Although it was only days away from Christmas as Tim parked up in the cobbled courtyard beside a mud splattered Land Rover Defender, Jules was struck by the lack of festive lights and decorations.

"Here we are, Penhallow Farm," Tim declared proudly, jumping out and running around to open the passenger door for Sheila. The collies leapt after him bounding and barking.

The farmhouse door swung open. A broad-shouldered figure was framed against the light.

"There's Dad!"

Tim waved at him. The figure waved back and whistled to the dogs who bounded to his side.

"Dad! We have visitors in dire need of your towing skills," Tim called.

"I'll get my boots on," his father called back. "Have they skidded on the ice?"

"Is your dad psychic?" asked Tess.

Tim laughed. "No, this happens a lot up on the moor. Dad's quite the expert on pulling cars out of ditches. He's normally the hero of the hour! Come and meet him."

He held the car door expectantly, but Sheila's backside appeared glued to the seat as she stared, ashen faced and saucer-eyed, at the farm house. Now Jules came to think of it, she hadn't uttered a word since they'd turned from the moorland road into the sunken lane. Was she ill? Hypothermic?

Alarmed, Jules leaned forward and laid a hand on the older woman's shoulder.

"Are you all right, Sheila? Are you feeling ill?"

But Sheila didn't reply. She seemed in another world altogether and her whole body was shaking.

Tess flipped the driver's seat forward and slid out.

"Maybe she's cold?" she offered doubtfully as she peered in at Sheila.

This explanation seemed highly unlikely since Tim had cranked the heating up all the way and his dogs pumped out enough hot breath to heat the whole nave at St Wenn's.

"I'll put the kettle on. Tea will warm her up," said Tim.

"Perhaps it's shock from the skid?" worried Tess.

"Maybe she needs a brandy? Dad has some," said Tim.

Sheila was shaking like a leaf in an autumn gale and her face was pale. Jules was worried. Had tonight been too much for her strait-laced friend? Yet Sheila had appeared to be having so much fun, she'd sung and danced and given every indication of having a marvellous time.

"She can't seem to get out of the seat." Jules gave Sheila a little shove but to no avail.

"Come on," Tess urged, taking Sheila's arm and trying to pull her from the Mini. "You need to come inside and warm up. We'll fetch some sweet tea."

"Or something stronger if you like?" Tim offered kindly.

Sheila shook her head.

"I can't," she whispered. "Please, don't make me. You don't understand. I really can't."

"They might not but I do, ma'am. These youngsters have no idea how it feels to have to haul yourself out of a car, but they'll find out soon enough it comes to all of us." Tim's father, a tall man with a thatch of white hair and gentle, lined face, was sympathetic to the new arrival's plight.

"Allow me to assist," he said gently, slowly bending down and reaching in to help haul Sheila out of the bucket seat. From her back-seat perch Jules saw his lined eyes widen when he caught sight of this passenger and all of a sudden she understood exactly why Sheila hadn't been able to leave the car.

She wasn't ill or shocked or wedged in a low-slung seat.

She was totally and utterly terrified.

"Sheila!" Tim's father took her hands, clasping them tightly in his as though afraid she might float away, and stared at her in wonder. "I can't believe it! It's really you! After all these years you're back at last!"

Chapter 11

Tuesday 22nd December

"Do you two know each other?"

Tim looked from his father to Sheila, puzzled.

"We certainly do," Mike said, easing Sheila from the passenger seat as though she was made of spun glass. "We were friends a long time ago, way before you were born, son. Back in the dinosaur days."

"Speak for yourself," said Sheila. Her voice sounded all breathy and funny, a bit as though Marilyn Monroe was playing a sixty-something church warden and her face was no longer pale but flushed.

Jules glanced at Tess who raised her eyebrows. It was clear from Sheila's shock, and from Mike's warm welcome, he and Sheila had been far more than friends. No matter how much time had passed some memories would remain as fresh as the moorland wind. Suddenly, Jules remembered the sad tale of Sheila's lost love and the pieces fell into position. Hadn't Alice said all the local lads had their noses put out of joint because her fiancé wasn't from Polwenna but Bodmin way?

Bodmin Moor way? Was it possible this elderly farmer was Sheila's long-lost fiancé?

"We haven't seen each other in what? Forty years?" Sheila was still breathless and although she was safely out of the car, Mike still held her elbow as he escorted her across the icy farmyard to the house. He seemed to be in no rush to release her.

"You haven't changed a bit," he told her gallantly.

Jules waited for Mike to be knocked back with one of her verger's usual scathing replies or stern rebuttals, but Sheila sighed heavily.

"I think we both know that isn't true."

"So I'm a little greyer and I've got a few more wrinkles than the last time you saw me? I'm still twenty-one inside, you know, and you'll always be that age to me."

"You too," Sheila said quietly. "Oh, you too."

These softly spoken words were so heartfelt and the expression on her face so tender that Jules's eyes prickled.

"You two really know each other?" asked Tess incredulously. "What's the chance of that?"

Slim, Jules thought, and yet maybe not? Events seemed to be conspiring in a very odd way this evening…

"Oh it was a long time ago now, before Sheila became a nun, but yes, we did once - although Sheila's probably forgotten all about it," Mike told her. "We were even younger than you, maid. She'll have had hundreds of suitors since!"

Sheila's salt and pepper head pinged up as though on elastic.

"Don't be so ridiculous! I'm not a nun, and of course I haven't forgotten!"

"I was joking," he said, gently. "You always were so easy to wind up, She!"

"And you were always a great one to tease, Michael Penhayes!" Sheila shot back huffily. "You haven't changed a bit, have you?"

He twinkled at her, delighted by this response.

"What did I tell you? Of course I haven't! Come on, let's get you inside and warmed up. Then I can show you I still know how to drive a Land Rover."

Nobody needed asking twice. The temperature had dropped even further, and a storm was blowing up. According to Mike, snow was forecast up country and Jules hoped it wouldn't drift west and maroon her friends. Neil was also due to drive back from Mull and snowfall would make his journey hazardous. Romantic as the notion of a white wedding set during a white Christmas was, she really could do without it.

Once they had retreated from the cold to the toasty farmhouse kitchen, the only warm room in the whole place according to Tim, Mike settled Sheila into the armchair by the gurgling Aga, quickly whipping some socks and pants off the rail first, while Tim filled the kettle and the dogs squabbled over a bowl of kibble, nosing it over the flagstones with a clatter. Mike fetched a knitted blanket from the sitting room which he draped over Sheila's knees before pouring a glass of brandy which he pressed into her hand.

"For the shock."

"It wasn't a big skid," Sheila said, and he laughed.

"I wasn't taking about the ice! I was referring to the shock of seeing me again after all this time. I'd have a drink myself except I'll need a clear head to tow your bus out of the marsh."

Sheila sipped the drink without a single protest, which was even more unusual, while Mike glugged more brandy into glasses for Jules and Tess.

"Mind if I make a call?" Tess asked Tim. "I think I need to let my partner know we're going to be late. People will be getting worried."

"I'm afraid there's not much signal here but you're welcome to use the house phone," Mike told her. "It's a dreadful relic, I'm afraid, and tethered to the wall in the hall."

"I'm always telling him to get a cordless," Tim sighed, sloshing strong brown tea into mugs and sliding them across the table. "Or one of those carelines round his neck, but will he listen? Will he, heck!"

Mike's outraged face folded into a scowl, skin creasing like laundry.

"I'm not quite there yet, son!"

"You say that, Dad, but how will I know if anything happens to you now Mum's not about to keep an eye?"

Mike shrugged. "The dogs would howl the place down when they didn't get fed. Anyway, you'd look for me when I didn't turn up for milking."

"That's great! And who's going to help me here when you're in hospital with a broken hip? Oliver? I know he's only a baby, but he'd be all the help I could find."

This was clearly a well-worn argument running along familiar tracks and they bickered amiably for a minute or two before Tim shook his head.

"I give up!" he said, spreading his hands in exasperation. "Come and make your call, Tess, but bring the hot drink with you or you'll turn into an ice pop. I'll fetch some ropes and start the Landy up and we can get going."

Tess went to make her call while Jules drank her tea and listened to the whistle of wind sweeping down from the moors and around the old house. Sheila looked down at her drink, uncharacteristically quiet, while Mike stared at her and shook his head disbelievingly. Had she sat as this table before, Jules wondered, in another life time when she was twenty, and pretty and the future stretched before her like a path of untrodden snow? Did the smell of dog and woodsmoke and damp mingle with the heartbeat of the clock and the shift and sigh of the old building to become a portal transporting her back in time? It certainly felt as though the atmosphere was swelling and crackling and Jules felt certain if she wasn't present Mike and Sheila would have been deep in conversation.

Goodness. Jules would have never imagined a situation where she felt like a gooseberry around Sheila Keverne and a man. Life really was full of fascinating twists and turns!

"I expect you're wondering how we know each other?" Mike said finally.

"Well, yes. I am rather curious," Jules admitted. She thought it best not to mention that Alice had told her a little of the sad story. Sheila was very private and although Alice was well-meaning, she might take exception to having her personal life discussed.

"Do you want to tell the story or shall I?" Mike asked Sheila.

Sheila glanced up and their eyes met in the way the eyes of couples who know one another well always meet, which all the shared memories and short cut codes of gestures and habits that exist between them. Jules loved sharing this with Danny. He could tell what she was asking just from a fleeting look, be it needing rescuing from an overbearing parishioner or requiring another biscuit from the tin. This was the language spoken by people who knew each other well.

It was the language of long-established lovers.

"You don't need to explain anything," she said quickly.

There was a tiny hesitation before Sheila exhaled.

"Mike and I were courting once. A long time ago."

"Come on, Sheila, don't be shy," Mike said, and Jules noticed he was dangerously bright eyed. Were those tears? "We were a bit past *courting*, weren't we?"

Sheila's answering smile made Jules's heart ache. It was a sad one, speaking of missed chances, regrets and echoed with the pain of long-ago partings.

"Very well. It's not a secret, Jules, and just ancient history to young folk but Mike and I were engaged to be married. I expect that surprises you? I wasn't always an interfering old biddy."

Jules flushed. "Nobody thinks that."

"Thou shalt not lie, remember?" said Sheila, her twitching lips telling Jules she could tease as just as well as Mike. "I once had a fiancé and I thought my life was all mapped out. I was set to settle down and be a farmer's wife. Me, can you believe? It seems impossible now."

"Life doesn't always happen quite the way we think it will. I think tonight proves that in all kinds of ways," Jules said thoughtfully.

"You're right," Mike agreed. "It has all kinds of strange twists and turns along the way but what an amazing ride. It beats Alton Towers!"

Jules had never been a theme park kind of girl. She felt queasy watching a merry go round. Call her boring, but she would have liked life to proceed on an even keel - even just for a few hours.

"Anyway a few months before the wedding, my father became ill and I began to realise I couldn't possibly leave my parents to marry Mike and move to the farm," Sheila continued, swirling her brandy as though she could see in its dark depths the girl she had been and the life she might have led. "Of course there was no way he could leave the farm and move to Polwenna, so we called the wedding off. We both knew our duty was to care for our parents."

"I expect this sounds strange to you, doesn't it?" Mike said to Jules.

"I know it was a different time," Jules said carefully. Alice had once told her a similar story about why she and Jonny hadn't been able to marry when they were young. They'd finally got there at almost eighty years old which was quite a wait by anyone's standard.

"We were raised to do our duty back in those days," Sheila explained, "and even if it was painful we loved our parents and wanted to do what was right."

Jules understood. Refereeing Linda and Alistair wasn't really that far removed from Sheila's sense of obligation and responsibility. The reality was both her mother and her father deserved an almighty telling off for their behaviour but because they were her parents and she loved them dearly, Jules would move Heaven and Earth to make them happy.

"It must have been hard to make that choice," Jules said.

"It really was," Sheila agreed. "But what else could I do? I didn't drive back then, not many women did you know, and there was only me to look after my parents. I couldn't leave them."

"And there was only me to take care of the farm so that was it; the decision was made for us and we called the wedding off. There was no acrimony or anger, just a lot of sadness," Mike finished softly. He turned to Sheila and lay his knotted farmer's hand over hers in a tender gesture which almost made Jules weep. "It did get easier. Time passes and life moves on because these things have to, but you never forget and you always wonder what if and how the other person is doing. A few years after Angela died I thought about getting in touch, but I didn't want to upset your life, Sheila. It was all so long ago."

"It was," Sheila agreed. She didn't move her hand away, Jules noticed. "And we were very young."

Mike inclined his head. A silence fell and from the hall Jules could hear Tess's excited voice rise and fall as she explained to Zak what had happened. The kitchen clock ticked, one of the dogs whimpered as a gust of wind rattled the windowpane and the old house seemed to hold his breath.

"That's a really sad story. I'm so sorry," Jules said eventually. Sheila and Mike's story sounded exactly like a plot line from one of her favourite Nicholas Sparks novels. Lovers from a past era torn apart by family commitments and duty. Lives unlived. Dreams of family life shattered. Questions unanswered for a lifetime. An emptiness filled with *what if?* Her throat tightened and she wished Danny was beside her. She missed him enough just being away from him tonight and just the thought of being parted from him for a lifetime, as Sheila and Mike had been, felt like a punch straight to her heart.

"It was a difficult time, but it was the right thing to do," Sheila said looking at Mike as she spoke. "I never regretted it. I was heart-broken, of course I was, but I couldn't have married at the expense of my parents' wellbeing. Selfishness is no basis for marriage, is it?"

"Gosh, no," said Jules.

Maybe Sheila ought to be taking the marriage classes at St Wenn's? She seemed to have a lot more insight than most thought Jules, who knew – on paper at least - all about marriage being a symbol of Christ's union with the church. Being unselfish and loving was at the heart of the matter and Jules felt ashamed for having often lazily dismissed her verger as a sour old spinster. This was another thing she'd need to ask her Boss to help her work on. The list was getting longer.

"You have to look at the good that came from it too. If we hadn't called our wedding off I would have never met my Angela and had so many wonderful years with her and raised our boys. Life's a strange thing, cruel sometimes too, but you have to work with the hand you're dealt," Mike said with a gentle smile. "That's what counts in my book."

Jules nodded but she also wondered how Sheila felt about the hand she'd been dealt. Her life hadn't been easy by all accounts and to see her tonight, sitting beside this gentle farmer with the soft voice and wise eyes, was to a catch a glimpse into the life she might have led if circumstances had been kinder. Still, it was odd they had ended up here tonight of all places, and odder still that if Jules hadn't asked Sheila to be her maid of honour they would never have driven this way or broken down. Sheila and Mike might have lived for the rest of their lives only thirty miles apart but never reunited.

Was this her Boss and His mysterious ways again?

"Zak's going to let the others know what's happened. Can you believe they are still in the restaurant? Nobody was at all worried because they hadn't even missed us!" Tess joined them, hands wrapped around the mug of tea and looking distinctly chilly.

Jules slipped from her seat. "We should get going. The girls will be getting worried about us, even if the boys are oblivious."

"Ropes are in the Landy and she's running and warm for you, Dad. I'll follow in the mini." Tim stood in the doorway jingling his keys. "Time to get you ladies back on the road."

The journey to the minibus took less than ten minutes. Tess and Jules jumped in the mini while Sheila rode in the Defender with Mike. Jules couldn't imagine the short journey was nearly long enough to catch up on over forty years, but it was a start.

"So she's Dad's 'one who got away'," Tim said to Jules as the mini bounced along the rutted drive. "Mum always used to tease him about that. What are the odds, eh?"

"It's a strange coincidence," Jules said thoughtfully although she was starting to think it was a great deal more than this.

"Bumping into her has perked him up no end. Christmas is always hard for Dad now Mum's gone. It's been a few years now, but I know he finds it difficult to get into the spirit of things."

Recalling the lack of lights and decorations, Jules now understood why this might be the case.

"It can be a hard time of year. Especially if you're on your own."

"That's what worries me. We're with my wife's family this year. I don't like to think of him alone but Dad's the type who'd rather die than think he was being a nuisance or putting someone out. He'll probably just have a Pot Noodle or something and go to bed early, which makes me really sad. Mum would have hated that. She loved Christmas."

Jules wasn't certain if it was divine inspiration exactly but all of a sudden an idea occurred.

"I'd love to invite him to my wedding as a thank you," she said. "It's on Christmas Eve and there's going to be lots of food, although no Pot Noodles."

"It's a kind offer but we haven't rescued anyone yet!" Tim pointed out.

"I'm not so sure about that," Jules said slowly. In her experience rescue could come when you least expected it and from the most unlikely direction. Often it wasn't even clear quite who was rescuing whom.

He nodded.

"Do you know, I think you could be right. I'm not promising anything, he can be a stubborn old soul, but let me see what I can do."

There was more they could have discussed but the minibus was ahead of them, lights on and engine running, and the hens were spilling out waving and cheering. Alice was bundled into the warmth of the mini while everyone else stood well back as Mike and Tim bustled about with ropes and straps. Mike's prowess with a Land Rover and a tow bar had not been underestimated and within minutes the minibus was free of the marshy dip and back on the road, none the worse for its adventure. The hens clapped and whooped and clambered back on board.

"It was good to see you again," Mike said to Sheila as he helped her back into the minibus.

"You too. Take care," she said, turning the key in the ignition. The engine roared into life and Mike stepped back, ready to slam the door but looking rather unwilling to do so.

What? That was it after forty odd years? No plans to meet again? No heartfelt words? Jules knew she read too many romance novels and watched far too many slushy Christmas movies, but even so! She couldn't let Sheila just drive away like this!

"You've done so much, both of you. You must come to my wedding on Christmas Eve," she blurted.

"That's kind but there's no need, maid," said Mike, sounding touched if a little bemused.

"There's every need! You've saved us from getting frostbite," Jules insisted. "It's at St Wenn's in Polwenna Bay at noon."

"It could be fun, Dad," Tim said. "You've not got much else on."

"I have the cows!" said Mike and his son rolled his eyes.

"I'll take care of them. You go and enjoy the wedding. If you're worried about being a nuisance it'll save me and Annie having to cook for you!"

"Email me! It's vicar@stwennspb.co.uk," Jules shouted over the engine and her cheering friends before the door slammed and the minibus rumbled away into the night. Was it her imagination or did Sheila study the rear-view mirror far longer than usual as they drove away? Jules didn't think so.

And she didn't think she'd ever seen the older woman quite so pink-cheeked and misty-eyed.

"You," Tess told Jules sternly, "are a hopeless romantic."

"Guilty as charged," she agreed. "Anyway, what's wrong with trying to spread a little love and cheer at Christmas time? It's the season of goodwill to all men."

Hopefully peace on earth would follow too, or at the very least peace in the vicarage between Linda and Alistair and amongst the residents of Polwenna Bay. So far Jules had survived parental skirmishes, the power cut at the carol concert and now her hen night. If things happened in threes she was home and dry.

Surely nothing else could go wrong?

As the mini bus crested a hill, and the red lights of the Caradon Communications Mast shone into the night, mobile phones began to ping into life. Hens delved into their bags or reached into coat pockets as calls and texts from their partners came through in a flurry. Jules's own phone vibrated in her pocket and pulling it out she smiled to see a text from Danny.

It would be a *I miss you* or maybe an *Only two days to go!* message, Jules thought as she opened it, because Danny was so sweet and thoughtful like that. Why some of the others were pulling faces and wincing, she had no idea.

But as soon as she opened the message Jules knew exactly why. She could have kicked herself for being too optimistic far too soon.

Got food poisoning. Pls pick up d and v medicine xDx

All the optimism in the world wouldn't help now. This was a job for Imodium!

"Oh my God! Alex is throwing up!" Kat wailed.

"So's Zak!"

"And Symon too. I told him not to eat at a rival establishment, but would he listen?" said Ella.

"And your father, no doubt, Ju Ju. He always made me eat shellfish and gorges on the stuff," shuddered Linda.

"Oh no! Luke's ill as well!" wailed Issie, staring at her phone. "And he says Dad is too!"

On and on it went as the members of stag party toppled like ninepins. Ushers. Groom. Father of the bride. Father of the Groom. All were suffering. Bad mussels, it transpired, were no respecters of forthcoming nuptials.

Jules turned to Sheila, any thoughts of lost love, matchmaking and romance totally forgotten in the race to save the stags from their volcanic stomachs.

"Would you mind making a slight detour, Sheila? I need to find an all-night chemist – and fast!"

Chapter 12

Wednesday 23rd December

The next morning saw Jules at Mariners having coffee with Mo Carstairs who, confined to the sofa and watched over by Ashley, was determined to attend the hen night vicariously by hearing every detail of the previous evening's adventures.

"And you thought *I* couldn't be trusted to organise something suitable!" she said, once she'd recovered from weeping with laughter at the thought of everyone arriving at The Rocky Horror Show by mistake.

"Yes, I take that back. I think even you would have drawn the line at men in fishnets," Jules laughed.

"Don't count on it," said Ashley who was loading up the wood burner. "You haven't heard what she was planning."

"Ignore him. There's nothing wrong with a fit young man taking his clothes off and asking you to squirt cream on his nipples and lick it off. It's all perfectly wholesome," Mo said.

"Cream is bad for you, Red. Cholesterol raises blood pressure," Ashley told her, sitting back on his heels and setting a match to a Firestarter. As flames surged into life and began to lick across the kindling he shut the door with a click.

"I wasn't going to be the one licking it off. I've not got the energy. I feel like I've swallowed a beachball," Mo grumbled, shifting on the sofa. "Jules is the bride. She would have been the one doing the licking."

"See what I mean? The Rocky Horror Show was definitely getting away lightly," Ashley said.

"And talking about getting off lightly, I can't believe you found Sheila's long-lost love. There's a man who had a lucky escape," Mo said with feeling.

"Actually, I don't think that's true. I think she would have been a very different person if things had worked out with him," Jules said quietly. "She gave up a lot to care for her parents."

Jules had been thinking a great deal about this and she was struck by just how easily a quirk of Fate, such as a sick parent, could change a person's life forever. Maybe a patch of black ice followed by an invite to a Christmas wedding could have a similar effect? She really hoped so. Seeing how Sheila had looked at Mike, a look which was certainly returned by the elderly farmer, she thought it was a chance worth taking.

"I'll take your word for it," said Mo doubtfully, tugging her blanket up to her nose and burrowing beneath it. "Brr. It's freezing in here, Ash. Is the heating on?"

"Cranked right up," he assured her. "The weather's exceedingly cold. Apparently there's snow forecast across most of the country. We're getting off lightly here in Cornwall."

Jules wrapped her hands around the thick ceramic mug and enjoyed the warmth. It was so bitter this morning that even Mariners with its underfloor heating, roaring wood burner and state of the art insulation was still chilly. Although bright sunshine poured through the floor to ceiling window and the sea sparkled just as brilliantly as on any summer's day, the world outside was iced with a thick hoar frost which refused to melt.

"And I'm glad you weren't there last night to be stranded up on the moor. That wouldn't have been good in your condition. You need to rest and avoid stress," Ashley was telling Mo as he placed a cushion beneath her feet and tucked in her blanket.

"What a bossy boots. See what I'm up against? Ash is a doctor now, apparently. Richard Penwarren had better move aside," Mo grumbled although she really loved every minute of being fussed over by Ashley.

"I don't think Richard's going to be moving far at all. Not judging from what Tara told me earlier on," Jules sighed. The village doctor was very poorly according to his partner and he wasn't alone. Most of the stags were suffering this morning.

"I've never been so glad I prefer steak to fish, although I am wishing I'd bought shares in Imodium!" Ashley said with feeling.

The stags' civilised meal out, which had seemed such a safe and sensible choice of activity had not ended happily. Across Polwenna Bay many of the village menfolk were in bed clutching their stomachs or dashing to the bathroom and Jules had been kept busy the night before delivering electrolytes and medicines. Luckily her father had been feeling off colour the previous night and plumped for a plain salad otherwise he too would have been in a bad way. Jonny St Milton had also decided he was far too old to party with the lads which was also a blessing because he was a big seafood lover and would have been very unwell. Nick Tremaine, who fished for a living, never touched seafood because he said it felt like eating chocolate when you worked for Cadburys and Jake Tremaine, the best man, had plumped for the steak pie. Perry Tregarrick, due to supply the bouquets and button holes was a vegetarian, as apparently so was Little Roger Pollard nowadays. There were enough key players still fit to keep the wheels of the wedding turning even though it was dreadful to know her poor fiancé and so many of their friends were suffering today.

Earlier on Jules had walked up to Seaspray to check on Danny and his father who were both feeling poorly, via Tess's cottage where Zak was also in bed feeling rough. She'd also delivered some chicken soup to Caspar James, another stag night casualty although quite how *he'd* ended up invited to the meal was a mystery. Jules suspected it was something to do with free food and drink and since there was no such thing as a free lunch then the same was doubly true of a free seafood dinner! Poor Caspar was certainly paying the price for his freeloading ways now.

It was starting to feel as though events were conspiring against her wedding, Jules thought. If only she'd stuck to her guns and insisted on a small do with no fuss. From rowing parents to bus breakdowns to food poisoning. Surely nothing else could go wrong? Could it?

If so, this didn't bear thinking about.

"Will they all be OK for tomorrow?" Mo was asking Ashley.

"I called Doctor Kussell earlier and he says this shouldn't last more than twenty-four hours. They'll feel a bit weak and wobbly but the worst of it will be over by this evening. Don't worry, Jules. The show will go on."

Part of Jules, a part she didn't dare admit to, was quietly hoping the wedding would need to be postponed so she and Danny might make it up to Gretna Green after all. She knew this was dreadfully mean spirited of her. She really needed to buck up. Danny had put a huge amount of effort into his wedding planning.

"While you're here, let's go through tomorrow's arrangements one more time," Mo said, reaching for her notebook and flipping it open. Jules groaned inwardly. They'd been over this a hundred times, but it seemed Danny wasn't the only member of the Tremaine family with a finely tuned sense of military precision.

"This is my cue to head for my office," said Ashley. "I'll leave Isla watching CBeebies in the snug, shall I?"

"She needs to get some fresh air, Ash. She'll get square eyes," Mo said. "Can't you take her for a walk?"

"My love, it's like the North Pole out there. The poor child will freeze."

"Nonsense. She's got a coat and a hat as have you," Mo reminded him. Then her blue eyes narrowed. "You want to work, don't you? You said you'd take Christmas off, Ashley! You promised!"

"It's only a couple of hours tops, Red. I need to check a couple of things before the markets close."

"I'll take Isla for a stroll," Jules said quickly before the Carstairs began one of their famous squabbles. She wracked her brains for a reason. "I was going to ask if I could pinch a bag of straw for the crib scene so I can walk up to the stables with her, if you like?"

"You can take carrots for Toffee." This was a smart move from Ashley who knew anything equine was guaranteed to deflect his wife's attention from what he was up to.

"Good idea." Mo looked much happier. "Penny took Isla up yesterday and she loved it. Thanks, Jules. Help yourself to straw and take as much straw as you need. It's in the far shed, behind the sand school. Penny should have put some salt down, so you won't slip."

"That's settled." Ashley kissed the top of his wife's curly red head and winked at Jules. "Enjoy your walk! Wrap up!"

The air outside was so cold it had felt like a saw against her face when she'd climbed up to Mariners, but it was beautiful day and Jules adored Isla. Besides, a walk would be a good way to take her mind off the fast approaching wedding and it was good to be out of the vicarage and away from Linda and Alistair's sniping.

With Ashley ensconced in his office, Mo turned her attention to finalising the arrangements for the wedding.

"Assuming everyone's up and running again, we're all set for the bridesmaids and parents of the bride to have breakfast at the vicarage. Morgan will arrive at nine to take the photographs of us all getting ready and Perry will bring the flowers over at ten."

Jules wasn't sure she liked the idea of have pictures taken while she got dressed but Mo had insisted this was all part of it. She reached for a biscuit and wondered whether there was such a thing as quadruple Spanxing it?

"Sounds good so far," she said.

"At half eleven your mum and the bridesmaids will meet Neil at the church while you have photographs with Alistair." Mo's head snapped up. "Where is Neil, by the way? Is he back yet?"

"He's due home today. It's a long drive from Mull."

"He does know there's snow forecast across the north?"

"I'm sure he does," Jules said. If he didn't, he would by now. The news was full of the heavy snowfall across the Pennines.

Mo chewed her pencil. "Photos outside the church of the bridesmaids. Then the Pollards will take the bride and her father on a brief tour of the village and, if you make it back in one piece, Morgan will take pictures of you arriving at the church. I must ask them to drive past Ivy's cottage so she can wave to you."

The Pollard cart was to be decorated and taken on a lap of Polwenna Bay. Jules was not one hundred percent convinced it was a good idea, but the Pollards were adamant they wanted to do this and any elderly parishioners who were housebound were looking forward to a glimpse of the bride. Jules would hate to disappoint them and if it meant risking her neck with the Pollards she knew this was a chance she'd have to take.

"Any sign of their turkeys?" Jules asked as Mo scribbled some more notes into her book.

"Nope. It's a mystery. Ash is going nuts. He can't find two more anywhere because all the super markets have been emptied. It looks like we'll be having pizza for Christmas dinner at this rate."

The steep walk uphill to Mo's yard did help to warm her up and Isla, who was chatting away, didn't seem to mind the cold in the slightest. Over the hedges they spotted Mo's horses, rugged up to the ears and wearing hoods like medieval chargers as they clustered around hay bales in groups like mothers gathered at the school gates. There was no sign of Penny at the yard this morning, although the tracks of her van suggested she'd already visited but, unusually, the main gate was padlocked. Undeterred, Jules and Isla clambered over it before slithering across the yard, Isla was having fun cracking the ice on the puddles and Jules doing her best not to slip over and break her leg. The way events were going she wasn't taking any chances.

Spotting Toffee, sporting muddy dreadlocks and standing at the gate in the manner of Oliver Twist holding an empty bowl, Isla's mittened hand slipped out of Jules's as she dashed off to pet him. Joining her with a bag of carrot sticks Jules, who'd lost all feeling in her nose, was tempted to crawl under his thick rug to defrost.

"Shall we go and find some straw for baby Jesus's stable?" she asked once Toffee was more carrot than pony. It was time to move or risk becoming an icicle.

"Birdies! Birdies!" Isla demanded, swinging on the gate and giving Jules a determined blue-eyed stare that was pure Mo. "Birdies! My feed birdies!"

Jules was confused. Did Mo have chickens? She hadn't mentioned it.

"We need to get the straw, Sweetie. Can you show me where it is?"

"No!" said Isla. "Birdies! My want to see birdies!"

She launched herself from the gate and into a frozen rut. Ice splintered with a merry crack and muddy water splattered her pink puffer coat. Isla splashed in it happily, spraying Jules's legs and coat, before zooming across the stable yard like a bobble hatted tornado.

"Isla! Come back," she called but the little girl had vanished behind the neat row of loose boxes.

Jules looked down at her sludge speckled jeans. Parenting was harder than it looked.

Calling Isla, who seemed to be unable to hear her hollers, Jules scurried after the little girl, slithering on the ice and almost tumbling several times. So much for Penny salting the yard, she thought as she somehow managed to make it across vertically. This place was like an ice rink. Nobody in their right mind would venture across to the barn. The things she did to decorate St Wenn's!

Isla was at the furthest barn where Mo kept a motley collection of jump wings in need of repair, wheelbarrows with flat tyres and bags of wood shavings. It was a bit of a family joke that she couldn't bear to part with anything even though Ashley could easily afford to replace it. "You never know when it might come in useful," was her favourite refrain and nobody had the heart to point out that in decades of being carefully stored Mo's 'treasure' had yet to find a purpose.

"Birdies!" Isla called as she stretched for the bolt.

But the bolt was too high for her to reach and secured with a padlock and a thick bicycle chain. How odd, Jules thought. Why on earth would Mo lock her junk away? Joining Isla, she rattled it just in case it was loose, but the padlock didn't yield.

It didn't need to. Jules already knew why it was there; the sudden cacophony of squawks, flapping and gobbling which rose up the moment chain bashed had against the door told her all she needed to know.

The mystery of the Great Polwenna Bay Turkey Robbery was solved.

"Birdies," Isla said, pointing at the shed. "My birdies!"

"You're right, sweetie," said Jules. "Birdies. About fifteen of them, I should imagine!"

As she stood outside the barn listening to Mr Wattles and Gobble and friends chattering away Jules realised she now had another riddle to solve: how could she put this right and keep everyone happy? Could she suggest that the Lord wanted the turkeys alive? Not really. You could also argue He must want the people of Polwenna Bay to have their Christmas dinners after all if the vicar had found them.

"Oh. Hello, Vicar."

Penny Kussell stood in the doorway of the opposite barn. Two filled hay nets were slung over her shoulder and she set them down on the ground, staggering a little as their weight swung her forwards. Her face was scarlet with a cocktail of guilt and effort.

"Birdies!" whooped Isla, dashing over and flinging her arms around Penny's jodhpur clad knees. "My see birdies!"

"I'm afraid your accomplice has given the game away. These are the Pollards' turkeys, aren't they?" Jules wasn't asking Penny. It couldn't have been more obvious if Mr Wattles had come out of the shed to perform a tap-dancing routine.

Or was this Sparky's talent?

Penny was nodding miserably. "Isla fed them with me yesterday. I didn't think she'd mind."

"I don't think she minds at all. They're a big hit," Jules said kindly. She'd always liked Penny, the girl had a soft heart and diligently toiled away for Mo without ever making demands. Jules was quietly impressed that beneath this mild-mannered and often overlooked façade lurked the genius mastermind of the Turkey Liberation Front - more evidence, as if she needed it, that judging by appearances was never a good idea.

"Am I in trouble?" Penny asked.

"There's a lot of people who are upset about their Christmas dinners," Jules said, "and technically you have stolen their birds since these were all paid for. It's going to take quite a bit of explaining."

"But they're going to be killed!"

There was no denying it.

"Yes," said Jules. "That's generally what happens to turkeys as this time of the year."

Penny's face now turned so pale her freckles stood out like a rash. She looked close to tears.

"What are you going to do, Vicar? Are you going to tell everyone?"

Jules thought for a moment.

"Look, how about I feed them with you while I try to work that out? Isla would really like it."

Penny swallowed. "But what will you do?"

Jules passed the question straight back. "What do you think I ought to do?"

"Tell Mo," whispered Penny. A tear tickled down her cheek and she dashed it away with the back of hand before pulling her hood up as though she wished she could vanish into it. "I'll lose my job, won't I? And Grandad will freak out."

Dr Kussell had been one of the villagers most vociferous about the turkey theft. Jules really felt for Penny. Christmas at their house would be … interesting.

"Let's take things a step at a time," she said gently. "First of all how about Isla feds them?"

Penny nodded and scurried into the feed room followed by Isla while Jules chewed her nails and gave up any hope of being a bride with manicured fingers. What was she to do about this? There was no Biblical precedent she could think of and as much as she felt for Penny, and deep down sympathised with her, she couldn't condone or cover up a crime.

Unless she followed a hunch?

Abandoning gnawing her index finger, Jules pulled out her phone and scrolled through the contacts list to locate Little Rog and fire off a rapid text message.

Get up to the stables now or Mr Wattles will meet the cranberry sauce!

Jules knew it was a low threat to make but the Pollards were notoriously good at ignoring her messages. It was amazing the amount of mobile signal black spots there were in Polwenna when tiles came off roof tops and churchyards needed mowing.

By the time Isla bowled into the yard, proudly bearing a heaped feed scoop of brown pellets, the message was zooming through the ether and Jules was in no doubt the Pollard quad was now hurtling up the lane. Sure enough by the time Penny unlocked the shed the roar of the quad engine echoed across the frozen valley followed by the thud of rigger boots running across the yard.

"Birdies!" beamed Isla as the door swung open and a sea of hungry turkeys surged towards her. "My feed the birdies!"

"Put some on the floor like I showed you and some in the feeder. Remember they can peck," Penny warned but, like her mother, Isla had no fear of animals and was happily fighting her way through the feathered mass loftily tossing pellets at them in the manner of a medieval king distributing pennies to his subjects. Jules was impressed because those beaks looked mean and the turkeys were massive. If they actually made it to Big Rog's customers, fitting them into the ovens of Polwenna Bay would be some challenge.

"I got your message, Vicar!"

Little Rog skidded into the yard, legs shooting out in all directions in his haste to reach them. His fluffy brown hair was standing on end and he appeared even more dishevelled than usual. He must have been half way through a painting job because his face was streaked Apache style and he was still clad in his overalls.

"Careful, Rog!" Penny cried, abandoning the turkey pellets to catch his arm and steady him. They clung to each other, a little longer than was strictly necessary Jules noticed with interest, before Penny released him.

"It's not Penny's fault!" panted Little Rog. "It's all because of me and I can explain everything, Vicar!"

Jules was so used to his father speaking for him it was something of a shock not to have Big Rog here to fill in the gaps. *That's right, my boy* seemed to hang unsaid in the air like a strange linguistic Christmas decoration.

"I'm sure you can," she said sternly and channelling her inner Tess because, no matter what the explanation might be, Little Rog and Penny had stolen these turkeys, "but first of all there's something I need to know."

Little Rog's Adam's apple bobbed nervously. "What's that, Vicar?"

Jules pointed at the turkeys.

"Which one is Mr Wattles, Rog? And can he really count to ten?"

Chapter 13

Wednesday 23rd December

If there was one thing Jules had learned during her time in the ministry, it was that a cup of tea solved a multitude of problems. Once she'd been introduced to each turkey, seen for herself that Mr Wattles could indeed count to ten and let Sparkles sit on her lap, Jules had ushered Little Rog and Penny into the old static caravan which doubled as Mo's staffroom, sat them down and put the kettle on. When they all had a mug of strong tea in front of them she gave Isla her iPhone so the little girl could watch Peppa Pig and leaned against the counter. It was time to find out was actually going on.

"So, who's going to tell me how fifteen Christmas dinners have ended up living in Mo's store?"

"They're not Christmas dinners —" Penny began to protest but Jules held up her hand and cut her off.

"No, Penny. I'm not asking you for a lecture. People bought these turkeys in good faith for their Christmas dinners, turkeys which *mysteriously* vanished when a rather convenient power cut took place at the carol service. Would anyone like to explain that?"

Little Rog and Penny exchanged a guilty look.

"Are we in trouble?" he whispered.

"You will be if you don't tell me what's going on," Jules said.

She waited for an explanation but neither party said a word. Both seemed to find the grubby caravan floor absolutely fascinating. Time for a different tactic.

"Fine. Maybe you'd rather Ashley dealt with this since it's his wife's property you've used to hide stolen goods. Two of the birds are technically his, I believe? Shall I give him a call?"

Their heads snapped up. Both parties looked very worried now and Jules didn't blame them one bit. Ashley Carstairs on the rampage was not a pretty sight.

"It was all my idea," Penny confessed. "I could see how upset Rog was about the turkeys when we were in the pub the other night. It was breaking his heart to know Christmas was coming because they aren't turkeys to him. They were pets. How could I sit back and let his pets be killed just so a few people can stuff their faces?"

"I always wanted a hamster, but Ma doesn't like vermin," Little Rog recalled sadly.

Penny tutted. "She should have let you have one."

Yes, she really should have, thought Jules. It might have saved a whole world of complications twenty years on if Karenza had put up with a hamster. There was no point trying to explain to Penny or Little Rog the turkeys weren't intended to be his surrogate pets or that they'd technically committed a crime. Anyway, now she'd seen Mr Wattles count to ten Jules wasn't sure she could have eaten him either.

"What did you do, Rog?" she asked.

"It wasn't his fault! It was my idea," Penny cried. "Please don't blame him. I said if he gave me the key to the harbour office I'd sort everything out. I knew there was a power switch in there from when the doctors did first aid training with the fishermen. All I had to do was turn off the lights run home to get my van and back it into the Pollards drive while everyone was distracted."

"So I gave her the key," mumbled Little Rog. He looked close to tears. "Pa will skin me alive."

"You were freeing the turkeys. You're a hero," Penny said staunchly, and Little Rog brightened in the glow of her admiration. Jules imagined he'd been called many things in his life and that hero was probably not amongst these.

"It took a few minutes to shoo the turkeys in and by the time the lights came on I was gone. I knew there would be no chance of Big Rog coming home if he thought he had to fix the lights. I'm sorry if it ruined the carol concert, Reverend Mathieson, but the turkeys' lives were at stake," Penny continued. "Anyone would have done the same!"

Jules doubted this but she was impressed by the audacity of the plan and Penny's attention to detail. She wouldn't have thought the quiet girl had it in her to rustle turkeys or divert the attention of the entire village. It went to show you never could tell and when people believed in something they could always take you by surprise.

"Roger had no idea what I was up to for deniable plausibility." Penny looked pleased with this although Jules wasn't convinced Little Rog knew what it meant. "All I had to do was hide the turkeys somewhere safe until Christmas was over. I knew Mo wouldn't be up here for while so it seemed like the perfect hiding place."

"And if it hadn't been for the pesky vicar you would have gotten away with it," finished Jules.

"Eh?" said Penny.

"Scooby Doo! That's what the villain always says at the end," Little Rog cried, delightedly. "When the police pull his mask off. I love that cartoon. You'd like it to, Pen. It's about a dog who solves mysteries."

"That does sound good," nodded Penny.

"We can watch it together, if you like? I've got all the episodes on DVD. I wouldn't bother with the ones with Scrappy Doo, though, because he spoils it."

Back to the turkeys, thought Jules sensing a Pollard tangent coming on.

"Technically it was Isla who gave the game away but that's not the point; you need to put this right," she told them. "People have paid for these turkeys and, whether or not you think they should eat them, it's caused a few headaches and a lot of extra Christmas stress. You are going to need to sort this out."

Little Rog's shoulders slumped.

"Do we really have to take them back?"

Penny crossed her arms defiantly. "It's too late to eat them now, Vicar."

"That's right, Pen, that's right," nodded Little Rog.

"There's nothing you can do now," Penny concluded. She sounded brave but her chin wobbled and her eyes were red. Years of managing Sheila and Co. had taught Jules well and she knew patience was the key here. If Jules insisted they returned the birds, Penny would only dig her heels in. The trick was to make the Christmas dinner snatching pair put things right themselves and in a way that would keep everyone happy.

Even the turkeys...

"That's not the point. You can't hide them here forever. Apart from the fact Isla's not much good at keeping secrets, Big Rog is blaming everyone and that isn't fair. I think it's best he hears it from you two first," Jules said calmly. "I do understand why you've done this, Penny, but unless you explain it soon I think it could cause all kinds of trouble."

"The Rev's right," Little Rog said sadly. "Pa accused Silver of putting a vanishing spell on them this morning. I really hope she can put one on me. He'll be right teasy when he finds out it was me who took them."

Jules thought *teasy* was putting it mildly.

Penny gulped. She knew she had no choice.

"What about Mo and Ashley? They'll be furious. Ashley really wanted to cook those turkeys."

This was true although Jules suspected once he was over the initial irritation, Ashley would find this whole episode rather amusing. She placed her mug in the sink and turned on the tap.

"I think if you explain it all to them exactly as you have to me, Big Rog and Ashley will understand. I'll give you an hour's head start and if you haven't made things right by then I'll have no choice but to tell them."

Little Rog jumped to his feet as though he could already hear the clock counting down.

"Thank you, Vicar. I owe you one."

"Hey! Wait for me! I'm coming too," said Penny.

"You're coming with me?" Little Rog asked, incredulously.

"Of course I am. We're in this together, aren't we?"

Little Rog turned the same colour as Isla's beloved bridesmaid's dress.

"Yes," he said hoarsely. "I suppose we are."

As she stood at the sink, scrubbing the mugs with a cloth of dubious cleanliness, Jules watched Polwenna's answer to Bonny and Clyde hurry to the quad bike. For somebody who had upset most of his neighbours, almost ruined the village carol service, wrecked Christmas dinner, and was about to have the biggest ever telling off from his father, Little Roger Pollard was looking very happy indeed and when Penny reached out to take his hand and squeeze it, Jules's heart lifted.

Aha! Those mysterious ways again!

"Tell me I'm not dreaming? You really found the Pollards' turkeys up at Mo's? If I've made that up, I'm in a worse state than I thought," Danny pleaded later on when Jules visited his sick room.

Her fiancé was still an odd shade of green and had been tucked up in bed with a hot water bottle. Summer, in role as nurse, had spent the whole morning running backwards and forwards between him and Jimmy while also doing her best to finish putting the wedding favours together, something she said wasn't easy to do when your fingers were half frozen and draughts insisted on blowing carefully arranged mounds of dried flowers away.

Jules sat at Dan's bedside listening to Seaspray's ancient radiators gurgle and splutter as they valiantly fought to combat the extreme weather conditions. The latest forecasts across the country showed snow was falling further north while the south-west was plunged in the grip of an unusual arctic blast. Gusts of icy wind pummelled the old house and rattled Big Rog's Christmas lights like a Newton's Cradle. As she looked out of the window Jules saw Eddie Penhalligan bent almost double as he walked along the quay to help Jake close the harbour gates.

"You heard me right. Even J K Rowling couldn't make it up," Jules said, sloshing Lucozade into a glass and passing it over. She was relieved to have found Danny sitting up and, although rather wrung out, on the mend.

Her fiancé shook his blonde head. "Who would have believed it?"

"Me. I saw Penny go into the harbour office. Fact." This comment from Morgan, cross legged on the bedside rug and fiddling intently with his camera, made Danny raise his eyebrows.

"Mate, are you sure? You were with us."

"I didn't say I'd seen her in *person*. My drone filmed it before the lights went off. I saw it on the screen," Morgan said with a weary patience which implied explaining obvious things to dim adults was a monumental bore. Jules guessed it was when you were as bright as Morgan Tremaine.

"You didn't say anything to us," his father said and Morgan shrugged.

"Nobody asked me to. Fact."

Danny groaned. "The spy drone strikes again. We could have saved ourselves a whole lot of bother if you'd told us, son, and we'd have still had a Christmas dinner!"

"Maybe we weren't meant to see her? Perhaps it's all part of a bigger plan?" Jules said thoughtfully as she smoothed the duvet and leaned Dan forward to plump up his pillows.

She had been really struck by this notion of a bigger plan ever since she'd seen Little Rog and Penny holding hands. The more she pondered it all the more the strange events of these past few days seemed to add up to make the sum of something far greater. While she'd walked back to Mariners with Isla, the frozen wind growing fiercer with every passing moment whippin white horses into a stampede across the bay, an email had pinged into her phone. To her surprise it was from Tim accepting her wedding invitation on his father's behalf.

Dad's not said much to me, but he was humming to himself during milking and this morning he said he was cutting down a Christmas tree for the front room. It means a great deal to all of us to see him looking happier. He said he'd love to come to your wedding and to thank you for the invite.

Another happy coincidence which had come from something which looked like a disaster, Jules had thought as she pinged back a quick reply. She may not have wanted a big wedding, but perhaps this wasn't really about her at all?

"If you can find a greater purpose in the groom's party getting food poisoning I'm all ears," Danny groaned, resting his hand on his stomach.

"You're wedding outfit will be nice and loose?" Jules suggested, thinking about her double Spanx plan with growing trepidation. Treble control pants it would be!

"I know! I know! It kept Grandpa Jimmy from getting into trouble before the wedding!" Morgan declared, shooting his hand into the air as though he was in class.

"That's a good point, mate," Danny agreed. "Even your granddad can't get up to mischief if he's feeling this rough."

"You'll be all right for tomorrow though, won't you?" Jules was worried because Danny did look really pale.

He reached for her hand and raised it to his lips, brushing her skin with his warm mouth and sending little shivers of longing rippling across every inch of her body.

"You bet I will, Miss Mathieson. Nothing is stopping me from making it to the church and marrying you tomorrow."

His good eye held hers and Jules knew he was also telling her nothing would keep him from their wedding night either. A lifetime of love was promised in that gaze and a treasure chest filled with sensations and wonders neither of them could wait to unlock.

"Unless you puke again, Dad," pointed out Morgan, ever practical and unmoved with the romance of the tender moment.

"Fair enough. That would rather spoil the day," Danny admitted. He adopted a Scottish accent *"Do you, Danny Tremaine, take this woman to be your lawful wedded wife? I d—* barf!"

"Don't," begged Jules, burying her face in her hands. "It could happen."

"So what? Don't you love me, puke and all? Sickness and in health, isn't that how it goes?"

She pretended to consider this. "I'm not sure. I'll have to think about it!"

Danny pulled a face at Morgan. "See what men are up against, son? Anyway, never mind our wedding. More importantly, what's happening with the turkeys? Did Ash pop a blood vessel? He's been obsessing about Christmas dinner since about June."

Jules laughed at all the questions. "Where shall I start first? The turkeys are still at the stables where I think they'll stay for a bit. As for Ashley, once he was over the initial annoyance he found it very funny there was a turkey rustling ring running from the stable yard. Anyway, as it turns out Isla's obsessed with the birdies and since he already owns two of them Ash says that's her Christmas present sorted."

Danny roared at this before clutching his stomach. "Ouch. It hurts to laugh. Well, it's too late to prep them for dinner now anyway and who wants to eat turkey at any other time of the year? It looks as though the bigger plan has given them a reprieve too!"

Regarding the fate of the other turkeys, Jules could only imagine Little Rog would have some explaining to do followed by some swift financial compensating. Maybe he would keep them and have some pets at long last. Personally Jules thought a hamster might have been easier.

"Hopefully everyone else has sorted out alternatives for Christmas dinner by now," she said.

"We're feeding most of the village on Christmas Eve anyway. I'd be amazed if anyone has room to eat more the next day," Dan reminded her.

This was true. By now Symon Tremaine would have prepped everything. The cake, lovingly baked by Patsy Penhalligan, was already on its stand and all the tables were set. Oh! She must add Mike to the guest list! And was Tim coming too? Jules felt a flutter of alarm. Now she understood why Danny had been so obsessed by the seating. It was a full time job.

"I've invited an extra guest and not told Ella!" she cried.

"Don't look so worried. I won't grass you up. I want you to live long enough to be my wife!" said Danny.

But Jules was plummeting into full panic mode, worrying about tables and seating and portions. Seeing her begin to spiral, Danny beckoned Morgan over.

"Hey mate, could you nip down to the kitchen and get me a piece of dry toast? I think it's time I gave my stomach a test drive. And maybe make a piece for Grandpa too?"

"I know you want to talk about grown up things without me hearing," Morgan said kindly. "I don't want to listen anyway. Fact."

"That boy is way too smart for his own good," Danny said admiringly once Morgan was safely downstairs.

"What did you want to talk about?" Jules asked. She flicked her gaze to the window and realised the light was starting to fade as the sun tugged the day into the white tipped sea. The harbour festive lights jived as the wind gusted spilling primary colours into the water. From the far side of the harbour Mo and Ashley's Christmas tree twinkled cheerily into the gathering dusk and their big window shone like a beacon over the bay.

Danny took her hand and pulled her down beside him on to the bed, drawing Jules close.

"You? Me? Our wedding?" he paused and, catching the note of hesitation in his voice, her heart quailed. He wasn't getting cold feet was he?

"Is everything all right?"

Danny's answer was a kiss so gossamer soft that it wove a spider's web of longing through her and Jules closed her eyes. There were no doubts at all. Tomorrow night couldn't come soon enough.

"Of course it is. I'm about to marry the woman I love," he whispered. "Oh Jules, I hope tomorrow is everything you've ever dreamed your wedding would be. I've done all I can think of to make this the wedding you've always wanted."

Her eyes snapped open. Dream wedding? Wedding she'd always wanted? Where on earth had Danny got these ideas from? Hadn't she always made it clear she'd like a low-key wedding?

"I'm marrying you which is all that's ever mattered to me," Jules said carefully. She wasn't sure what else to say. He'd worked so hard to make their wedding perfect. Surely this wasn't because he thought she'd secretly been hoping for a huge affair? It wouldn't be the first time they'd both got the wrong end the stick in their determination to make sure the other party got what they most desired. The last time this happened they'd almost ended up moving to London each mistakenly believing it was what the other party wanted.

Marriage was all about honesty and Jules had no intention of theirs starting with a misunderstanding. She needed to tell him she'd never wanted a big wedding and make Danny understand the only thing that mattered to her was the man who would stand at her side. Him. Danny Tremaine. The love of her life.

Outside the wind slammed against the house and down below the waves hurled themselves against the harbour gates as though frantic to break through. A massive gust caused a door somewhere downstairs to slam and something smashed. It all felt faintly metaphorical and, hoping she wasn't heading into a different kind of tempest, Jules took a deep breath just the exact second all the lights cut out.

The cosy bedroom plunged into a grey ocean as myriad variations of iron and pewter draped themselves over everything. The floor was awash with slate hued shadows. Sitting bolt upright, Jules realised the lights on the fish market had also been snuffed out and all the houses in the village, from the smallest quayside cottage to Mariners, were in total darkness.

"Great. A power cut. This is all we need," groaned Danny.

"Big Rog's Christmas lights?" Jules asked. It was what Sheila had continually predicted ever since the first humble strand was strung along Fore Street.

"I doubt it. They wouldn't take out the whole village and I don't imagine even Penny's capable of shorting out all of Polwenna to rescue a few more Christmas dinners."

"Maybe it will come back on in a minute?" Jules was hopeful but even in the gathering gloom she could tell the expression on Danny's face wasn't optimistic.

"I doubt it, sweetheart. Maybe it's the substation at the top? Or perhaps the wind's knocked a power line out? That will take an hour or so to fix."

Jules swung her legs over the side of the bed and reached for her bag.

"I'd better get back to the vicarage. Mum will be having a fit now the heating's gone off and if Dad tries to light the fire the whole place will go up in flames."

"That means I won't see you until tomorrow at the church. Stay for some dinner and invite your folks up. We can still cook on the Aga hotplate when the power's off."

"Absolutely not. It's bad luck for the groom to see the bride the night before the wedding," Jules reminded him.

Danny raised his eyebrows. "Isn't that kind of thinking a bit on the superstitious side for a Church of England vicar?"

"After the past few days I'm not risking anything." Jules was adamant about this. "Anyway, I can't leave Mum and Dad alone for much longer. They might murder each other without a referee."

But Danny wasn't interested in Linda and Alistair's skirmishes. He caught her wrist and pulled her back down beside him.

"They'll be too cold to fight," he murmured, rubbing the tip of her cold nose with his in an Eskimo kiss. "So in the meantime, why don't you just stay here a little longer to cheer a poorly patient up?"

Jules snuggled up beside him, melting as Danny pulled her close.

"Maybe I should have been a nurse rather a vicar?" she said. Then Danny kissed her and all thoughts of parents, power cuts and even weddings were totally forgotten.

Chapter 14

Wednesday 23rd December

Evening had crept in like the tide by the time Jules kissed her fiancé farewell for the final time before they'd meet at the altar. Seaspray, heated by the ancient wood fired Aga, was still warm and the candles Summer lit in the kitchen filled the place with leaping light and a sense of Christmas magic. Soup was heating on the hotplate and once she'd taken Danny up a steaming bowl and hunk of bread Jules felt happier that he'd make it to the church the next day.

Outside the old house, Polwenna slumbered beneath a thick blanket of darkness. Jules blinked as her eyes adjusted and for a moment the steep path down through the garden was almost too dark to see. The wind whistled past, whipping her hair against her face, and the thick bushes either side of the path seemed to press forward as though wanting reassurance that the lights would ping on very soon. In the blackness the suck and sigh of the waves seemed louder than normal and her own breath was an intrusive rasp in her ears as though compromising of one sense heightened the others. Even the bones of her feet made their presence felt, turning to shards of ice inside her boots, and her cheeks ached with the bite of the north wind. Jules inched her way down the icy path, her gloves brushing on the handrail as she felt her way and exhaling in relief when she made out the faint outline of the gate.

It was strange how the familiar could become alien so swiftly, thought Jules as she turned towards the village. Just the absence of a few weak streetlights was enough to transform Polwenna Bay into somewhere strange where midnight shadows were plunge pools and a well-known landscape shifted into foreign territory. It felt like falling back through time and it wasn't difficult to imagine smugglers slipping through Polwenna's warren of narrow streets and leading ponies laden with packs of lace and kegs of cognac. Normally December's deep darkness was soothed by the cheery beams of Christmas lights and the twinkle of the harbour tree and it was disorientating to walk home cloaked in darkness. Even the moon and the stars had been snuffed out as though their electricity supply had also been cut off.

"Oh, vicar, what a menace this power cut is! I've got lots of ladies in here having their hair done for the wedding."

Kursa Penwarren stepped out from the door of her salon. From the candles flickering in the window Jules made out the indistinct shapes of several Polwenna residents draped in gowns and with their heads wrapped in thick towelling turbans, shampoos and sets scuppered by the power outage.

"Any idea what's caused it?" Jules asked. The hairdresser's salon was second only to the village shop as a source of information.

"Kathy Polmartin at the shop said it's Big Roger Pollard and his lights again!" Kursa crossed her arms over her ample bosom and bristled with outrage. "Wait until I see him! He'll have the sharp edge of my tongue, all right! I've got my ladies booked in until seven o'clock tonight. Christmas is my busiest time and with a wedding too I'm double busy!"

"I don't think we can blame Roger Pollard this time. It's most likely a power line down in the storm," corrected a familiar bossy voice from beneath a towel headdress. Squinting into the gloom, Jules was surprised to spot Sheila Keverne beneath a drier with her hair set in curlers. Sheila's idea of hair styling was usually to scrape her salt and pepper hair into a bun and stab this with Kirby grips. Jules felt honoured Sheila was making such an effort for her wedding. Or was this sudden interest in hair styling not for the wedding at all but for somebody who would also be attending?

A farmer perhaps? From Bodmin Moor?

Maybe!

"Well, whatever's caused it I hope they fix it soon. The ladies of this village need their hair done," grumbled Kursa. "Ten at the vicarage still good for you tomorrow, Vicar?"

"I think so," Jules said although she didn't really feel this was necessary. Her hair was easy to style. She'd planned to simply pin it up with some flowers before Linda had engaged the services of the local hairdresser.

"Right you are," Kursa said. "Ooo! You must be getting so excited!"

Was she? Jules dredged her emotions and found some nervousness and quite a big chunk of worry but there wasn't a great deal of excitement about the wedding - although she could hardly wait for the marriage to begin. Jules was actually starting to wonder whether she and Danny had been at cross purposes with the whole shebang, but it was a little too late in the day to raise the topic now.

"I will be once the electricity's back on," she hedged.

"I'm sure it won't take long, love," said Kursa, optimistically.

"At least we've not got snow like up country," Sheila pointed out.

Kursa nodded. "It's certainly getting colder, though. I'd better shut the door before we all freeze. See you tomorrow, Jules!"

Jules waved goodbye and continued on her way through the village. The wind funnelled up Fore Street, its cold fists pummelling her back, and seemed to chase her past the bakery and along the edge of the green. The cottage windows were soft with candle light and even though it was splinteringly cold and windy, friends and neighbours chatted on doorsteps and holiday makers battled the elements to walk down to the harbour. The Ship was bound to be stuffed to the gunnels as locals and visitors alike gathered around the roaring log fire to enjoy drink and camaraderie. She was tempted to pop in for half an hour, not least because the vicarage would be freezing, but knowing her parents were bound to be squabbling over the best way to light the wood burner Jules continued on her way. She didn't trust Alistair and Linda not to burn the place down as they competed to win the title of 'most helpful parent'.

The climb up to the vicarage warmed Jules a little and she stopped half way to catch her breath.

"All set for tomorrow, Vicar? We've decorated the quad for you! It's a beauty!"

Big Roger Pollard loomed out of the night, arm in arm with his wife, and trailed by a balaclava wearing Little Rog still in disgrace and possibly, judging by his headgear, also in disguise – or else he'd joined the Cornish wing of the Turkey Liberation Army! Jules thought it was very lucky for Little Rog that the Polwenna residents now had bigger problems to contend with than the whereabouts of their Christmas dinners. Failing this, they wouldn't find him in the liquid darkness.

"How's Danny?" Karenza wanted to know. "On the mend, I hope? What a thing to happen! I hear they've all been dreadfully poorly."

"He's feeling much better, thanks." Shivering, Jules didn't want to stand around but Karenza was keen to chat.

"It's funny all the things that have gone wrong, isn't it? The breakdown, then food poisoning and now this power cut," she chuckled.

"Hilarious," said Jules.

"It's not a power cut, Ma. There's a tree down near the hotel and it's taken a line with it," said Little Rog from inside the depths of his balaclava.

"That's right, my boy," agreed Big Rog before remembering he was still angry with his son. "Not that I'm talking to you, mind. Not after what you've done."

"Oh, leave the boy alone. I'm proud of him for standing up for his principles," said Mrs Pollard.

"You won't be so proud when we're all looking at an empty plate on Christmas Day. Principles don't taste nearly as good with cranberry sauce," warned her husband. "And I've had to pay everyone back too so don't come mithering to me about no presents this year."

"So you own all the turkeys now?" Jules said.

Big Rog grimaced. "Bleddy things."

"What we'll do with them, I don't know Vicar," sighed Karenza.

"Take the money for them out of the boy's wages for a start," said Big Rog.

"Maybe they could go to a petting zoo?"

Jules was joking but Little Rog lit up like his father's Christmas display.

"Emmets love a petting zoo, Pa! They'd pay a fortune to see the turkeys."

"That's right, my boy. That's right," said Big Rog slowly.

"And we could have other animals. Penny knows this lady who wants to re-home a lama and a pig," Little Rog added.

Jules opened her mouth to say she hoped these weren't about the materialise at Mo's yard because Ashley would have a complete sense of humour failure, but it was too late: Big Rog was up and running.

"*Pollards' Polwenna Pets*. It has quite a ring to it."

The ring of tills, Jules thought wryly.

"That was a joke," she said but neither father nor son was listening; they were far too busy planning their next venture.

"Many a true word spoken in jest, Vicar," Big Rog said sagely. "Anyway, can't stand here all night gassing. We're heading to the pub to warm up. It's going to be a while before the electricity board sorts Polwenna Bay. There's trees down all across the south-west. I'll be amazed if it's back in time for Christmas. Dreckly, see?"

"Rubbish! It'll be back on by the morning," Karenza said quickly, catching sight of Jules's horrified expression.

Leaving the Pollards deep in discussions about the future residents of their petting zoo, all fallings outs forgotten in the pursuit of new money-making ideas, Jules continued up Church Lane. The wind was howling in earnest and the sea roared as it flung fistfuls of brine onto the beach. It was a wild night and the wild weather felt Shakespearean. As she unlocked the vicarage door and called a welcome to her parents, Jules hoped Karenza wasn't right. These things did feel rather like signs.

Oh, she was being daft. Of course they weren't! The electricity would soon be back on, the weather would calm down and the wedding would go smoothly. There was nothing to worry about. In the meantime she'd light the wood burner and fetch some blankets so the three of them could keep warm until the power was restored. It was the last evening they'd probably ever spend together as a threesome and it might be nice to sit together and chat – if Linda and Alistair could manage this?

The narrow passageway was dark but a warm orange glow from the far end and the rise and fall of voices revealed the whereabouts of her parents. At least they were talking, Jules thought, which meant they hadn't murdered each other in her absence.

"Ju? Is that you, love?" Linda called.

"We're in the living room," Alistair added.

To her great surprise Jules found her parents hunkered down by the wood burner. They'd dragged the sofa as close to the leaping flames as was possible and burrowed beneath a mound of duvets. A pan of soup was simmering on the top and plates of bread and cheese were balanced on their knees as they enjoyed a makeshift supper. Every single scented candle she possessed was blazing merrily on the mantlepiece and the room smelt delicious as the aromas of cinnamon, tomato soup and Christmas tree mingled together like merry guests at a party.

But best of all there was not a pool of blood or strangled parent in sight.

"Is everything all right?" Jules asked. She felt rather unnerved.

"We're fine, just keeping warm," said Alistair, who was wearing his coat and a stray bobble hat Morgan had left in the porch. "It looks as though the power might be down for a while, so it made sense to pool resources and body heat. Your mother fetched the duvets while I sorted the fire."

"We thought we ought to eat something hot to keep us warm," Linda explained. "So I found the soup and your father buttered up the remains of the loaf. I don't usually eat carbs, but I think this cold might require a few extra calories."

Linda and Alistair had worked together, and Jules was lost for words. This was the Mathieson family's equivalent of a Christmas Day football match in No Man's Land. It was amazing what a power cut and plummeting temperatures could achieve, she thought as she wedged herself next to Alistair while Linda sploshed soup into a mug for her, and maybe, just maybe, those mysterious ways in action again?

After a few hours the soup and bread had been consumed, the room was heated to a toasty warmth and even a few fond stories of Jules's childhood had been told. The soup pan was refilled with mulled wine and after a few generous mugs, her parents began to grow merry and a little nostalgic.

"I can't believe my little baby's about to get married," Linda sighed, dabbing her eyes with her coat sleeve. "It feels like five minutes since we brought her home, doesn't it Ally?"

Ally? Jules was taken aback because Linda hadn't called him this in years. *That git* or *your father* were far more common epithets. How much mulled wine had her mother consumed?

"It really does." Alistair crunched an indigestion tablet and looked wistful. "You were such a little scrap of a thing and I was terrified when I first held you. I thought you might break. I almost passed out with the sheer enormity of becoming a father."

"More like you almost passed out when you had to change her nappy," Linda sniffed but Alistair only laughed at her tart words.

"Oh yes, that was a shock! And the broken nights."

"Boiling terry nappies!"

"Trying to write a thesis while rocking a crying baby!"

"And remember the time she had us worried sick at the hospital and it turned out to only be wind?"

"We must have looked a right pair of idiots!"

They smiled at one another, laughing and shaking their heads as the memories came in a torrent. The howling wind and bitter weather were soon forgotten as Jules listened to tales of her childhood and the early days of her parents' marriage. She'd never heard any of this before because Alistair and Linda were usually far too busy sniping and point scoring to recall anything about their former relationship with fondness. Having a new picture painted of happy family times was the best wedding present either parent could have given Jules because it was clear there had once been so much love between them. This seemed obvious now; such anger could only come from disappointment and broken dreams. It was a lesson to her to always communicate with Danny and to work through the problems and upsets that life would, without doubt, fling their way. As she listened to Linda and Alistair reminiscing, Jules prayed with all her heart that her marriage to Danny would be the start of a new and happy chapter for her family.

"I'm sorry I wasn't there more for you, Linda," Alistair said when his ex-wife came to the end of a story about how she'd tried to clean the porch and got herself stuck when her ladder toppled over. "You had to do so much yourself. It must have been hard."

The flickering candle light softened the taut lines of her father's face and Jules thought he looked less austere and far younger than he had for a long time. He wasn't old, of course, mid-sixties at the most, but for so much of her life he'd been a distant and rather intimidating figure. She felt moved to picture him as a young father, holding his child for the first time and feeling overwhelmed, and was filled with compassion for the conflict he must have felt as he did his best to provide for his family. Yes, he'd worked long hours and Linda had felt neglected at home with a small child, but Alistair had done his best in the only way he knew how. Wasn't that all any of us were doing?

Jules held her breath, waiting for Linda to put the (leopard skin spike heeled) boot in, but to her great surprise her mother just patted his duvet swaddled knee.

"It was a different time, Alistair. It wasn't easy, and I did struggle, but you always provided for us. Anyway, look at our daughter all grown up and about to get married. I don't think we did too badly in the end, did we?"

They looked at one another and Jules knew something had changed. Something *huge*.

"I'll be a very proud father tomorrow," Alistair said finally.

"You'll still walk me down the aisle?" Jules hardly dared hope.

"I always intended to. I just found it hard to jump off my high horse," he confessed.

"Honestly! You always were a stubborn one," tutted Linda but there was affection in her voice and Alistair laughed.

"I think we both are, Lin. Poor Danny doesn't stand a chance if our daughter takes after us."

"He's a lucky man in my book," Linda said firmly, and Alistair nodded.

"He certainly is."

Jules glowed at this unexpected praise. A companionable quiet fell as they watched the flames dance and listened to the wind gust before Alistair's attention turned to his Kindle and Linda gave herself a candlelit manicure. Jules closed her eyes and drowsed as the fire crackled and the wind howled. She couldn't remember ever sitting this peacefully with her parents or seeing them so at ease with one another.

Miracles, it seemed, could still happen at Christmas.

Chapter 15

Christmas Eve
The Wedding Day

It was the squabbling gulls which woke Jules. At first she wasn't sure where she was because her back ached, her neck was cricked, and the tip of her nose was icy. A spring dug into her left buttock and as she shifted to stretch her cramped limbs she almost slipped onto the floor. Blinking away sleep, she opened her eyes and saw the thick blackness of the night had thinned down to greys and blues which picked out fireplace and drew a narrow outline around the curtains.

The living room! Of course. When the power failed to return Jules and her parents had decided to camp out by the wood burner, loading it up with logs and piling the chairs and sofa bed with all the duvets and blankets they could find. It wasn't quite the wedding eve Jules had anticipated but as she rubbed her eyes and sat up she recollected the entente cordiale of the previous night and knew she couldn't have asked for a nicer start to her special day.

There was a soft snore. Beside her Linda was fast asleep on the sofa bed, snuggled into her fluffy white coat and dead to the world. There was no sign of Alistair. The arm chair he'd chivalrously insisted upon sleeping in was empty and a pile of blankets was neatly folded up on the arm. He'd always been an early riser, usually up at five to ambush the new day, and as a child Jules had always padded downstairs to find him listening to Radio Four and munching on a bowl of Cornflakes. She had a feeling that if she wandered into the vicarage kitchen right now something very similar would be taking place.

The big day was here. At last! Jules wasn't sure whether the little tingle deep in her belly was excitement or nerves, but she did know she couldn't wait to see Danny in St Wenn's. She wondered whether he was up too and feeling the same way? She'd text him in a moment – this didn't count as seeing the groom before the wedding, did it?

Outside the wind had dropped and pink dawn was stealing across the village. Braving the cold since the fire had died down, Jules slipped from her nest of duvets to pull open the curtains and look out across the bay where the waves were still white tipped and cantering merrily towards the shore. Was it her imagination or did it feel not quite as cold as yesterday? There was a heavy frost but it didn't appear as thick as it had the previous few mornings. Already the daylight was spreading across the water as though somebody celestial was colouring in the sea and Jules watched as the waves turned from silver to rose to gold. It was going to be a bright and beautiful midwinter's day and perfect for a wedding.

Although it was early the fishermen were already busy on the quay checking bow ropes and bailing out small tenders. There were no lights on the fish market though and all the cottages were still in darkness. Jules's heart sank and when she flicked the light switch her fears were confirmed: the power was still out.

This was out of her control, she told herself as she draped one of Alistair's blankets around her shoulders and crept out of the room. There was nothing she could do about this. Surely the electricity board would fix it soon? And what was the worst that could happen if they didn't? St Wenn's had a good stock of candles!

The hall way was icy and a knife edge draught gusted around her ankles. She'd refill the log basket, lay a fire and heat a saucepan of water to make tea, Jules decided. It wasn't quite the Prosecco and smoked salmon breakfast Mo had planned but it would warm her up and a couple of chocolate digestives wouldn't go amiss either.

"Good morning, love." Alistair was sitting at the kitchen table measuring Gaviscon liquid into a table spoon. "I'd offer to make you a coffee but the power's still off."

"I'll sort the fire and make us some tea. Are you feeling poorly?"

He grimaced. "Just a touch of heartburn. One of the joys of getting old. That soup didn't agree with me and I've got a bit of back pain from sleeping in the armchair."

Jules rummaged in the saucepan cupboard and dragged out a small pan which she filled at the sink.

"None of us expected to be camping in the sitting room," she said over her shoulder, "but I'm glad we did. It was nice wasn't it? Just the three of us?"

He nodded and rose to his feet. "Give that to me. I'll sort the tea and the fire. This is your wedding day and you've got more important things to do than run around us."

"Thanks." Jules didn't argue. The kitchen clock said it was coming up to seven am and Mo was due to arrive at nine. This didn't give her long to call Danny, have a wash and start to prepare herself for the day ahead.

Alistair patted her arm. "It's the least I can do. I'm so glad I came, Jules."

She swallowed. "So am I, Dad. I really am."

"And after this, when you and Danny are settled, maybe you can come and stay with me in Oxford? I could show you around? If you like."

"I'd really like that," Jules told him warmly. "We both would. I love you, Dad."

"Mmm. Yes. Same here." Alistair mumbled. He was hopeless at showing his feelings, probably another reason why it hadn't worked out with her mum, but Jules knew he loved her.

While Alistair went to do battle with the fire and collect logs from the woodpile, Jules fetched her iPhone from her bag. She only had a half the battery left and had switched it off to conserve what remained and as soon as she turned it on texts and messages came buzzing through. One was from Danny to say he couldn't wait to see her, and Jules pinged an answer straight back telling him she felt exactly the same. There was another from Sheila with a list of instructions, which Jules ignored, as well as three from Mo along similar lines. She already had a timetable blue tacked to the fridge with the day mapped out practically to the second, although Jules suspected events were about to go seriously off piste.

She scrolled through her messages, most of them from friends who couldn't make it to Polwenna wishing her well, but when she saw Ella St Milton's name appear and the urgent nature of the message, Jules was alarmed.

Call me – I can't get hold of Danny.

Ella was usually cooler than the chilly temperature in the vicarage. Anxiety curled through Jules like ivy and hit the green phone icon with trepidation.

"Jules!" Ella sounded breathless when she answered her phone. "No! Not there, you idiot! What do I have to do to get something done properly?"

From Ella's end came the sound of raised voices and clattering. The air of panic was tangible.

"Ella? Is everything all right?"

"Not really," said Ella, her tone even more brusque than usual. "There's no easy way to tell you this so I'll just come out with it. The hotel kitchen's out of action."

Jules leaned against the work top.

"Of course. The power cut."

"Power cut?" Ella echoed, sounding puzzled. "Oh yes, that. It's a major pain in the neck but if that was all we could have got around it."

All. Could have?

"It'll come back on soon, surely? South West Electricity won't leave us without power much longer. There's ombudsman rules about that kind of thing," Jules said.

"Half the county's without power," Ella told her tersely. "The storm last night took a lot of old trees down and the cold weather has caused accidents everywhere. The roads are in a terrible state."

"Oh," said Jules faintly. Neil was driving back, due this morning. She hoped he was safe.

"Sy said the electric company's surveyor will attend the fallen line first thing, but they'll need to keep the electricity off while they work on it." Ella always had the facts at her well-manicured fingertips. "Anyway, that's not the issue. Not directly anyhow but it was so cold last night the pipes froze here. *Don't open the bloody freezer, you absolute moron*! Sorry, not you, Jules! Look, I'll cut to the chase. A pipe burst's and water's somehow tracked into the main consumer unit and utterly fried it. The hotel's electrics aren't safe and the wiring's shot to bits. We can't possibly open while it's like this."

Jules couldn't believe what she was hearing. "What does that mean?"

Ella paused for a beat and Jules spotted the signs of someone searching for a gentle way to break bad news. She braced herself.

"I'm really sorry, Jules, but the reception can't go ahead, or not here at least. It's a health and safety issue. The hotel will have to close until it's certified safe to open again."

Jules had the sensation she was whooshing downwards in a fast lift.

"You can't close! We have over one hundred people coming to our sit-down reception."

"Yes, I'm well aware of that since I'm the wedding planner," said Ella, her clipped voice sharp.

"And what about everyone who's staying there tonight? And the food? How will we cook the food?" Jules was helter-skeltering into full blow panic. "And the band? The dancing? Are you sure there isn't a way? Doesn't Sy cook on gas?"

This was actually a wild stab in the dark. All Jules knew about chefs came from watching Gordon Ramsay. Swearing, wielding huge knives and tossing onions over leaping blue flames was about the size of it. Would the St Wenn's gas barbeque do?

"We have gas hobs but the lights and the extraction and the fire alarms are electric. I'm not sure the insurances cover the staff under these circumstances," Ella said slowly. "I'll look into it asap. Maybe check your wedding insurance too?"

"My what?" Jules had never heard of such a thing. It was bad enough finding the cash to get her old banger covered third party. You could actually insure a wedding? Seriously? And *now* her wedding planner thought to tell her this?

Ella sighed. "Look, you're going to have to leave this with Symon and me to sort out and we *will* sort it, I promise. He's trying to call Danny right now but I need someone's permission to make any necessary decisions about the food and the venue."

Jules couldn't have made a decision now if her life depended on it. Ella could make them all as far as she was concerned.

"Yes, yes. Of course. Do whatever you can."

"Will do," Ella promised. "*I said leave the canapes in the fridge, you idiot!* Look, Jules, I've got to go, but trust me, we've got this. Symon and I will sort out a wonderful reception for you and Dan. Somehow. It's going to be fine."

"Maybe we could draft Nick and Meg in with their seafood shack?" Jules suggested. It was a joke, but Ella pounced on it with worrying enthusiasm.

"Fabulous idea. That's just the kind of blue sky thinking we need. Their outfit runs on gas and so does Chris the Cod's mobile van. I'll give them all a bell. And anyone who has a wood fired range we can cook on. I'll start with Seaspray and call Alice. Nobody knows the Aga better than her. All hands to the pumps!"

She rang off while Jules collapsed at kitchen table with her head in her hands. Ella and Symon were going to cook the wedding breakfast in a chip van and all over the village on assorted Agas? It sounded insane.

It *was* insane.

Maybe her Boss would like to revisit the five loaves and two fishes miracle this afternoon, updated for the twenty-first century palate with canapés and filet mignon? Jules thought hopefully. And if He could throw in a venue too Jules would be really grateful. The village hall was big enough, but it was cold even when all the ancient heaters were cranked up to the max and with its 1970s orange curtains and peeling paint it was in dire need of decorating. Some balloons and streamers might go some way towards disguising the worst of it if she and the bridesmaids dashed over first. Was there time to do this? Jules glanced at the kitchen clock and wailed because the hands seemed to be whizzing around at double speed. How could it be almost quarter to eight already? And who was hammering on the front door like a scene straight from Macbeth?

She took a deep breath and wondered whether it was bad form for the bride to hit the bubbly before the bridesmaids arrived?

"Only us," carolled Mo, waddling into the kitchen with her left hand pressed into the small of her back. Ashley followed her, his arms full with dresses and a giant wicker picnic hamper slung over the crook of his arm, and little Isla, already in her hot pink bridesmaid's dress, was dragging a wheeled makeup case behind her. Morgan Tremaine brought up the rear and catching sight of Jules began to click away with his camera.

"Not yet!" Jules cried, blinking at the flash in the style of Dracula confronted with daylight and flinging up her hands. "I'm not ready, Morgan!"

"I'm making a record of the whole day from start to finish. This is the start. Fact," stated Morgan still snapping away and turning to Isla and Ashley who beamed at him obediently.

"I know that, love, and it's a great idea but I'm feeling a bit overwhelmed," Jules said. Her voice was shaking and even Morgan, not always the most sensitive to other people's emotions, shot her an anxious look.

"Morgan, can you take Isla outside and get some pictures of her? And maybe Jules's mum and dad? Informal ones?" Mo said quickly.

Morgan sighed. "You mean can I leave Jules alone while you find out what's wrong?"

"Yes," Mo admitted. "That's exactly it."

Morgan frowned.

"You're still going to marry my dad, aren't you?" he asked, not looking at Jules at all but studying the kitchen floor intently.

"Morgan! Of course she is! This is a wedding day thing.," said Mo. "All brides get stressed but this is even worse for Jules because there's no electricity and the hotel's in a state – which I totally blame Ella for by the way – and Neil's stuck in Bristol."

"What?" said Jules. There was a rushing sound in her ears and she was glad she was sitting down.

Mo's blue eyes widened in horror and she clapped her hand over her mouth. "Oops!"

"Bit late now for that, Red," remarked Ashley, untangling the bags and slipping them onto the floor. "Maybe just take your hand away so you can fit the other foot in?"

"What do you mean, Neil's stuck in Bristol?" Jules stared at Mo in horror. "How is he stuck? He's meant to be here opening up the church."

There was just over four hours until she was meant to be walking towards her curate at the altar and Bristol was at least two hours east on a good day. On an icy Christmas Eve with holiday traffic and trees down on roads he might as well be on the moon.

"Don't panic," Mo began but it was far too late because Jules was already buying a one-way ticket to Panic Town, via Meltdown City and catapulted from her chair to make a beeline for the fridge where the Prosecco was chilling.

Jules was through with worrying about the niceties; she needed a drink.

"Don't panic? You've just told me Neil's over a hundred miles away."

She fumbled with the cork and wordlessly Ashley took the bottle from her and popped the cork effortlessly before sloshing foaming bubbles into a Mickey Mouse mug.

"Have a sip," he advised, "but not so much you keel over. Nobody wants to see the bride staggering up the aisle, it's not a good look."

"If you think I'll even get that far," Jules said darkly but sipped anyway. Luke warm bubbles burst across her tongue, a bit like the way her wedding plans were also popping.

"Of course you will," Mo said staunchly. "Neil's just had a tiny accident. Nothing to worry about."

"Accident? What's happened? Is he OK?" Jules gasped, snorting bubbles and almost choking.

"Don't ever work for the diplomatic service, my angel," Ashley said to his wife while the bride to be coughed and spluttered. Patting Jules between the shoulder blades, he added, "Neil's fine. He skidded on some black ice and the bonnet's a mess. When he called Danny he was waiting for recovery and failing that he said he'd leave the car and catch a train."

"But the wedding's at half past twelve!" Jules wailed. What else could possibly go wrong? Was her Boss trying to tell her something?

"Neil will be here," Ashley said firmly. "You need to start thinking about getting ready. I'll take Mo's dress upstairs and leave you to it."

"Please don't decide to go into labour," Jules said to Mo once Ashley had left them. "I don't think I can take any more drama."

"I fully intend to keep cooking this baby. Anyway, I'm not missing your wedding reception. I want to see how Evil Ella sorts it out."

"She was going to see if the food could be cooked elsewhere," Jules said.

"There's enough folk with wood fired Agas who can cook stuff," declared Mo, with great confidence and as though she wasn't famous in the family for being able to burn water. "Anyway, it's not your problem. Your job is to sit by the fire, pop a face pack on and relax with your bubbles. Summer and Sheila will be here any minute and Perry's on his way with the flowers."

"What about washing? I can't have a bath," Jules fretted. It was easier to focus on the smaller things.

"Elizabeth the First only took one bath a year. In comparison to her you're positively fragrant."

"That's your solution? I have to adopt Tudor personal hygiene?"

Mo grinned. "I'm teasing! Ashley's getting Penny to bring my hot horse wash over. I'll even lend you some Frisky Filly mane and tail shampoo and some Coat Shine if you want?"

Jules started to laugh. Only Mo would come up with such a crazy but clever idea. The hot horse wash was a butane gas camping shower and a perfect solution.

"Yes to the horse wash but I might pass on the shampoo."

"You don't know what you're missing," Mo said. "Anyway, you can pamper yourself for a bit – Summer's on her way to do your nails and Kursa's bringing butane gas curling tongs to style our hair. Between us we'll get this wedding sorted."

"What about Danny?"

"Does he need his hair curled?"

"Mo! I meant is everything all right at Seaspray?"

"I'm sure it is. It's easy for the boys, isn't it? They only have to wear a suit. Far more work for us but fear not. I've got enough horses ready for the show ring at yards with no electricity." Mo picked up the bottle and sploshed more into Jules's mug. "Drink up, Rev! We've got this!"

They had got this, Jules told herself as she sipped her champagne and watched Mo unpack the picnic hamper, laying out smoked salmon and cream cheese onto sliced bagels, of course they had! She exhaled and allowed herself to relax a little, or at least relax as much as it was possible to relax with Morgan snapping away, Linda fussing about and Mo determined to get her drunk before nine am. Behind the scenes Jules knew everyone was doing all they could to make sure the wedding went according to plan. Ella was sorting the reception, Symon relocating the cooking and Neil doing his utmost to travel across the storm ravaged south-west as fast as possible so he could conduct the ceremony. They said things came in threes, didn't they? So her wedding was more than covered.

Surely nothing more could go wrong now?

Chapter 16

Christmas Eve
Still the wedding day

"We're nearly there. Not much longer." Kursa Penwarren stepped back and appraised Jules through narrowed eyes, tweaking a curl and pinning it more securely. "There! Perfect."

The hairdresser had been hard at it with her curling wand and had worked her magic to transform Jules's wild mop into a cascade of shiny ringlets artfully arranged on the crown of her head to frame her face and brush her shoulders. The elaborate do was woven through with the white roses and ivy Perry had delivered and threaded with white ribbons. Linda had done her makeup, thankfully avoiding the full Kardashian, and her wedding dress fell in graceful folds to the tips of her white sparkly DM boots. Somehow, and against all the odds, she'd been transformed into a bride. Michelangelo couldn't have looked prouder when he'd laid his chisel down on completing David than Kursa did as she stepped back and appraised Jules.

"Wow. Thank you!" Jules said, tilting her head and admiring her reflection. Was she preening? Usually more of a drag a brush through it and run kind of a person, Jules didn't think she'd ever preened before a mirror in her entire life but if you couldn't do so on your wedding day, then when?

"You brush up a treat love!" said Kursa. "It's amazing what a little bit of base and the right lippy can do, Linda."

"I know! She looks lovely! So feminine," said Linda.

"I hardly recognise you, Vicar!" cried Sheila, clasping her hands and shaking her head.

Backhanded compliments aside, Jules could have said exactly the same about her chief bridesmaid, with her hair no longer bullied into a salt and pepper bun but tonged into a bouncy halo of gold curls. And was she wearing blusher or were her cheeks just flushed?

Interesting, Jules thought. Was this transformation down to a certain farmer's imminent attendance at the wedding?

"Sounds like they're surprised I didn't crack the mirror beforehand," Jules said to Summer who was applying a final top coat of pale pink to the bridal nails.

Summer looked up from her task. "You're gorgeous, Jules. That's what they are trying to say!"

"Of course it is," Linda said, her eyes bright and her voice wobbling. "You make a beautiful bride and I'm so happy we've managed to do you justice in spite of everything."

Linda was right because it hadn't been the easiest few hours. It was incredible just how much extra work everything became without the things you took for granted but the bridal party had improvised. Mo's horse wash was hooked up to the outside tap and buckets of hot water carried upstairs to the bathroom to be tipped into Jules's tub as she channelled her inner Downton Abbey. Her wedding dress hung over the steaming water so the creases could drop out - saving on ironing was always a bonus, Mo pointing out as she waddled in to hang up the bridesmaid's dresses.

The bright winter sunshine made up for the lack of electric lighting and Jules had sat in the window of the living room while Linda and Kursa worked their magic. Alistair kept the wood burner fed and although the weather outside was still freezing, the room was warm and the bridal party were in high spirits.

As Kursa turned her attention to Mo's hair and Summer screwed the lid back on the nail varnish, Jules checked her phone for the umpteenth time just in case there was any news of Neil's whereabouts, but the screen remained worryingly blank. Oh! Where was he? Never mind electricity or hot water; there was no way they could have a wedding without the priest!

"There's still no word from Neil," she said.

"Mind your nails! They're still tacky!" warned Summer.

But Jules had more important things on her mind those wet nails.

"We can't get married without Neil! He has to be here."

"If the worst comes to the worst maybe Eddie Penhalligan can marry you on the deck of his trawler," Mo grinned.

"Could your Dad actually do that?" Jules asked Summer. Never mind grasping straws; she'd grasp whatever it took to save her wedding - even Fishy Eddie in his oilskins and wellies!

But Summer was laughing. "No, definitely not! You might as well ask Big Rog!"

"Don't suggest it. He'll get himself certified as a registrar and be St Wenn's competition in no time. Turkeys are so yesterday!" said Mo.

"What's happening with those turkeys?" Kursa asked. "Tara's meant to have one, you know. If our Christmas dinner is ruined I'll have the Pollards' guts for garters!"

There was an image Jules could have done without.

"They're still in my barn. Ashley's promised to sort it but Isla's obsessed with 'the birdies' and he's terribly soft where she's concerned," said Mo fondly. "But don't panic, Kursa. He's sent Penny to the supermarket with strict instructions nobody who put their faith in Pollard's Poultry will goes without their Christmas dinner if she wants to keep her job."

"If not, goodness knows what we'll all eat tomorrow," Kursa grumbled, jabbing kirby grips into Mo's thick red hair.

"Pizza!" declared Morgan from the far side of the room where he was taking pictures of the bridal party. "And chips!"

"Chips! Chips!" Isla shrieked, jumping up and down on the sofa and brandishing her posy. "My want chips!"

"You can't have pizza and chips for Christmas dinner!" cried Sheila.

Morgan's brow crinkled. "Why not?"

"Yes, why not?" Mo said.

"Because it isn't traditional, Morwenna, as well you know. Christmas is all about tradition," Sheila sniffed.

"Like going to midnight Mass?" Morgan suggested.

"Exactly," Sheila agreed, delighted with this response. "It's just like going to church and singing carols!"

Morgan thought about this for a moment before turning to Jules.

"Did Jesus eat turkey at Christmas?"

"Not as far as I know," she said, trying not to laugh.

"There may have been one at the stable though," said Summer kindly.

"Don't be silly. Turkeys don't live in stables," scoffed Sheila.

"You'd be surprised," Mo told her.

But Morgan was still puzzled. "If Jesus didn't eat turkey at Christmas why can't we have pizza and chips? Everyone would rather have pizza and chips than turkey. Fact."

Jules quietly agreed with him and she was certain Mr Gobbles and friends would too.

"It's just one of those things," she told him, but this sounded lame even to her own ears.

"That's weird," Morgan said but he didn't question it and Jules supposed he'd concluded the adult world made absolutely no sense at all. Fact.

And he was pretty much on the money.

There was just over an hour to go until the wedding. As well as having no word from Neil, Jules was also waiting to discover what was to become of her wedding reception since Ella and Symon hadn't been in touch. They were talking to Summer and Jules knew behind the scenes everyone was flat out to pull some kind of reception together. There was little she could do but trust all would be well. Somehow. The village was still without electricity and likely to remain so for some time since the power line was badly damaged and replacing it meant keeping the supply turned off. From the little Jules could glean from the whispers hissed between her friends in the furtive style of Roman senators plotting to accost Caesar, most of Britain's roads were in chaos this morning courtesy of the bad weather and the festive getaway. She twisted her engagement ring anxiously and tried to slow her breathing. Everything was going to be just fine.

"Have you got you something blue?" Mo asked.

Jules pulled up her skirt to reveal the frilly garter. "Check."

"All you need now is your cape and your bouquet and that's it," Summer said. "Morgan, can we have a picture of Jules with all of the bridesmaids and then one with her parents?"

While Morgan shuffled everyone into position, Jules looked into the mirror and hardly recognised the young woman who smiled back at her. She was thrilled with her dress and her hair and she hoped Danny would be too. She looked like herself but a more polished and girly version, which was the whole point.

"Where's your dad, Jules? I need him for the next ones," Morgan said once he'd snapped his fill of the bridesmaids and Jules hugging Linda, resplendent and festive in a clinging crimson velvet dress edged with green. Huge hooped earrings and armfuls of clattering bangles completed the outfit, along with the towering pair of stiletto heels with bright red soles which had made Kursa's jaw drop when she'd spotted them.

"He was here a moment ago." Jules glanced around the sitting room but there was no sign of Alistair. Hadn't he been in the arm chair, dressed in his suit and crunching Rennies?

"That was at least ten minutes ago," Summer said.

"He's gone outside for a sneaky smoke, if I know him. Some people never change! I'll find him for you, Morgan," sighed Linda and tottered from the room hollering for Alistair.

Jules smiled fondly. The pair had still been bickering all morning but without the usual bitterness. She'd even detected a fondness in their war of words and was hopeful her wedding day marked a lasting ceasefire. If she and Danny had children, something they'd quietly talked about, it might be much nicer for everyone concerned if their grandparents weren't starting World War Three each time there was a family gathering!

Jules was about to pick up her beautiful bouquet and pose once more for Morgan when a scream slashed the gentle chatter and laughter to ribbons. Seconds later, Linda stumbled into the room, hands outstretched and eyes wide with terror.

"It's Alistair! He's on the kitchen floor! I think he's having a heart attack!"

Jules had always dismissed the old cliché of blood running cold as the type of exaggeration beloved by hammy writers like Caspar, but Linda's words were like a drenching from a bucket of icy water.

Sheila was already on her feet.

"I'm a first responder so I'll go to him. Morwenna, call an ambulance," she ordered.

For once, Mo didn't argue; Sheila was well known in the village for her first aiding ambitions and most of the Polwenna residents had been bandaged and practiced on at some point. While Mo whipped out her phone Sheila strode to the kitchen and Jules, grabbing handfuls of cream silk into her fists so she could move quickly, tore after her. She felt as though she might faint; fear and control underwear were not a great combination.

Alistair Mathieson was sprawled by the kitchen sink, clutching his chest and gasping. His face, although shiny with sweat, was dreadful waxen shade and his breath was coming in sharp wheezing rasps. A bottle of Gaviscon had rolled from his hand and gloopy liquid pooled across the floor. Without a thought for dresses or nails or weddings, Jules was kneeling at his side in an instant.

"Dad! What's wrong? What is it?"

"Chest hurts," gasped Alistair, his hands curled into claws and his eyes closed. "Can't breathe. Feel…bad."

"Let me through. I'm a first responder." Sheila placed a hand on Jules's shoulder, gently but firmly moving her aside. She crouched beside him. "Can you hear me?"

He groaned which Sheila took to mean yes. She checked him over and turned to Jules.

"Do you have any aspirin?"

"Yes, I think so," Jules said. Her legs had turned to over cooked spaghetti.

"Fetch me one as quickly as you can. He can have it under his tongue," ordered Sheila. "Help me sit him up. Let's lean him against the kitchen units."

While Jules rummaged in the old ice cream tub where she kept a mish mash of painkillers and plasters which acted as her first aid kit, Sheila and Summer hoisted Alistair into a seated position. He groaned and clutched his chest but didn't protest. Jules wasn't sure this was a good sign; usually her father argued about everything.

"The paramedics are coming." Mo stood in the doorway, one hand pressed into the small of her back and her phone in the other. "They want to speak to you, Sheila."

Usually Mo was rather scathing of Sheila but the older woman's calm air of authority and clear knowledge of what was happening had changed everything. Jules, who usually thought of herself as calm under pressure, felt close to hysteria and Linda was distraught.

Sheila took the aspirin from Jules's shaking fingers and slipped it beneath Alistair's tongue. She reached for the phone, tucking it beneath her chin while she loosened his tie.

"Male, early sixties," she said. "Yes. Yes. Already given him 300mg. Chest pain. Sweating. Struggling to breathe. Suspected heart attack."

Suspected heart attack? Jules met Linda's gaze across the kitchen and saw her own shock reflected in her mother's eyes.

Sheila had finished her call. "Not long to wait. They'll be here in twelve minutes."

As she crouched by her father Jules could have kicked herself for not realising what was really going on with him. She'd done enough first aid courses to know the signs of a coronary. No wonder Alistair was knocking back the indigestion remedies and complaining of shoulder and neck ache. Of course. These were all classic symptoms of a heart attack.

"This is a suspected heart attack?" Linda said, her face paler than Jules's dress.

"It could be severe angina," Sheila offered but Linda wasn't comforted in the slightest by this.

"Alistair! Stay with us!" She dropped to her knees and bent over him, mascara running in sooty rivers as she wept. Gaviscon spattered all over her designer dress and her tights were already laddered. "Don't go down the tunnel, Ally! Stay away from the light!"

It was a sign of just how unwell Alistair Mathieson was feeling that he didn't tell Linda there was no light or mutter that she was merely referencing a shared cultural myth deeply engrained into the human psyche in order to explain the closing down process of a dying brain. This alarmed Jules even more and when his eyes closed, his chin slumping towards his chest, she was beside herself with fear. Suddenly all her worries about receptions and weddings were placed well and truly into context.

Please help him! She begged her Boss. *Please!*

Aloud she said, "The ambulance will be here soon, Mum."

"How can they get an ambulance up here? The streets are far too narrow," Linda wailed.

"They're sending the air ambulance. They'll land it on the beach and the Pollards can collect them with that quad of theirs. It's high time it made itself useful." Sheila said, handing the phone back to Mo. "Can you call Jake and ask him to make sure the beach is clear? And if the Pollards have their quad on standby?"

Mo usually bristled whenever Sheila asked her to do anything but today she nodded. Everyone was very happy to have Sheila at the helm, Jules realised. She was a funny old soul, and dreadfully bossy, but Sheila was *exactly* the kind of person you needed in an emergency.

Mo stepped away into the hall and moments later Jules heard her speaking to Jake. The thought of Danny's calm and capable brother taking control made her feel marginally less terrified. Jake would know just what to do.

"I'll go down to the beach and help Jake." Summer, winter coat draped over her bridesmaid's dress, was pulling on her boots. "As soon as the Pollards are on their way up with the paramedics, I'll text you."

"Thanks," Jules said. She didn't think she'd ever loved her friends more. She squeezed Alistair's hand. "The Pollards are going to give you a lift to the ambulance in their quad. As if things aren't bad enough, Dad!"

She tried her best to joke but Alistair was in too much pain to hear her, let alone crack a smile. He was looking worse by the minute and time had never seemed to move so slowly. Jules heard the front door slam and felt a chilly gust of air swirl around her haunches.

"Summer's gone and I've phoned my Richard," said Kursa, peering into the kitchen, her plump face creased with worry. "Tara's coming to take Morgan home."

"He'd better not take any pictures of this. Fact," said Jules. "Right, Dad?"

But Alistair's answering grimace could have been a smile or pain, it was hard to tell. She stroked his grey hair from his clammy forehead.

"Hold on, Dad. The doctor's coming. It's going to be fine."

"Danny's on his way over," Mo said, joining them. "He'll be here any minute."

Jules almost wept with relief at just the thought of her fiancé's calm presence.

Sheila, taking Alistair's pulse, looked up with a frown.

"Any sign of the paramedics?" she asked Mo.

"Ash says he can hear the helicopter approaching." Mo replied, glancing at her phone. "Jake's down on the quayside and Big Rog is ready. Any second now, I think."

"Not long now, Dad. They'll be here soon," Jules promised Alistair. "It's all going to be fine."

But her father was looking worse and she could tell from the way Sheila kept glancing out of window that the faster the air ambulance arrived the better it would be.

"The lengths you'll go to in order to stay out of a church," Jules teased Alistair and was relieved to see a faint smile.

"Not ready to see if you're right just yet," he gasped.

The bang of the front door followed by hushed urgent voices announced the arrival of Ricard Penwarren, Kursa's son and one of the village GPs. A calm man with a gentle manner, Richard always inspired confidence and it was with great relief that Jules stepped back to let him examine her father while Sheila filled him in. The portable defib he placed beside her father was also reassuring as much as she hoped desperately they wouldn't need it.

"You've done exactly the right things," Richard told Sheila, kneeling down beside his patient. "Very well done, Miss Keverne."

Sheila swelled with pride.

"I would have been a nurse if my parents hadn't needed me at home."

"You would have been great," Richard said firmly. "Hello, Mr Mathieson. I'm Dr Penwarren. Where's the pain?"

Alistair's eyes were closed, and his breathing was ragged. "Middle of my chest hurts. Thought it was indigestion. Heart attack?"

"I'm afraid that's not my call to make, sir. They'll start to run some tests in the ambulance to find out more. You may be having a severe angina attack which would account for the chest pain you've thought was indigestion, but they'll be able to explore that and make you more comfortable."

Although Richard's voice was steady and his tone was calm, Jules saw his gaze flick to the kitchen clock and knew he was willing the paramedics to hurry. Even Danny's arrival and the comforting pressure of his hand in hers didn't quell the roiling panic in Jules's chest. Each passing minute felt like a lifetime. By the time the red helicopter was hovering above the beach, spraying the quayside with sand and water, she feared Alistair Mathieson wasn't the only one in danger of having a heart attack.

Like the well-drilled professionals they were, the air ambulance crew landed the helicopter neatly on the beach while the Polwenna residents watched from their houses and the far side of harbour. Jules and Linda sat with Alistair while Danny gave a running commentary from the living room window to keep them up to speed with the developments and relay what Jake was telling him via the mobile. Although all her attention was focused on her father, Jules was able to picture the red-suited paramedics dashing across the sand and sprinting up the beach steps and when Danny announced they were on board the Pollards' quad bike and heading up Church Lane she could have wept with gratitude.

"Not much longer now, Dad. Hold on," Jules said but Alistair didn't answer. All his effort seemed to be focused elsewhere and she was terrified he was slipping from them.

"They're here!" Danny called as the door rattled voices and footsteps could be heard in the hall. "Come through. He's in the kitchen."

After this time seemed to bend and twist on itself and to Jules the scene became almost dream like. Danny drew her away gently, pressing a kiss onto her pinned up curls. Together they watched as the paramedics got to work and Jules prayed as hard as she had ever prayed in her life that Alistair would make it. He was grouchy and difficult and stubborn, but he was her dad and she loved him dearly. They'd only just begun to build bridges; surely this couldn't be the end?

"Who's his next of kin?" One of the paramedics asked while her colleague and Richard conferred in hushed voices.

Danny's hand slipped to the small of Jules' back and he gave her a gentle push. "That's you."

Goodness. Jules supposed it was since her parents were long divorced.

"I'm his daughter. What can I do?"

If the paramedic was surprised to find herself talking to a bride, albeit a Gaviscon splattered one, she didn't show it.

"We're going to admit your father to hospital. There's room for you to come with him, if you're happy to fly?"

Jules didn't need to think twice. All the arrangements which had seemed so desperately important only half an hour ago couldn't have mattered less.

"Of course!"

"I'll meet you at the hospital." Danny said, kissing her swiftly as Alistair, already on a stretcher, was carried from the kitchen. Jules had never loved her fiancé more than she did at this moment. Danny hadn't hesitated for a nanosecond even though he'd spent months planning this wedding in the most minute detail and all his work was ruined. She cupped his face in her hands.

"I love you."

"And I love you," he said softly. "So, so, much. You're absolutely stunning, too. The most beautiful bride in the world and I'm the luckiest man alive. Apologies for letting the show down but I was only half way through dressing when Mo called."

Jules had been so intent on what was taking place with her father she'd scarcely noticed much else. Now she realised that underneath his waxed jacket Danny was still in his jogging bottoms.

"I'd marry you no matter what you were wearing," she said, kissing him back and hurrying after the stretcher. Danny followed, snatching up her bag from the hall table.

"Take this and go!"

The Pollards had parked their quad outside the vicarage. The trailer was painted white and beautifully decorated with streamers, ribbons and white roses and the sight of it brought a lump to her throat. Big Rog and Little Rog gave her a lot of headaches, but they had gone to a huge effort to make her wedding day transport special. Richard and the paramedics were already in the trailer with their patient, resting rather incongruously beneath a canopy of flowers, and it was left for Jules to hitch up her skirts and flash her blue garter at the world as she rode pillion behind Big Rog.

"Danny! Wait! I'll come with you!"

Linda, heels abandoned and feet thrust into a pair of Jules' wellies, ran through the garden and out into the lane after Danny who was already striding down the hill. As Richard gave Big Rog a thumbs up and the quad bike's engine roared into life, Jules turned her head to gaze back at the vicarage and the stunned friends and family who were standing in the frozen garden watching the scene unfold. Mo had her arms around Isla and Tara held Morgan's hand as he stood motionless with no sign of his beloved camera.

"Drive carefully," Sheila ordered Big Rog and for once he didn't argue with his old adversary but just nodded. Jules imagined word was spreading fast that Sheila Keverne was the hero of the hour.

"I will, Miss K, don't you worry. I'll treat this passenger like glass."

Jules clung onto Big Rog tightly as the quad rattled down the lane and through the village. Window boxes were missed by centimetres and festive holiday makers leapt back to avoid being squashed, eyes widening when they realised a bride was on board.

"Out the way! Emergency coming through!" Big Rog hollered, tooting his horn. Jules suspected he would have loved a siren and flashing lights because this was his big moment and he was determined to rise to the occasion. Roger Pollard Senior would deliver this patient to the air ambulance – never mind how many other people he injured in the process.

The cold air slapped Jules' cheeks and make her eyes water. By the time the quad stopped most of her headdress had blown away and all of Kursa's handiwork was undone. Her stockinged legs were blue and shaking, although this was with terror as much as from the temperature.

She followed the paramedics down the beach steps and across the wet sand, barely noticing that the hem of her long skirt was sodden or how the cold wind was slashing through the thin silk of her dress. All Jules could focus on was the stretchered figure being lifted into the helicopter. Richard stepped back as she reached it.

"Good luck," he said. "I'll be thinking of you."

She hugged him quickly. "Thank you, Richard. Will he be all right?"

"If he's half as determined as his daughter, I'd say he stands a good chance," was all the doctor would say and Jules understood just how much was hanging in the balance for her father.

The engines were spooling up as the air ambulance prepared to take off. Jules took a deep breath. Richard was right. She *was* determined – determined her father would be fine. Nothing else mattered except for this. Jules took a deep breath and climbed inside. Moments later the blades began to rotate and the helicopter rose from the beach, flinging sand into the air and ringing the sea with ripples. All Jules's worries about lost curates, electricity cuts and reception venues felt like quaint concerns from a golden and care free age. All that mattered was that her father was taken to the hospital as quickly as possible. The rest of it could wait.

Hundreds of feet below, Polwenna Bay was shrinking to model village proportions. Jules could sense the eyes trained on the air ambulance and the love and good wishes of all her friends who were watching her depart. As the helicopter rose into the bright blue sky of what should have been her wedding day, Jules watched the paramedics working on Alistair and prayed as hard as she had ever prayed in all her life. Why had she been so worried about things which really didn't count at all? Who cared whether the reception was held in the village hall? Or whether the food was able to be saved? Even her worries about the Spanx seemed shallow. Who gave a hoot if she was thin or curvy? Suddenly, it was crystal clear what was important.

And all that mattered now was getting her father to the hospital as soon as possible. Everything else would have to wait.

Chapter 17

Christmas Eve
Still the wedding day

Along with most of the villagers, Alice and Jonny St Milton watched the air ambulance rise from the beach and circle Polwenna Bay before hovering over the roof tops and sweeping over the crest of the hills behind the valley. The sound of the blades grew fainter and fainter as the helicopter bore Jules and her father away and soon only the marks where it had rested on the sand and a faint ringing in their ears betrayed the fact it had ever visited.

"My goodness." Jonny put down his phone which he'd been using to try and video the drama. "Do you feel as though you've just had a surreal dream?"

Alice nodded. "I've only seen it land on the beach a few times before. They must be very worried about poor Alistair."

As the drama unfolded instant messages had whizzed back and forth through the ether as Jules and Danny's family and friends did their utmost to help. The Tremaines already had their own family WhatsApp group, which Mo had been updating to keep them all up to speed, and *The Only way is Polwenna!* Facebook group was exceedingly busy with well wishes and messages of concern.

While Johnny went to fill the kettle, Alice sank into the arm chair by the fire and reached for her reading glasses. She scrolled through the feed, touched by the outpouring of love for Jules and Danny and their extended family. Polwenna was a family in its own right and all the villagers had been looking forward to this wedding for months. Each post was filled with worry for Jules and her father, good wishes and the hope all would be well. The lack of electricity and disappearing turkey dinners had swiftly paled into insignificance and Alice couldn't help smiling to see how swiftly the Pollards' fortunes had reversed following their mercy dash to transport the patient from the vicarage to the air ambulance. From turkey stealing villains to village heroes took some doing and she shook her head admiringly; they really did have a habit of falling into the manure and coming up smelling of roses!

The village Facebook page had already been busy this morning. Even before this latest and most shocking development, Polwenna's residents had been posting suggestions for alternative venues and offers to help cook the reception food on wood fired Agas and camping stoves. Chris the Cod had located several generators to power the village hall and was busy setting up there. His mobile chip van and the Crab Shack his daughter owned with Nick Tremaine were on standby, and the oil-fired space heater from the marina workshop was already blasting the chill away. Nobody in Polwenna would let Jules and Danny's wedding be affected by the power cut – not least, Alice thought wryly, because they were all looking forward to a good party and some free booze!

Danny's father had set off for Bristol several hours ago in Ashley's plush Range Rover, outwardly on a mercy dash to rescue Neil Cavendish in time for the wedding. Alice rather uncharitably suspected Jimmy wanted an excuse to drive such a flash car and also to avoid having to lug tables and chairs from the hotel to the village hall. In the meantime the WI had stormed the new reception venue armed with as many decorations as they could find, and Tess had rounded up her pupils to blow up balloons and drape tinsel everywhere. Even Jonny's idle grandson, Teddy, had stepped up for once and was busy helping the hotel manager ring around to reassign wedding guests some alternative accommodation. The electricity company was optimistic all power would be restored by the afternoon and as she had dressed in her elegant grey trouser suit Alice had been wondering whether she would be regretting the thermals she'd worn beneath. She'd never dreamed for a moment the temperature would be the least of her concerns.

Alice sighed and lay the phone down on the arm of her chair. Even with all the good will in the world a wedding without a bride or groom was beyond salvaging. Her heart broke for Jules and Danny who had been looking forward to this day for so long and she was fearful too for Alistair. Poor Jules must be absolutely beside herself.

There wasn't going to be a wedding now. Everyone in the village must realise this but ought she to say something? Post it on *TOWIP*? Station the ushers at the church door to turn the any guests away? And what about the reception and all the food? What on earth could they do with food for over a hundred people? With the best will in the world, Alice had a big family and even she would struggle to know what to do with it all.

Her head was starting to ache and with another heavy sigh she reached up to pull off her hat. She knew it wasn't the weight of her headwear causing her temples to throb but there seemed little point sitting in her house looking as though she was dressed up for Ascot.

"Tea." Jonny placed a steaming cup on the table beside her and lowered himself into his usual straight-backed chair. "Drink up, Ally. It cures all ills."

"Even tea might struggle to sort this lot out," Alice said sadly. She picked up her phone once again and opened up her chat app. "Danny's messaged. He and Linda are on their way to the hospital. He says can we let everyone know the wedding's off." Tears burned her eyes. "Oh, love, what a dreadful thing to happen. He and Jules were so excited."

Jonny didn't say anything for a moment, sipping his tea thoughtfully and watching the flames leap in the hearth. He placed his cup back in the saucer with a rattle and exhaled slowly.

"The thing is, Ally, I'm not so sure they were."

Alice was outraged. "What are you talking about, you silly old fool? They can't wait to be married."

"I didn't say they weren't keen to be *married* but I'm not convinced either of them are massively into this big wedding they've somehow ended up with. It's run away with them is my guess." He took off his glasses, polished them on his sleeve, and regarded her over the top of them with quizzical blue eyes. "Have you ever heard Jules say she wanted a big do? Or Danny?"

It was funny but now he'd mentioned it, Alice hadn't.

"No," she admitted.

"Do either of them strike you as the type of people who would want a big song and dance made? Ella, for example, is going to want to put Harry and Meghan to shame and I can imagine Zak having some kind of showbiz bash, but Dan and Jules?" He shook his head. "I've always thought they'd be happier with a small affair and a family party."

Sometimes Jonny's observations took Alice totally by surprise because they were so insightful and made her wonder why she hadn't thought of them herself. This was one such occasion. Dan and Jules were very unassuming people who loved their friends and family and each other.

"You could be right," she said slowly.

"Did either of them ever ask you about holding their reception at the hotel?" Jonny continued. He leaned towards the fire, warming his hands by the leaping flames, and when he leaned back and looked at her, Alice saw he was troubled. "Ally, is this my fault for assuming they'd be pleased with our offer? Did I start something they couldn't stop because they didn't want to hurt our feelings?"

"It was a joint decision," Alice said staunchly, but the more she thought about it the more she seemed to recall Jules had originally been planning a modest wedding. Alice had assumed this was down to budget and it had seemed a no brainer to offer the hotel as a venue. Alice tried to recall Jules ever saying she wanted a big sit-down reception but as hard as she tried to dredge up the memory no such conversation had ever taken place. Oh dear. Had she and Jonny inadvertently put pressure on the couple? Jules had seemed very worried about the size of today's affair, but Alice had taken these concerns to be no more than the usual jitters a bride felt on the run up to the big day.

"What did we want when we got married?" Jonny asked and Alice sighed.

"A small gathering."

"And what did we get?"

She laughed despairingly. "The total opposite, but wasn't it fun? Besides, I've got a huge family and I'd waited almost sixty years to marry you!"

He reached across to take her hand in his and raise to his lips. Although it looked very different to the smooth skinned hand he'd first held when they were sixteen, Alice knew when Jonny looked at her he still saw the girl she'd once been.

"It was worth waiting for you," he said gallantly.

"Flattery might get you another cup of tea," said Alice, but her stomach still fluttered when he looked at her and although his eyes were cloudy these days the love in them hadn't changed a bit.

"Our wedding suited us, but I do suspect Dan and Jules would have been happy if it was just them. I fear they may have been caught up in village wedding fever," Jonny concluded, releasing her hand and reaching for his newspaper.

He was right, Alice realised. Neither her grandson nor his fiancée had ever shown the slightest inclination towards a big wedding and thinking back to the far-off time when Dan had married Tara, Alice recalled he had only plumped for the full shebang to make his new wife happy. Tara was not the kind of girl to make do! Had he feared Jules might be missing out if they had a small wedding? Although divorced, Danny and Tara had remained friends and now Alice actually thought about it, Tara had made several comments which suggested she was keen to ensure Jules never felt second best or missed out on her special day. Jules, of course, would never want to disappoint Danny by not going along with his plans and she would have hated to seem ungrateful or risk hurting Alice and Jonny by turning their offer down…

It was as though the final piece in a jigsaw had dropped into place. While Jonny turned his attention to the crossword Alice looked out of the window and prayed hard that Alistair Mathieson would pull through and that maybe, just maybe, some part of Jules and Danny's wedding day could be salvaged.

It was the least the young couple deserved.

The hospital waiting room was trying valiantly to be festive. An artificial tinsel tree with a bad case of alopecia had been set up in the corner and a strand of jaunty fairy lights threaded through its bare branches. Ropes of garish green and hot pink tinsel were wound around the clock face and pinned to the notice board. Jules, sitting on a plastic orange chair across from this, had already diagnosed herself with several nasty illnesses and head lice – although in all likelihood her scalp itched because of Kursa's liberal application of hair spray and pins – and was trying hard to distract herself by thumbing through dog-eared gossip magazines. Unfortunately there was a limit to how much the woes of a Kardashian or antics of the junior royals could take a girl's mind off the terrifying reality that her father was having a heart attack.

Nobody had confirmed yet this was what was happening but neither had they denied it. The journey to the hospital had passed in a blur and as soon as the air ambulance had touched down a team of medics had been waiting to transfer Alistair onto a trolley and race him across the tarmac and into the Emergency Room. The last Jules had seen of her father was a supine figure surrounded by a blur of blue scrubs as he was wheeled through a set of double doors into a room alarmingly labelled *Resus*. Head spinning from the speed of events, Jules had tried to overhear the handover conversations but since all of her medical knowledge was gleaned from watching *Holby City*, none of it made a great deal of sense and as Alistair vanished she'd felt even more alarmed.

Was he going to die?

Nobody Jules asked had seemed able to give her any concrete answers. They were all so kind, offering to find somebody who might know and promising her faithfully Alistair was in good hands, but Christmas Eve in the casualty department of a major NHS hospital was a busy time. The medics in their jaunty festive badges were rushed off their feet, unable to stop for a moment as they raced about. Tubs of *Quality Street* and *Celebrations* placed at the nurses' stations went untouched and Jules recognised the focus needed to concentrate on doing a difficult job with both compassion and efficiency. She tried her best to remember that the doctors and nurses saw lots of patients like Alistair and knew exactly what they were doing. He couldn't be in better hands and while they worked on him she'd been gently but firmly steered into the waiting room to chew her nails and watch the hands creeping slowly around the tinsel edged clock face. With each passing minute Jules felt as wilted and dejected as the dusty spider plant on the coffee table.

She should have been exchanging vows with Danny right now. Maybe they would even have been Mr and Mrs Tremaine? And if things had gone according to plan Alistair would have been sitting in the front pew, no doubt looking disgruntled, but present nonetheless to pose for the photos and bicker with Linda. What Jules wouldn't have given right now to hear him make a sarcastic comment or roll his eyes at something daft his ex-wife had said. Her dad was a difficult customer, but he was *her* difficult customer and the only Dad she had. Last night, as she'd listened to Alistair and Linda's stories from the long ago days of their courting, Jules has really felt as though she was starting to get to know him properly and for the first time allowed herself to believe the hurt which had troubled her small family for so long was finally starting to heal. It seemed unfair and cruel beyond belief that she might lose him now.

He couldn't die. She needed her father.

She loved him so much.

If the other occupants in the waiting room were intrigued by the sight of a bride they were too polite to stare for long. Anyone with a friend or relative spoke in hushed tones while those who waited alone turned inwards, focusing on their own fears while running through an internal inventory of terrible scenarios. If anyone's eyes did meet they would smile awkwardly before settling their gaze somewhere safer, such as on the tips of shoes, hands resting in a lap or an outdated magazine story. The tension was palpable and each time the squeak of rubber soled shoes heralded the arrival of a nurse heads and pulses shot up in tandem, only to plummet when somebody else was called.

"Jules! Any news?"

Danny strode into the waiting room with Linda scurrying in his wake. As he pulled Jules against him and held her close to his racing heart, she knew she had never been so pleased to see him in her life.

"Not yet. He's still in resus," she said.

"No news is good news, isn't it?" Linda was asking, her fake fur coat and jaunty fascinator at odds with tear stained cheeks and wellies.

Jules had no idea. She hoped so, but maybe no news meant Alistair was too poorly to leave?

"Absolutely," Danny assured her mother. "Sit down, Linda. They'll call us when there's news."

They settled down beside her. While Linda flicked through a magazine Dan took Jules's hand in his.

"I'm here," he murmured. "In sickness and in health. Always."

"That's meant to be our health, not my father's," Jules half-laughed and half-sobbed.

But Danny was serious.

"I'll always be there for you, no matter what life decides to chuck at us. I'll love you through rubbish bits and the sad bits as well as the good times. Isn't that what the marriage service is really all about? The suits, the dress and flowers are the easy parts. Anyone can have those. It's the rest of it, the behind the scenes nitty gritty, which really counts. I don't need to be standing in a church to promise you I'll always be here for that."

Their fingers knitted together, and Jules knew beyond all doubt this man was her rock and her absolute anchor. Without him beside her she had felt no more substantial than the grey flakes of ash which whirled upwards and away from winter bonfires.

"Reverend Mathieson?"

A young man in scrubs stood in the doorway, Staff Nurse Paul Wise according to his flashing festive ID, and nodded at Danny.

"If you'll come with me, I'll take you to see your father now."

"This is Reverend Mathieson," Dan said, nodding at Jules. "I'm her fiancé."

Staff Nurse Wise began to apologise but Jules took pity on him.

"It's fine. I have a different hat on today," she said. "It's a long story but we were meant to be getting married but my dad was taken poorly. How's he doing?"

"He's comfortable but come and see for yourself. Sorry, only two of you at the moment," he added when Linda stood up too.

"You two go. I'll wait here," Danny said at once. He reached for a magazine. "Go! I'll still be here reading about Kim Kardashian when you come back so don't worry about me! Heavens! That backside's never real?"

His silly remark lifted the atmosphere. As Jules and Linda followed the nurse along the corridor and through several sets of double doors she felt more hopeful than she'd dared allow herself to feel since they'd arrived. If there was something seriously wrong, they would have said so surely?

"I'll find a doctor to have a chat with," said Nurse Wise, ushering them past several bays and various patients on trolleys or hooked up to drips. "Here's the patient: cubicle four."

Alistair was propped up in the last bed at the end of a bay filled with oxygen-masked patients linked up to a variety of machines. He was wearing a hospital gown and had a mask over his face but was sitting up and even though he seemed frail and lost amid several monitors showing wiggly lines and all kinds of mysterious information Jules was thrilled to see his gaze was as sharp as ever.

"How are you doing?" she asked.

Alistair lifted his drip tethered arm.

"Do you need to ask?" he wheezed.

Better then, thought Jules. Out loud, she said, "You gave us a real fright."

"It wasn't much fun for me either," he retorted. "You must be devastated, Linda."

Linda leaned forward. "Why?"

"Because I'm still alive."

"Dad!" said Jules, horrified. "Mum was really worried. She came straight here."

But Linda was smiling. She pulled out a chair and sat down next to him.

"Yet again you don't deliver. I hadn't even finished my face!"

"This is the hospital," he wheezed. "You've no business frightening people to death without wearing your make up!"

"I didn't have time. I needed to make sure you were really shuffling off," Linda retorted, and his lips twitched. "I'd have had to give Jules away, I suppose."

"Over my dead body," he said, closing his eyes.

"Almost. You always were an attention seeker. Anything for a free helicopter ride."

Jules listened to them banter but as much as she felt relieved to see her father was looking brighter, she was alarmed by the wires and machinery he was hooked up to and eyed the monitors warily. There was no point trying to make sense of it and the days of notes being clipped to the ends of beds were long gone.

Thank you that he's still here, she said to her Boss. *Thank you!*

Jules had spent the entire flight to the hospital praying hard, and not just because she wasn't a fan of heights. Alistair might not believe in God, but Jules did and as the air ambulance made short work of the thirty miles between Polwenna and Plymouth she prayed as hard as it was possible to pray. That her father was sitting up, albeit wired up like Robocop, and bickering with Linda was a miracle.

She was beyond thankful.

The wait for a doctor was lengthy but it was Christmas Eve and there were plenty of people passing through the Emergency Department. Nurses continually checked on her father and ran ECG tests, and several cleaners swished by to battle superbugs with mops and disinfectant wipes. By the time they were joined by a young doctor, the sky outside was streaked with apricot and pink and the buildings beyond shifted into a silhouetted cityscape. Her wedding day was almost over, Jules thought wistfully. Now she wished she had enjoyed the run up more rather than wasting so much time worrying about it.

The doctor drew the curtains for privacy and consulted an iPad.

"How are you feeling now, Mr Mathieson?" she asked.

"Fine. Nothing wrong with me," Alistair replied but his pallor and laboured breathing told a different story.

The doctor frowned.

"I disagree, Mr Mathieson, and so does the data I'm looking at. The electrocardiogram results, along with your bloods, suggests an attack of severe angina."

"Angina? But that's not serious is it?" said Linda, surprised.

"Actually, it's very serious if it isn't treated. If a severe attack continues for over twenty minutes it can cause serious and lasting damage. It can also be a symptom of other serious heart conditions, including blocked arteries and heart disease. You've been exceedingly lucky in my opinion, Mr Mathieson, and you need to take this episode as a big wakeup call."

It was a sign of just how shocked Alistair was that he didn't pull this young whipper snapper up by pointing out he was a professor and not a mere *Mr*. His hands, clutching the sheet, trembled.

"So it's a warning?" Jules asked.

The doctor nodded. "That's exactly what it is. Had the attack continued for a prolonged period, things might look a great deal worse this afternoon. Your father's also exceedingly fortunate somebody had the medical knowledge to administer aspirin and call an ambulance. That certainly bought him some extra time. You must have a guardian angel, Mr Mathieson!"

Jules waited for Alistair to scoff at this notion but, most unusually, he said nothing. If anything he looked a little thoughtful.

"I was praying for you all the way here, Dad," she said and for once her father didn't roll his eyes or make a pithy remark.

"I knew that, Jules, and believe me I appreciated it. More than you'll ever realise," he replied. "I'm so very proud of you."

These words meant more to Jules than anything; they were an acceptance of her faith and acknowledgement of who she was. She screwed up her eyes and focused hard on the grubby hem of her dress, determined not to cry. It was odd how something she'd hoped to hear for her entire adult life could reduce her to a weeping heap, especially when it made her so happy. Alistair might not share or understand her faith but to know he was proud of her, and that she had been able to offer him some comfort when he most needed it, meant the world.

Her wedding might be ruined but seeing her parents chatting amiably, knowing Alistair was proud of her, Jules thought she wouldn't have changed a thing.

"Sheila Keverne? An angel in disguise?" Linda was saying incredulously. "It's lucky she was your maid of honour, Ju-Ju. I did think she was an odd choice at the time, but I stand corrected."

Jules sent her Boss a silent thank you she'd agreed to let Sheila be maid of honour. Everyone had thought she was crackers at the time, but here were those mysterious ways again. Bossy boots Sheila might have saved Alistair Mathieson's life.

"What happens now?" Alistair asked.

"We'll need to monitor you closely for at least twenty-four hours and start a course of treatment. As soon as there's a bed free you'll be transferred to the coronary care unit for more tests. You'll be here for a few days while the specialist keeps a close eye on you."

"But is the worst over?" Linda was still looking worried.

"I'd suggest this was a big warning of what could happen if you don't make some changes such as quitting smoking and avoiding stress. If he follows our advice your husband should make a good recovery," the doctor said.

Linda opened her mouth to say they were divorced but Alistair was even quicker.

"Her husband's in Spain and as far as I know he's absolutely fine," he wheezed.

Jules raised her eyes to the strip lit ceiling.

"Ignore Dad. My parents are divorced!"

"And is it any wonder why when he has such a dreadful sense of humour?" Linda added. "It's amazing I haven't had a heart attack having to put up with it!"

The doctor smiled although Jules knew she would be privately thinking to herself they were utter lunatics. Jules recognised that expression of pained politeness; she used it a lot herself!

"You'll be in for a while, Mr Mathieson, but you should make a good recovery," she told him.

"Not quite ready to meet your maker?" Linda remarked once the doctor had moved on to the next bay.

"I'm all for testing hypotheses but maybe not that one just yet," he said.

"Maybe don't try it for a while?" Jules suggested. "I'm not certain my nerves can take it!"

Chapter 18

Christmas Eve
Still the wedding day

Still a little shaky from the events of the day so far, Jules went to relay the prognosis to Danny. Thrilled to hear the good news, he messaged Alice in order to update her and pinged another text to Mo and Ashley. They could let everyone else know what was happening and would take care of all the logistics of sending guests home and packing away the reception, he said. This was not going to be something Jules needed to worry about. All she had to do was focus on her father.

Jules loved him for lifting this burden. Her mind was spinning around like Kylie and she didn't think she could have made any sensible decisions feeling so strung out. It had been bad enough planning the wedding; dismantling it would be even worse. She felt weak and wobbly and close to tears. This was not the wedding day she'd had in mind.

"You need a cup of tea and some food," Danny decided, sliding his phone into his pocket and taking her hand. "I know just the place. Trust me, I've spent a lot of time in this hospital and they do the best iced buns in the canteen. They're the size of plates!"

He frog marched Jules along through a maze of corridor which eventually opened out into the hospital's vast canteen. Feeling wobbly had a lot to do with lack of food as well as worry, Jules realised as she sat at a table by the window while Danny joined the queue, and she hadn't eaten anything more than a slither of smoked salmon. The canteen smelled of turkey and gravy as the cooks dished up festive fare and her stomach rumbled while her spirits lifted to hear Christmas carols and happy chatter. All would be well.

Somehow.

"Hello again."

An elderly gentleman had paused by her table and was down smiling at her. He was rather familiar with his thick mop of white hair and twinkling eyes, but Jules struggled to place him. Oh! She hated it when this happened! Where had she bumped into him before? Was he a Parishioner? Clergy member? Jules couldn't quite recall, although she was certain he was something to do with the church.

"We met in Truro Cathedral," he explained with a kind smile which instantly put her at ease. "You were admiring a painting."

Of course! It was the old man she'd poured her heart out to on that last shopping trip. Now Jules recognised him.

"I'm so sorry! Of course. I hope you're well?" Jules said, feeling bad. She hoped he didn't think she'd forgotten him. Quite the opposite. She'd recalled his words quite a few times and mulled them over.

"Oh, I'm fine my dear. Just passing through," he said, leaning on his stick. "You look a little fraught, though?"

She laughed. "That's one way to put it! It's been quite a day so far. My dad's been taken unwell. Right before my wedding actually."

"My dear! How dreadful. I hope he's feeling better now?"

"They've moved him to a ward for observation, but I think he's on the mend, thanks. Mum's sitting with him while my fiancé and I grab some food," Jules explained.

He raised a white eyebrow. "I seem to recall your parents don't get on."

Jules was impressed. "You do have a good memory! Usually my parents make Tom and Jerry look like friends but funnily enough since we chatted in the cathedral things have changed quite a bit. They actually called a truce just in time for the wedding."

He nodded slowly but didn't appear very surprised.

"Didn't we say to have faith and believe?"

Jules stared at him. "Actually, you said that."

"Ah yes, so I did. And how about the big wedding?" He inclined his head towards her white dress. "Did it go well?"

"As I feared it ended up being totally out of our hands, although not quite in the way I'd imagined," she said. "We've missed the whole thing because we've been here with Dad. There wasn't a wedding at all, so I was worrying about nothing."

"Ah, but remember what we also said? That things have a funny way of working out for the best, especially when you put others first?" he reminded her. "Especially at Christmas time. Have faith and believe, my dear."

"I'm trying," sighed Jules although sometimes this was easier said than done.

"And that's all anyone can do even though it's often the hardest thing in the world," he said firmly. "Anyway, I must be getting on. Merry Christmas, my dear. I'm sure it, and your wedding, will still be everything you and your young man hope for."

Jules was quite sure it wouldn't be, but it seemed rude to disagree.

"Won't you join me for a moment and have a cup of tea?" She indicated the seat opposite. "Danny won't be long. I'd love you to meet him."

But the old man shook his white head. "No, no. I must get on, my dear. I've a lot to do today, but I'm sure we'll meet again. All will be well, I'm certain of it. Have a very merry Christmas!"

"Will you be at the cathedral?" Jules called but he was already on his way, walking stick tapping a route through the tables as he headed for the canteen exit, and probably couldn't hear her above the clatter of plates and George Michael singing about giving his heart away at Christmas. She watched him depart, feeling a little puzzled, before checking on Danny's place in the queue. Maybe she could wave Dan over and introduce them quickly? She turned back to see where the elderly gentleman had got to in his slow progress but there was no sign of him, and Jules felt rather annoyed at herself because once again she hadn't even asked his name.

In fairness she did have a lot on her mind today!

It was a real coincidence bumping into him again. While she waited for Danny, Jules reflected on what the elderly stranger had said both this afternoon and on the last occasion they'd met. He'd seemed to see straight into her heart and had understood exactly what was troubling her. It was almost as though he'd already known what would happen and how everything would work out perfectly if she would relax and have faith.

Have faith and believe.

Jules sat bolt upright. Impossible! It couldn't be! She'd watched too many Christmas movies!

Abandoning her seat, she dashed through the canteen to the door, looking each way but the corridor was empty. A lift call pinged from somewhere and a trolley piled high with laundry was wheeled past but there was no sign of him. Feeling disappointed, she returned to the table.

"Let's hope my stomach's up to food!" Danny set down a laden tray and sat opposite Jules. He reached for a bun, adding, "Who were you just chatting to?"

"It's a really strange coincidence, but I just saw the elderly man I bumped into in the cathedral," she said slowly.

"The one who was looking at the painting?"

"That's right. He gave me lots of advice about trusting things would take their natural course when I was stressing about the wedding. He was right; worrying was a waste of time."

"Things haven't quite turned out as we'd thought, have they?" Dan agreed. "Not really much of a coincidence seeing him here. Elderly people visit hospitals an awful lot. Jonny and Alice practically have season tickets."

"Mmm," said Jules. He was bound to be right but she still had the strongest feeling the old gentleman wasn't visiting the hospital for medical reasons. She sipped her tea and mused on his words. It was crazy but they'd felt like a message meant especially for her.

"Not quite the wedding day we had in mind," Danny remarked, tipping a sachet of sugar into his tea and stirring it vigorously.

"I'm so sorry, Dan."

"Sorry? What on earth are you apologising for? None of this is your fault. It's just one of those things. What is it they say? An act of God?"

Jules looked up from her bun, struck by his choice of expression.

"What do you mean? What's an act of God?"

"All this? Your dad's heart problems and the wedding being off. Nobody could have predicted it. Isn't that what they call an act of God?"

"I suppose so," Jules said slowly. Was it?

"Anyhow, I'm just glad your dad's OK." Dan pushed his plate aside and took her left hand, turning the engagement ring around tenderly. "That he's going to be all right is the only thing that matters. The rest of it can be rearranged."

"But you worked so hard, you really did. I also know what it meant to you having everything perfect for today," Jules said sadly.

"What it meant to *me*?"

"The big wedding with all the guests. The reception. The party." She bit her lip. "I can't bear it you did all this for nothing. You must be so disappointed to have missed it."

"Can we rewind for a minute, sweetheart?" Danny asked, a frown crinkling his brow.

"All the work you've done," she repeated. "I know how much this meant to you. You've been so busy making sure it runs smoothly."

He released her hand and massaged the crease between his eye brows.

"Do you think I pressed to arrange the wedding the way we did because it's what *I* wanted?"

Jules knew marriages had to be based on honesty if they were to last. Quite how much honesty should be involved was a matter for debate, but she also knew their marriage had to be built on truth.

"Didn't you?"

"Err no," said Danny, seeming surprised she might think such a thing. "I'd have been happy to marry you on the quay and with pasties on the beach as the reception! None of the trappings bother me at all as long as you're the woman I'm going to spend the rest of my life with."

Jules was unable to believe her ears. "What?"

"I thought *you* wanted the full works. Isn't that what all women really want?"

"No, absolutely not! The fish quay would have been fine by me too. More than fine."

"You didn't want a big white wedding?" Danny's mouth was hanging open.

"I'd marry you anywhere! In my jeans and hoody with a fish and chip shin dig at the village hall would have been my dream wedding," Jules gasped. "I've been terrified for months about what ours has turned in to."

"Me too!" Danny said with feeling. "It felt like a runaway train."

"With us tied to the tracks," she added.

He laughed. "Exactly! So, let me get this clear, neither of us wanted a big wedding but we were too worried about letting the other down to say what we really wanted?"

"I thought it was your dream and you thought it was mine." Jules picked the icing from the top of his cake and crumbled it thoughtfully. "Danny Tremaine, do you even know me at all? Do I strike you as the kind of girl who dreams about white frocks and obsesses over seating plans?"

"Not for a second but Tara said—" Danny stopped abruptly.

"Tara?"

But Dan had clammed up like a scallop.

"Don't stop there when it's just getting interesting," Jules scolded, wagging her index finger at him. "Come on, Daniel Tremaine! What exactly did your ex-wife say?"

Danny groaned. "Oh Lord! What was I ever thinking listening to Tara? I must have been crazy, but she seemed so sure about what you wanted."

The last time Jules looked, Tara Tremaine was a restaurant manager and not a psychic. Jules liked her very much, but they weren't close friends. How on earth would Tara have a clue about the kind of wedding Jules wanted? As far as she recalled, they'd never once discussed this.

"So what did Tara, who never once spoke to me about it, think I wanted my wedding to be like?" Jules asked him.

"She said you were only saying you wanted a small wedding because you were worried about me having been married before and feeling awkward," Danny explained. "Tara says deep down every woman wants a massive white wedding and she said I'd be wrong to deny you that just because it wasn't what I wanted. So I decided to pull out all the stops because I love you so much and I couldn't bear to let you go without. It seemed a plausible theory when I was talking to Tara and caught up in it all, but now?" He pulled a face. "Now it just sounds plain crazy."

"Yep," said Jules. She couldn't deny it.

"Why on earth didn't I just talk to you?"

"For the same reason I didn't tell you how I was feeling. Neither of us could bear to hurt the other," Jules replied slowly. "What a pair we make."

Danny grinned, the boyish lopsided grin that always made her feel as though the sun was peeking out through clouds and bathing her in sunshine. Her own mouth curled upwards in reply.

"We're idiots, aren't we?" he said. "Fact!"

"Fact," agreed Jules. "But, Dan, in the future can we absolutely promise to be upfront with each other? Even if it might be difficult, or even painful, in the first instance? I think it might save a whole heap of trouble."

"I think we should shake on it," said Danny, offering his hand. "And also let's make a deal that the next wedding we plan is small and just the way we want it."

"Amen to that," Jules said.

They shook hands over the debris of cooling tea and half eaten buns, laughing and unable to believe they'd planned a wedding neither of them wanted in order to keep the other party happy.

Dan was right, Jules concluded. They were idiots!

Fact!

More tea, much discussion and several iced buns later, Dan and Jules left the canteen to visit the patient in the CCU, tucked up in bed with an impressive bank of monitors surrounding him and Linda fussing over his pillows. Alistair was comfortable and, according to the nurses, doing really well.

Outside the small side room, night had fallen in earnest and the harsh strip lights were reflected in the shiny window and into infinity. Beyond the wail of ambulance sirens and bleep of monitors, Plymouth stretched into the darkness, a thickly sprayed mass of glimmering lights stretching between the squat hospital buildings before thinning out towards the feet of the sweeping tors of Dartmoor. Jules gazed out and imagined families across the country wrapping up last minute presents, or cuddled up on the sofa to watch *The Snowman* by the twinkling lights of the Christmas tree, and she was suddenly struck by the realisation that this was the first Christmas Eve she'd spent with both of her parents in over twenty years. Maybe it wasn't exactly the way she might have planned but they were all together and peacefully, just as she'd hoped.

Have faith and believe, the old man had said, and he was right.

It was strange how things worked out. This might not be how she'd ever imagined her wedding day but to see the colour returning to her father's face and listen to her loved ones chatting easily, Jules didn't feel cheated or sad. Quite the opposite. She was with Danny and always would be because he was there for her come what may; Jules didn't need a ring on her finger to know this was true. Marriage was about deep and steadfast love, not dresses and parties.

"Which one is for Grand Theft Auto?" Danny was surveying the monitors surrounding Alistair's bedside.

"None because we're going to watch a carol service," teased Jules. "How about that, Dad? Are you up for it?"

"Are you trying to give me a relapse?" Alistair grumbled, but he was smiling as he spoke.

"Absolutely not! I couldn't go through all that again," Jules shuddered.

"I know they say weddings are stressful, but I had no idea just quite how stressful today would be!" Danny joked. "If I still drank, I'd be hitting the pub as soon as we were back."

"I'm so sorry. I never wanted to cause either of you any stress or ruin the wedding," said Alistair quietly.

"Most people just wait for the part when the vicar asks whether anyone knows of any just or lawful impediment," Jules deadpanned.

"Your father wouldn't do anything so traditional. He much rather call the emergency services," said Linda tartly.

But Alistair was being serious, and he shook his head. "I know in the past I've made some things a little more *difficult* than I needed to, and I know I have some strong opinions about marriage as an institution, but I promise stopping your wedding was never my intention. I can see how happy you are and, Danny, there's nobody I'll be prouder to have as my son-in-law."

"Thank you, sir," said Danny. "Your daughter is a wonderful woman and I promise I will do everything in my power to make her happy."

"Yes, she is wonderful," Alistair agreed. "I might not have said it in the past, Ju, but I am incredibly proud of you. I want you to know that."

Jules had waited her whole life to hear her father say this and it had been worth every long moment.

"Thanks, Dad," she said, choked.

Alistair settled back onto his pillows. "And that's all the emotion and excitement I can cope with in one day. You three need to go home and I need to rest, which I can't do with Linda fussing non-stop. I've no idea why David puts up with it."

Linda winked at him. "Oh yes, you have!"

Alistair clearly did have a very good idea because he flushed, spluttered, and started to cough. Green lines darted up and down on one of the monitors and something pinged loudly, summoning a nurse who scuttled over to check on him.

"You need to rest now, Mr Mathieson. No more excitement."

Alistair closed his eyes. "Hear that? Now go away, the lot of you, and leave me in peace!"

"Maybe we can salvage something from all this?" Danny said quietly to Jules once they were all in the lift whizzing back to ground level. "We've got all that food going to waste and Christmas is a really tough time for lots of people. We could donate it all to community kitchens and shelters in time for Christmas Day meals. What do you think?"

For an answer, Jules rose onto her tip toes and kissed him.

"I think I couldn't love you more, Danny Tremaine," she said. "And I cannot wait to marry you. I really hope we don't have to wait too long to rearrange it."

Chapter 19

Christmas Eve
Still the wedding day

By the time Danny, Jules and Linda arrived back, night's curtains were well and truly drawn. Stars blazed across the heavens in a celestial display which rivalled that of the very first Christmas Eve two thousand years ago and echoed the sparkling frost already covering the shivering earth. The landscape was pared down to a palette of indigos and deep blues and midnight black and the glazed world seemed to hold its breath as though waiting for the heavenly host to rock up. This was the only hope the villagers had of a Christmas party, thought Jules, since the power wasn't restored yet.

At the top of the hill, just before the main road twisted right and dropped into the narrow valley where Polwenna's cottages had huddled against the elements for centuries, was a small lane which led to the hotel. It was here the power line had come down and the junction was teeming with electricity workers, all in orange hard hats and working double time as they toiled to restore electricity. Lights blazed from their trucks and when Jules wound the window down she heard the rumble of generators.

"This doesn't look good," grumbled Linda from the back seat. "I thought they'd have sorted it by now."

"I think it's a lot more complicated than we first thought," Danny told her. "Jake says they've had to do some major repairs which means cutting off the whole village for most of the day."

"I wanted to have a hot bath," grumbled Linda.

"At least the wind's dropped," Jules said. There. Have a silver lining, she added silently.

After the fright with her father, a power cut seemed a small thing to worry about. Ditto weddings and receptions and dresses. Truth be told, she could hardly wait to get back to the vicarage and change into her jeans and hoody. Several pairs of control knickers had been consigned to the bin in the hospital loo and now Jules could sit down without feeling as though her circulation was about to go the same way as Polwenna's electricity supply. There was an awful lot to be said for this and she'd already decided that when they rearranged the wedding she would prioritise comfort over a slimline look. Jules couldn't imagine anything quite as dramatic as this was likely to happen again but with her luck you never quite knew!

"According to Jake they'll have the power back tonight even if they have to bring in generators," Danny was reassuring Linda. "It's going to be fine."

He'd called his brother as they walked through the hospital car park to the car to fill his family in on Alistair's progress. Jake had warned him to drive really slowly since the roads were so icy and Danny, whose adapted car wasn't built for speed, had appreciated his brother's concern. Today was a day for holding loved ones close and cherishing them. As Dan's car crossed the Tamar Bridge, the Pollards had texted Jules with the offer of ferrying everyone up to the vicarage to and save them a cold and steep walk. For once, Jules hadn't worried about Big Rog's erratic driving and accepted with gladness; people cared about and wanted to help and this meant the world. Her friends and neighbours had been incredible today.

Linda leaned forward and tapped Jules on the shoulder anxiously. "But what about the guests and the reception?"

"All taken care of and absolutely nothing to worry about," Danny said.

"Really?" Jules asked. She hadn't allowed herself to start fretting about this. Her head would explode.

"Really. I told Jake we wanted to donate as much of the food as possible to the hostels and community projects and he said he'd get Tess on the case."

Jules smiled. "That means it's already done."

"Exactly! I didn't ask the details because I was in a rush to get us home, but I think any hotel guests have been shuffled about into alternative accommodation too. It's all fine. Even Neil's back safely. Dad went to all the way to Bristol to rescue him."

Jules was impressed. Jimmy Tremaine was usually the last person you could count on in a crisis. Everyone was pulling out the stops. As she settled into her seat for the final sweep into the village her phone rang. Mo.

"Where are you?"

"Just coming down the hill and heading into the top car park," Jules said. There was a lot of noise in the background and what sounded like a guitar tuning up. "Where are you, Mo?"

"Oh! You're breaking up! It must be the power cut! Bye!"

"I can hear you clear as a bell—" Jules began but Mo had gone. She put her mobile down, puzzled. Surely the outage didn't affect mobile signal?

"What was that all about?" Dan asked, swinging the car into the car park. His headlights swept over the quad parked up at the entrance where the Pollards were waving. They seemed to have made up, Jules noticed, which meant another scheme was bound to be cooking.

Unlike their last one!

"Not sure." She waved at Big Rog, at least Jules assumed it was Big Rog waiting beside the ribbon festooned vehicle although it could have been anyone buried beneath all the layers of coats and scarves. "Just Mo being Mo."

Dan reversed into his parking space. "Why does that fill me with alarm? And talking of alarm, are you willing to chance the Pollard express?"

Given the choice between walking up hill in the cold or hopping into the Pollards' trailer, Jules plumped for the quad. Soon they were all onboard and whizzing through the quiet streets and up to the vicarage. The cottage windows were lit with candles and the ruffled sea was silvered by moonlight. The frozen air kissed Jules's cheeks and snatched her breath. Even in a thick coat she was chilled to the marrow and when Big Rog pulled up outside the vicarage gate Jules wondered whether she was frozen to the trailer seat.

"Right," Bid Rog said, clapping his gloved hands. "Here we are. Delivered to the church as promised."

"Promised?" Jules asked.

"I mean as promised to you. When you asked me to be the wedding transport!"

"Right," Jules said. She was too tired to question him further. Sometimes you just needed to have faith and believe!

When they arrived back at the vicarage the doorstep was folded up in the darkness. Danny held up his phone torch for light while Jules scrabbled for her keys. Before she could find them the front door swung open.

"Here you are! At last!" Mo stood in the hall and tugged Jules inside. "Right! Let's get you sorted. In here!"

Jules was confused as Mo trundled her into the living room.

"What's going on?"

The room was lit by flickering candles and glancing around Jules spotted Ashley with Isla on his lap and Morgan, camera in his lap, perched on the window seat. Seeing her, he jumped up and began to snap away. The flash made Jules blink and she covered her eyes with her hands.

"Morgan! No! Not when I look like this!"

"Or me!" shrieked Linda, covering her face with her hands. "I've got no makeup on!"

"It's a record of the day and it has to be authentic," protested Morgan. "Fact."

"That's true, mate, but maybe let Jules catch her breath? It's been a long day." Danny put his arm around Morgan's skinny shoulders.

"But Mo said I've got to —"

Mo jabbed Ashley in the ribs so violently that he yelped.

"Ash. You need Dan to do that thing, remember?"

"Eh?" said Ashley. "Oh, yes! Can I borrow you for just ten minutes, Dan? I need you to look at the hot horse shower."

"Seriously? Can't it wait?" Danny said, eyeing the armchair hopefully.

"Not if you want any hot water," said Mo.

"Come on, mate." Ashley tipped Isla gently onto the floor. Danny looked puzzled but he didn't argue. Jules was instantly suspicious.

"What are you up to?" she asked Mo. It had better not be the Chippendales. Apart from being inappropriate, Jules was far too exhausted to appreciate them!

But Dan's sister tapped the side of her nose with her index finger before handing Jules a pile of clothes and a powerful torch.

"Pop these on, brush your hair and maybe I'll tell you."

Jules knew better than to argue. She started to unfold the garments which comprised of a white hoody with *Bride* written across it in silver sequins, her favourite pair of jeans and a thermal vest.

"What's this in aid of?"

"Mostly comfort," said Mo, lowering herself into a chair with a grunt. "I thought you'd be happier in jeans and a hoody? That's what you normally say."

This was a fair point and as much as she loved her wedding dress Jules couldn't wait to step out of it. The hem was filthy, the skirt speckled with stains and at some point she must have trailed one of the sleeves in her coffee. The sad ruined dress felt rather metaphorical of her whole wedding day and the idea of lolling by the fire in her jeans feeling comfortable was most appealing.

Taking the torch, she made her way upstairs and changed as quickly as possible. It was bitterly cold away from the wood burner and she was glad of the thermal vest. Jules pulled out what pins were still embedded in her hair and raked her fingers through the knotted curls. It was a dreadful shame Kursa's handiwork had been ruined but something of the style remained so Jules she pinned her hair back up again as best she could. She braced herself for a wash with cold water - which certainly revived her even if she almost turned blue.

By the time Jules returned downstairs she was feeling a little less frayed around the edges and looking forward to a catch up but only Mo was left.

"Where's everyone gone?"

Jules glanced around. There was no sign of her mother, Isla or even Morgan with his camera.

"They've decamped to the pub."

"The pub?" Jules echoed in disbelief. "It's Christmas Eve."

"Adam's got gas burners apparently so food is on the cards. I said we'd join them."

"Oh, Mo, I don't think so. I'm exhausted. Besides, what if there's a change with Dad and the hospital needs me?"

"Take your mobile," Mo suggested, already half way out of the room. "Come on, everyone wants to see you and they're so disappointed about missing the reception. They've clubbed together to buy you some champagne. Danny and Ash have gone ahead with your mum."

Jules was so tired she could have fallen asleep in the hall, but she didn't want to look ungrateful and besides Linda might have a few too many and need looking after. With a sigh, she reached for her coat and followed Mo into the night.

Outside, the air was cold enough to splinter and Jules's breath rose in little puffs as she walked up the path. She couldn't wait for the warmth of the pub.

"I've had a thought." Mo stopped so abruptly in the darkness that Jules almost tripped over her. "Let's light a candle for your dad before we go the pub."

Like many churches St Wenn's had a rack filled with tea lights which, for a donation, could be lit in memory of a loved one or to symbolise a prayer. Although not strictly Biblical Jules had always liked the idea. To her it represented the light of the world and the flickering flame of hope which faith kept burning even when life seemed at its darkest. This seemed especially meaningful today.

"Dad doesn't believe in God," Jules pointed out.

"So what? You do," said Mo. "Anyway, I'd like to light one for Chewy."

Sometimes Jules found Mo impossible to keep up with. "Chewy?"

"Isla's hamster, gone but not forgotten. God made hamsters, right?"

Jules couldn't deny it. "Yes."

"Well, then," said Mo. "Let's do it."

For a heavily pregnant woman, Mo certainly walked fast and Jules had to stride out to keep up.

"Careful! The path is icy," she warned but Mo didn't slow down and by the time they reached the church porch Jules was panting. She bent double, hands resting on her knees, and recovered while Mo pushed open the heavy oak door.

"She's here! She's here!"

Whispers and excited voices rippled through the stillness and Jules saw that, far from being in darkness as she'd expected, St Wenn's was lit with hundreds of candles. This was how the building must have looked centuries ago, long before gas or electric, and when the altar candles were for more than just decoration, she thought, and it was beautiful. The stained-glass windows were warmed with endless leaping reflections, the flowers on the sills and draped at the ends of pews glowed and the brass gleamed from more than the WI's elbow grease. But what really snatched Jules's breath was realising the church contained many dear and familiar faces, all of which turned her way and smiled delightedly as the door swung open. Wide-eyed, she spotted her mother sitting in the front pew beside Alice and Jonny while various members of the Tremaine and Mathieson family were scattered into others. The only people who weren't members of her family were Sheila Keverne and Big Rog, one holding out Jules's bouquet and the other already mopping his eyes with an enormous spotty hanky.

"Please can I take a picture now?" demanded Morgan, hopping from foot to foot desperate to get on with his task. "Wait until the bride's arrived, you said Mo. She's here now."

"She flipping well is so go for it," said Mo. "And don't forget the bridesmaids."

"Here are your flowers, Jules." Sheila passed over the bouquet which Jules, still reeling, clutched tightly. "I'm so glad your father's going to be fine. What a terrible fright for you. For all of us."

"It was," Jules said, dazed. She turned to Mo. "What's going on?"

Mo pointed to the front of the church. "Your wedding of course! Don't keep Danny waiting!"

Jules squinted into the dim light, her heart contracting with love when she saw the outline of the dearest of figures, broad shouldered and with close cut hair glinting gold in the candles' glow, standing at the altar. Danny! And there was Jake beside him, equally broad shouldered and deep in conversation with Neil Cavendish dressed in full clerics robes and who, on noticing Jules, grinned from ear to ear. He must have whispered something to Danny because moments later her finance turned to smile at her and the current of love that flowed between them was all Jules needed to feel wide awake and energised.

This was real! She was getting married!

"You didn't think we'd let you miss your wedding, did you?" said Mo.

"Not in a million years," added Summer.

Jules's eyes filled and each candle flame wobbled. The man she loved was waiting for her, their closest friends and family were gathered here to bear witness, and she was even wearing jeans and a hoody. This was the wedding she had always dreamed of and although she was sad Alistair wasn't here to give her away, Jules also knew if it wasn't for her father none of this would have happened. It was as though all her wedding wishes had been granted this Christmas Eve, that most wonderful of nights when the stars shone above St Wenn's and yuletide magic spread over the world in a festive embrace.

"I'm needed to play the organ, so best of luck – not that you'll need it," Sheila said, kissing Jules's cheek. She smelled of a beautiful floral scent rather than her usual lavender and her eyes sparkled from far more than candlelight. There was magic all around this Christmas, Jules realised as she clutched her bouquet and smiled for Morgan.

"Ahem!" The sound of loud throat clearing from Big Rog interrupted these thoughts. "Excuse me, vicar, who's going to give you away?"

Eager to join Danny, Jules hadn't thought of this. She'd probably have charged along on her own or perhaps Linda could have been called upon?

She was about to suggest this when the hopeful look on Big Rog's face brought her up short. He was also wearing a suit and even his sparse grey hair had encountered a tub of gel and a comb. Big Rog caused Jules no end of headaches, and it was thanks to him she'd had cold baths for almost a year and no turkey for Christmas dinner, but he'd flown to her father's aid without being asked twice and it was down to the Pollard quad that the medics had reached Alistair so fast. Big Rog had also helped to save Alistair's life?

"I could help out? If you like?" he added hopefully. "You're a bit like a daughter to me, maid."

Jules was touched to hear this, although she wasn't sure she needed Little Rog as a sibling. She also knew there was only one answer to Big Rog's question. Besides, he reminded her a little of Alistair - neither man ever listened to a word she said and were both as determined and as difficult as each other!

"I'd really like that, Roger," she said. "If you don't mind?"

The electricity board could have lit Polwenna Bay with the brightness of Big Rog's smile.

"Mind? I'd be honoured, maid!" he beamed, offering Jules the crook of his arm and waving to Sheila. "Ready when you are, Vicar!"

Jules had heard the opening bars of *Here Comes the Bride* hundreds of times but as Sheila's fingers touched the keys, and St Wenn's swelled with the stirring notes, her skin was dusted with goose pimples. Today she wasn't an observer. Today she wasn't a priest. Today Jules was the bride and by the time this music ended she would be standing beside Danny Tremaine, ready to make sacred vows before their family, friends and God as they became husband and wife. When Jules stepped forward she would be doing far more than walking down the aisle of a church; she would be embarking on the biggest adventure she would ever know.

She took a deep breath and raised her chin, seeing in Danny's face the reflection of her own happiness, one thousand promises and an eternity of love. Danny Tremaine was the love of her life. He was her soul mate and her best friend.

There need be no more waiting.

"I've always been ready," she said.

The ceremony was shorter than originally planned but for Jules it flew by. One moment she and Danny were facing one another and repeating the age-old vows, knowing this was the ultimate celebration of the love they shared, and the next they were exchanging rings and Neil laughingly telling Danny he could kiss his bride. Applause rippled through the church, phone cameras flashed, and Jules saw Linda dabbing her eyes with the handkerchief offered by Jonny. At last they were husband and wife and against all the odds.

"Didn't I always say I'd be happy to marry you in jeans and a hoody?" Danny whispered, squeezing her hand.

"Too late to change your mind now," Jules teased, not wanting to let go even for a moment.

"I love you Mrs Tremaine," he said. "And that's something I know I will never, ever change my mind about."

Chapter 20

Christmas Eve
The Wedding Evening

The register was signed, Tess and Jake witnessing the signatures while Zak sang an arrangement of Ave Maria beautiful enough to melt even the icy world outside, before Neil gave a final blessing and the new Mr and Mrs Tremaine walked through the church while Sheila thumped Mendelssohn's Wedding March out on the organ.

Linda and Alice were both crying, Big Rog was nodding as proudly as any father of the bride and even Mo was misty eyed as she smiled up at Ashley. As she accepted the congratulations of their friends and family and wove her fingers with those of her new husband, Jules knew without any doubt she was the luckiest woman in the world. Dreams did come true and there were happy endings, or perhaps more appropriately in this case happy beginnings?

The night was still glacier cold but somehow this no longer mattered as confetti snowed down and congratulations filled the air. It was still pitch black without street lights but this night the stars seemed to shine more brightly than Jules could ever recall, and the moon smiled at her from high above.

Jules had expected the evening to end at this point, it was Christmas Eve after all and the day had been a strange one by any stretch of the imagination, but when she and Dan finally reached the church gate Little Rog was waiting with the quad and trailer, Penny riding pillion with her arms wrapped around his waist and, Jules suspected, not just because she wanted to keep warm.

"Your chariot awaits to take you to the reception," Big Rog announced, waving at the ribbons and flowers which he must have replaced after the morning's mercy dash.

"Reception? Is the hotel up and running?" Danny asked, surprised.

"In our dreams!" Symon Tremaine dragged a hand through his shaggy red mane. "We've had to think fast."

"You mean I have," said Ella, coolly beautiful in a floor length white velvet coat and black fake fur hat. At least Jules hoped it was fake. "I seem to recall you just ranted and raved that your creations were ruined!"

Symon laughed and pulled her close. Ella's acerbic tongue never phased him. He looked at his girlfriend the way Danny looked at her, Jules realised, and Ella wasn't nearly as spiky as she made out.

Maybe she and Danny had started a trend when it came to unlikely pairings?

"Yes, all right! I had a tantrum and you sorted it!" Symon agreed.

"With some help from me!" Tess huffed, arms crossed and giving Ella her best teacher look. "And the villagers who are all there right now. Tara did lots too."

"Where are they?" Jules asked but Symon tapped his nose.

"You'll see!"

"We've found somewhere and although it's not quite what Dan had in mind, I think you'll be pleased," Tess added.

"Come on, you two lovebirds! It's bleddy freezing out here. We need to warm up before we're back for midnight mass. Into the wedding carriage," ordered Big Rog, rubbing his hands together and stamping his feet.

Jules and Danny did as they were told and before long were tucked beneath a thick blanket and rumbling through the village. It wasn't a long ride because after several minutes Little Rog stopped the quad outside the village hall where Chris the Cod's mobile chip van shone into the night, the air was thick with the aroma of chips and all their friends and neighbours milled around, swaddled in coats and with their hands wrapped around Styrofoam cups as they listened to music.

Jules turned to Danny in disbelief. "I don't believe it! They've managed to get a reception together. Even Zak's band's here!"

"How long have you lived in Polwenna, Mrs Tremaine?" he laughed. "You should know nothing stops a party in this village!"

Danny was right. Everyone was here and somehow there was food and drink and music. Spotting the bridal party, a big cheer rose into the cold air and there was applause and cries of congratulation. Jules spotted Kathy Polmartin and Silver Starr handing out nibbles, Teddy St Milton doing the rounds with champagne and more of her friends and neighbours than she could count. Nick Tremaine and his girlfriend Meg had towed their crab shack over and fired up the gas cookers to heat mulled wine and cook bowls of thick chowder mopped up with hunks of Patsy's bread. Even Sheila's long-lost beau, Mike, was here, chatting away to Eddie Penhalligan. All their old romantic rivalries were long forgotten! Jules wondered whether Mike's presence accounted for the light in Sheila's eyes? Jules really hoped so; everyone should be as happy as she was!

As Danny helped her down from the trailer, and their friends surged forwards to hug and congratulate them, her heart swelled with love. Oh! This wedding was everything she'd ever wanted! A fish and chip supper at the village hall with her friends and family. There were no speeches and no formalities, just love and laughter and celebrations. Nobody would feel left out or wrongly dressed. This was perfect!

What was it the old man had said to her about trusting and things having a way of working out? How had he known? Jules still wondered, and she suspected she would never know the answer to this, but maybe somethings were better staying as mysteries?

"Jules! Danny! Congratulations!" Tara Tremaine hurled herself at the newly-weds and hugging them while Richard, not quite as demonstrative, shook Danny's hand before kissing Jules's cheek.

"Congratulations," he said. "And I'm so pleased to hear your father's doing well, Jules."

"Thank you so much, Richard. Thank you for coming up to be with Dad and for all this too." Jules knew her thanks were inadequate. Nothing she could say would ever come close to describing just how much the quiet young doctor had helped her earlier on. She could never repay him.

But Richard waved her thanks away. "Just enjoy yourselves now. You both deserve it after what you've been through today."

"And by the way, I'm never taking wedding advice from you again," Danny told Tara, pulling a mock stern face. "Big wedding, indeed? Did you even speak to Jules? The poor girl was having kittens! She wanted a small do all along."

"Oops," giggled Tara, turning pink.

"Oops indeed," agreed Danny but he was laughing too.

"Anyway, you won't ever need wedding advice again from me or from anyone. I'm so happy for you both. Maybe it'll be us next, Richard?" Tara threaded her arm through the doctor's and batted her eyelashes at him. "How about it?"

"Only if I can be in charge of the planning!" Richard said. "I'm not letting you near it!"

Before long Jules was drinking champagne and tucking into a pile of golden chips. Warmed by the marina workshop's space heater, the village hall was toasty and cosy with candles wedged into bottles. The Tinners played, people ate and chatted, and Jules realised Danny was right; there was nothing the Polwenna residents liked so much as a party! The inconvenience of power cuts and missing turkeys were long forgotten and as she watched Little Rog and Penny, holding hands, oblivious to anything else except one another, Jules smiled. It seemed those turkeys were responsible for a lot more than some Christmas dinner headaches!

Across the village hall, transformed from a dusty utilitarian space into a dancing hall festooned with streamers and balloons, Sheila was twirling around, long skirts flying while Farmer Mike held her hand and matched her step for step. It might have been the soft candle light which wiped away the years but somehow Jules didn't think so. Candle light wasn't renowned for tinting cheeks pink and making eyes shine! She had never seen Sheila laugh so much or look so carefree. Maybe this wedding would be the beginning of a new chapter for more people than just her and Danny? Jules really hoped so.

"That was such a beautiful wedding," Linda said when she joined Jules and Danny at the crab shack. Holding out her cup so Nick could refill it with chowder, she added, "I think it was actually far nicer just having a few of us. I do wish your father had been able to make it. Even an old misery like Alistair would have enjoyed this."

"Any news from the hospital?" Jules asked.

"No, all quiet which is good news. You heard what the doctor said. A couple of days of being monitored and some lifestyle changes. No more smoking and as little stress as possible and he'll be fine, if still stubborn and incredibly annoying. Still, I suppose medicine can't cure everything!"

"You two seem to have buried the hatchet?" Dan ventured and Linda nodded.

"Isn't it funny? Once upon a time all I would have wanted to do was bury it in his head. Alistair will always drive me round the twist but I'm glad he's going to be fine. How can I be angry with him when we have our wonderful daughter? We didn't make the distance but we definitely got something right."

Jules hugged her. "Thanks, Mum."

"Mind the soup! This dress is a Valentino!" Linda, never one for sentiment, backed away hastily. Jules sighed, reminding herself that although she'd learned recently to love her parents exactly as they were, this didn't mean it would be easy. They would always drive her crackers!

"Shall we find a seat, Mrs Tremaine?" Danny suggested, seeing Jules's hurt expression. "We can't afford to start married life with a massive dry cleaning bill!"

His use of her new name made Jules smile because knowing it was hers at long last made it impossible to feel anything but happy. Linda meant no harm. She was just being Linda!

They carried their chowder into the church hall where Alice and Jonny were sitting with the Carstairs family and watching Isla dancing.

"This is a lovely wedding!" Alice St Milton announced when Danny and Jules joined them. Danny's grandmother was sitting on one of the primary school chairs Tess must have organised and tapping her foot to the music.

"Thanks," said Danny. "I can't take the credit for any of it but I totally agree."

"I think it's by far the nicest wedding I've ever been to," Alice continued. "I can't think of a single one I've enjoyed more."

Jonny was outraged. "Hold on! What about ours?"

"Don't be difficult. You know exactly what I mean. I didn't *go* to ours did I? I was *at* ours! No, this has been just so…so…" Alice paused as she sought the right word. "So friendly and relaxed!"

Jules was delighted.

"That's what I'd always wanted our wedding to be like. It's so strange but I've ended up with my perfect wedding after all."

"In spite of power cuts and air ambulances and floods?" Mo asked.

"Absolutely," Jules said. "Or maybe even because of them?"

"Perhaps all of that was meant to be?" Alice said slowly. "In my experience things have a funny way of turning out the way they're supposed to. In any case, love, I'm thrilled for you and Danny. I know you'll be very happy together."

"Just like Ashley and me," agreed Mo. "Isn't life odd? You never thought we'd end up married when I stopped you bulldozing the woods, did you Ash? But look how happy you are now."

"I'm absolutely ecstatic , my angel, especially each time I carry the shopping half a mile up to the house," he said drily. "And talking of that, I've just about lugged everything up for Christmas dinner tomorrow. You two will be there, won't you?"

"You guys can't miss Ashley's Christmas Dinner. He's been slaving away. I've told him bread sauce comes out of a packet but apparently not," Mo said fondly.

Ashley grimaced. "You utter heathen. You'll be telling me gravy's made from granules next!"

"Of course we'll be there. Our honeymoon won't start until Alistair's discharged," Danny said.

"There's not much use for bread sauce without turkey," Jules pointed out. "Unless Mr Wattles is on the menu after all?"

"Ella's saved the day for Mr Wattles and our family Christmas Dinner," Ashley said, shooting Mo a stern look when she opened her mouth to protest. "Yes, she did, Red. If Ella hadn't decided to donate the contents of the hotel's freezers to the Community Centre at the same time Sy took the reception food, she wouldn't have come across those catering sacks full of chicken nuggets. It's not quite turkey but I'm going to improvise and make festive fajitas because if I've learned anything from today it's that things don't need to be perfect to be perfect!"

Jules was delighted. She *loved* fajitas. And she loved it even more that Mr Wattles and his chums would live to gobble another day.

"So what's going to happen to the turkeys? I imagine they'll be a little surplus to requirements after tomorrow?" she asked.

Mo rested her hands on her vast stomach.

"Tell her, Ash! It's sweet, if slightly bonkers."

"You'll shatter my hard man Cashley image for once and for all," Ashley grumbled but he was smiling too. "I did it for Isla. She really loves those birdies."

"So you say, you big softy," said Mo, ruffling his hair fondly, "but I think she gets it from you!"

"Don't keep me in suspense!" Jules pleaded. She really hoped it would be good news for the birdies. They'd been a part of this most strange and wonderful of weeks and it seemed fitting that even Little Roger's turkeys might have a happy ending.

"I've rented one of Perry's fields and ordered a big shed so Penny and Little Rog can start an animal rescue centre. I couldn't bear their long faces a moment longer and how could I look my little girl in the eye if I didn't keep those birds?" Ashley shook his head in despair at his own tender-heartedness. "I'll probably live to regret it, but you're looking at the major share-holder of the *Polwenna Bay Wild Life Park!*"

"You can all guess who their first residents will be," Mo said. "What next? Will Rog and Penny rescue lobsters from Nick's crab shack?"

Ashley groaned. "Don't even joke about it. I'm going to have to set down some strict ground rules."

"Starting with Big Rog. He's already taking about film crews and tie in merchandise," laughed Mo. "Perry needs to watch out because the Pollards have big ambitions. They'll turn Polwenna Manor into Longleat before he knows it. Hippos and lions here we come!"

Jules flicked her eyes across the church hall and spotted the gangly and slightly dishevelled Perry Tregarrick deep in discussion with Penny and Little Rog. Maybe this idea wasn't as crazy as it sounded? Perpetually broke Perry was a sweetheart and could do with a little luck. Sometimes it was the craziest ideas and the oddest combinations that ended up making the most sense. Look at her and Danny for instance. Who would have ever imagined the handsome soldier hero and the shy village vicar would go together like tea and biscuits?

Sometimes you just had to have faith and trust everything would work out the way it was always meant to.

The rest of the evening passed in a whirl of dancing, heaping plates with food, and catching up with relatives and friends who'd travelled all the way to Cornwall for the wedding. Billeted in houses and B and B's around the village, everyone was in high spirits and having a wonderful time in spite of all the upheaval. David's free bar had been a huge hit and Caspar James had miraculously risen from his sick bed in order to make the most of it. Bobby and Joey Penhalligan had passed out hours ago and only the hard-core fishermen were still standing, or in Eddie's case throwing some interesting shapes on the dance floor. Finally Patsy unveiled the wedding cake, a giant chocolate affair smothered in rich buttercream icing and sprinkled with curls of dark chocolate, and Jules and Danny cut it slowly, their hands clasped on the knife's handle as the posed for Morgan.

"Speech! Speech! Speech!" demanded Nick Tremaine and everyone joined in.

Danny looked at Jules. "Me or you?"

"Oh you, absolutely. They've all heard enough of my sermons!" she said.

"Too right!" called Neil (who was not, to the great disappointment of most of Polwenna's women, wearing a kilt). "You've all got to get to Midnight Mass!"

Dan grinned. "Short speeches are best in my book anyway. My wife and I—" There was a round of applause at this and he waited for it to fade away before continuing, "my wife and I would like to thank you all for everything you've done today. This wedding and reception wouldn't have happened if it wasn't for all of you and Jules and I will never ever forget that. You're the best family and friends anyone could ever have. I'm the luckiest man alive – and I don't say that lightly as you'll all know."

His voice choked up and Jules knew he was recalling his long and hard road from injury and rehabilitation to this very moment. She squeezed his arm, a touch which said how much she loved him and would always be there for him, and Danny inhaled sharply before thanking individuals and raising a toast to his new wife.

Ashley raised his glass. "To Danny and Jules! Long life and happiness!"

As his words were echoed, glasses and paper cups raised and the room rang with cheers, there was a sudden flicker from above and without warning all the lights blazed on. Unaccustomed to the abrupt brightness, everyone blinked in the relentless glare of strip lights and for a moment there was confusion as the entire village was illuminated once again by thousands of coloured lights from Christmas trees, Big Rog's festive decorations and the orange glow of street lamps.

The power was back! Christmas was saved and Jules couldn't help but take this as a sign. After all, the Bible was full of such things so why not in Polwenna Bay as well as the Holy Land?

"Let there be light!" she smiled and in answer Danny, pulled her close and kissed his new bride soundly.

The church hall rang with cries of delight and after this the party began to break up as people hurried home to make sure their preparations were underway before putting carrots and milk out for Santa or walking up to Midnight Mass. They called Merry Christmas to one another as they parted outside the church hall and Linda, who had been invited to stay with Alice and Jonny, kissed Jules and held her tightly.

"I'm so proud of you, Ju Ju. You're the best daughter anyone could ever have and I'm the luckiest mum."

Jules hugged her back, filled with love for Linda.

"I'm the lucky one," she said. "Happy Christmas, Mum."

There were more goodbyes and cries of *Happy Christmas* and Jules soon lost count of how many people she had kissed and hugged. Her eyes felt heavy and as she leaned into Danny she realised just how exhausted she was. It wasn't very rock and roll of her, but she longed for nothing more than to crawl into bed and sleep. They may not be destined to spend their wedding night in the plush honeymoon suite, but Jules couldn't wait to unlock the front door of the vicarage, make a cup of tea and snuggle under the duvet with Danny. It was hardly the stuff of Mills and Boon, but she couldn't think of anything more romantic!

"Shall we go home, Mrs Tremaine?" Danny said softly, his lips grazing hers. "I don't know about you, but I'm shattered. It's been quite a day."

"I'd love nothing more, but shouldn't we help tidy up? We can't leave it all to Sy and Ella," Jules said, worried.

"Yes, we can! It's our wedding and Ella's the wedding planner. We'll catch up with it all tomorrow. Besides," he gave her a sideways look which made her skin ripple with anticipation. "I want my bride to myself."

"I think that can be arranged," Jules said softly. "Fancy coming back to my place, Mr Tremaine?"

Dan grinned. "I thought you'd never ask!"

Hand in hand they slipped out of the village hall and out into the deep-frozen night. With the restoration of the power, Christmas had returned in full force and it was almost a shock to see the village ablaze with colour after the intensity of the darkness. Now reflections danced in the still waters of the harbour and shivered on the wet sand while every cottage window bloomed with light. The moon rode high in the indigo sky, frost sparkled from the roof tops and somewhere a solitary owl hooted. It was utterly magical that Jules's breath caught in her throat even though she had looked on this scene a thousand times. On her first Christmas as Danny's wife the whole world sparkled with beauty and wonder, and Jules knew this was a night she would remember until she closed her eyes for the last time.

"I'd carry you over the threshold if I had two arms," Danny told her as they let themselves into the vicarage.

"You'd give yourself a hernia, the amount of chips I've guzzled, or put your back out which wouldn't be a great start to the honeymoon!"

"But I still wish I could."

"You carry me in a million other ways," Jules said fiercely.

The vicarage was already warming up, the radiators gurgling away merrily, and Jules switched on the lamps and the Christmas tree. The wood burner's glow lit the sitting room and Danny sank onto the sofa with a groan of bliss.

"Come here," he said, patting the seat beside him and Jules didn't need asking twice. She leaned her head on his shoulder, basking in the warmth of the fire and of Danny's love. They could have a little rest before heading out to Midnight Mass, was the last thought that flickered through Jules's mind before her eyes closed and she tumbled into sleep at exactly the same time her new husband's breathing grew deeper. Oblivious to the voices of worshippers walking up the lane to the church, they slept on with their arms around one another and the warmth of the fire caressing their faces.

As their wedding day drew to a close, the frost sparkled across the moonlit village and the bells of St Wenn's rang out for Christmas Day. The new Mr and Mrs Tremaine drowsed contentedly in front of the fire, dreaming of the life which lay ahead and more at peace than they could have ever imagined when Alistair lay in the kitchen surrounded by medics and their wedding plans were in tatters.

The clock ticked away the most holy night of the year and Jules snuggled into Danny, smiling in her sleep. In spite of everything her wedding had been everything and more than she'd ever imagined. As she slept, she dreamed an elderly man with thick white hair and kind wise eyes had slipped into a pew at the back of the church, joining the villagers to welcome the birth of the Christ child and listen to the age-old words about angels and wise men and bright guiding stars. In her dream his appearance in St Wenn's was nothing unusual or even unexpected. Now she was in the mysterious hinterland between waking and sleeping Jules realised he'd been here many times before.

Of course he had! Finally, she understood...

A log shifted in the fireplace. Danny reached out to pull her closer and then the dream was gone. By the time daylight stole beneath the curtains, and the shrieking gulls announced the dawn of Christmas Day, only fragments remained to be snatched from all recollection like fallen leaves whirled out of reach by the wind. Yet the sense of contentment and peace this dream had brought remained as pink light seeped beneath the curtains and the gulls began to squabble. As Christmas Day dawned Jules knew beyond all doubt that her new life with Danny was going to be wonderful and filled with love and laughter. If she had faith and believed, if she could trust, then all would *always* be well.

And knowing this was, Jules thought as she lay in her new husband's arms, the best wedding present anyone could ever ask for.

Epilogue

Christmas Day

Christmas Day dawned as cold and frost freckled as any film director could ever wish. As the bells of St Wenn's rang out across the village, each peal a glad tiding of joy and hope, villagers out walking called out cheerful greetings before hurrying home to peel vegetables and, like Ashley Carstairs, improvise Christmas dinner from whatever they had managed to find from the deep freeze. Children peddled new bicycles through the streets, wobbling in a perfect imitation of their parents after several festive sherries, and second-homers sporting brand-new Christmas jumpers enjoyed a pre-lunch stroll by the tide's edge.

Polwenna Bay was a magical place all year round but on Christmas Day it was particularly wonderful Jules decided as, hand in hand, she and Danny wandered through the village. Cottage windows twinkled with tree lights, doors were festooned with holly wreaths and woodsmoke huffed from the chimney pots to coil up and away into a vivid blue sky. Now all power was restored the Christmas illuminations blazed from the quay and pierced the water with jewelled shards of light. Seagulls danced in the sky, shrieking and wheeling as though in celebration of this most special of days, and as the sunlight turned their wings to purest white Jules thought if you squinted they could almost be snowflakes tumbling and whirling down on this greetings card scene.

"It's pretty special, isn't it?" Danny remarked when they paused halfway up the path to Mariners to catch their breath. From this point the track grew steeper as it zig-zagged above the beach on its relentless climb to the headland. The village was spread out before them, a patchwork of white washed cottages, narrow cobbled lanes and velvety soft lichen roof tops, and in the middle was the harbour and the pièce de résistance, a perfect scoop of water circled lovingly by the granite arms of ancient walls. The tide was in and the boats rose and fell with the gentle swell of the waves in a rhythm as old as time. Now and then a villager walked along the quay side to tighten a rope or check a bilge pump and Jules found it comforting to know that even though her life had changed forever, and in the most thrilling and soul-blending way possible, the timeless world of Polwenna continued as it always had and always would.

"Happy?" Danny asked, pressing her gloved hand against his cheek.

Jules almost melted at his question. *Happy?* That word wasn't enough for the deep sense of wonder thrilling her to the very core of her being. *Happy* was too brief, too bland and came nowhere close to describing the rich and utter completeness she felt at becoming one with the person who truly was the other half of her heart. When dawn had thrown pink light across the living room and the fire died down to little more than a glow, Jules and Danny had crept upstairs and finally begun their married life. Oh! How Jules wished she could dredge up a new word to do justice this shimmering, glorious sensation which consumed her today! All the romance novels she'd read late at night, the tear-jerking rom coms she'd watched alone and endless wistful pop songs that made her heart ache were nothing, *nothing*, in comparison to this emotion! Today it was as though Jules finally saw the world in vivid colours rather than greyscale.

And it was wonderful!

"I'm really happy. Fact!" she told him. "How about you?"

Danny's reply was a tender kiss as the church bells pealed one last time, their golden tongued notes trembling in the air before fading as the village sank into an enchanted Christmas Day peace. The Pollard quad was sleeping in the now empty turkey shed and the engines of tied up fishing boats slumbered too. Shops snoozed behind closed shutters and even The

Ship was quiet as Adam and Rose Harper savoured a rare day off. The congregation flowed from St Wenn's, a colourful tide of coats and scarves and bobble hats, and chatter floated over the still valley. Jules spotted Alice and Jonny walking slowly along the path followed by Reverend Neil and finally the duffle coated figure of Sheila. She was always last to leave after locking up and was usually alone but today Sheila walked in perfect step beside a grey-haired man in a waxed jacket and tweed cap. Although Jules couldn't see her face from this far away she was sure the older woman was smiling, and something told Jules this Christmas would be the happiest Sheila Keverne had known for a long time. It just went to prove even a hen night which had seemed like a big disaster could turn into something wonderful.

The more she thought about everything, the more it seemed to Jules that this was the story of their wedding. Her Boss had been very busy making sure the wedding, and this whole perfect start to married life, had fallen into place exactly as Jules had secretly dreamed it might. From wearing her jeans and hoody to the ceremony, to fish and chip suppers in the village hall, to the wedding breakfast being enjoyed by those who needed it the most today; everything had happened exactly as it was always meant to.

Have faith and believe the old man had said, and he'd been right. Or should she say *He'd* been right? Jules knew this was fanciful but she liked to think that maybe, just maybe, something very special had happened for her this candlelit Christmas.

"I know a dash to the hospital wasn't quite the start to married life we had in mind," Danny was saying and, as always, reading her mind, "but, do you know what? I wouldn't want yesterday to have turned out any other way. It was the perfect wedding against all the odds, wasn't it?"

"It really was," she agreed.

"And it's fantastic your dad's doing so well," he continued. "It sounds as though he's rather enjoying being fussed over!"

"Unlike me, my parents love to be the centre of attention," Jules laughed.

It was good to be amused by Linda and Alistair rather than driven to despair. Another wonderful if strange turn of events that had blossomed from what had looked like a disaster.

Having called the hospital just before they set off to celebrate Christmas up at Mariners, Jules had been thrilled to learn Alistair was doing well and was likely to be discharged by the end of Boxing Day. He would need careful monitoring and rest, the consultant said, and should stay with family while he regained his strength. Danny had offered instantly to have Alistair convalesce at the vicarage when the consultant added he was delighted to hear the patient would be recuperating in Tenerife.

"Warmth and no stress are exactly what we recommend, and lots of salads and grilled fish will be most beneficial," he'd said to the new, and rather mystified, Mr and Mrs Tremaine. "A rest in the sunshine will be very good indeed."

It transpired that Linda had offered to have Alistair come to stay with her and David at their villa in Spain while he recovered. This was a kind gesture although Jules wondered privately if it was actually a form of subtle revenge? After all, Linda knew all about low fat diets and exercise. Alistair also had no hope of so much as a one puff on a cigarette with her around. At long last he would be at his ex-wife's mercy!

"Who would have thought your mum would be the one to offer to look after Alistair?" Danny said wonderingly. "Is this an example of those mysterious ways you're always talking about?"

Jules kissed his cheek.

"I'm sure of it," she said.

Like Danny, Jules had also assumed she would take care of her father. She would have offered to do so in a heartbeat even though it would mean cancelling their honeymoon, which Danny had revealed was the exact gentle retreat in a Cornish beauty spot she had hoped for. With roaring log fires, good food, walks on beaches and big beds piled with white pillows and plump duvets this was her idea of heaven. Jules hadn't thought she could possibly love her new husband more but when Danny offered to cancel the lot so they could nurse Alistair through his recovery, her heart had swelled almost to bursting. Love, Jules was learning fast, wasn't finite; the more you gave away the more you had and the more you felt. She knew she would love Danny more with every passing year. It was a mystery and a miracle and the biggest privilege of her life.

"Shall we start the hike up, Mrs Tremaine?" he asked her. "I don't know about you but I'm ravenous. Somehow I seem to have worked up an enormous appetite already this morning!"

She blushed and Danny smiled at her, a cheeky smile which brimmed with fun and promised so many new delights.

"I think we should, Mr Tremaine," she said. "Fajitas and pizza here we come. Morgan will be thrilled."

He certainly will. It's not just you and I whose hopes and dreams have come true this Christmas!" Danny laughed.

"No," agreed Jules, watching Sheila tuck her hand into the crook of Farmer Mike's arm as they walked away from St Wenn's. "It really isn't."

Hand in hand, they began the climb up to Mariners where Ashley would be dashing around the kitchen doing his best to improvise a turkey free dinner while Mo barked instructions from her sofa. Maybe Isla was out with Penny feeding her new feathered pets? As she padded downstairs to make tea for her new husband (how she loved being able to say that!) Jules had seen Little Rog and Penny walking along Church Lane. One of Penny's hands was clasped tightly by Little Rog, who looked as though he never wanted to let go, while the other swung a carrier bag crammed with green leaves. The Kussell family's lost Christmas lunch was Mr Wattles' gain and Jules, who wanted the whole world to be as full of love and happiness as she was, felt thrilled to see how happy Polwenna Bay's newest, and most unlikely, couple looked.

Perhaps the origins of this new relationship had been a little dubious, Jules reflected as she'd carried two mugs back upstairs, but one man's terrorist was another turkey's freedom fighter! She'd started to say something along these lines to Danny but when he tugged her back beneath the duvet all thoughts of turkeys, Pollards and pretty much anything at all vanished. There was only her new husband, a million wonderful sensations and the wonder of a world which had suddenly turned a thousand times brighter.

Fingers knitted together, and chatting easily about the events of the past few days, Jules and Danny continued their walk to Mariners where family and friends, but definitely no turkey dinner, awaited. Jules's first Christmas as Danny's wife, and newest member of the Tremaine family, was about to begin and with it the biggest adventure of her life. As she ascended the path, Jules's heart climbed too until it soared as freely and as joyfully as the gulls above the waves in the bay. Yes, this was exactly what happiness felt like and as she smiled at her new husband Jules Tremaine knew she was finally home. Home for Christmas and for the rest of her life.

The End

Ruth Saberton

I really hope you have enjoyed reading this book. If you did, I would really appreciate a review on Amazon. It makes all the difference for a writer.

Amazon UK

Amazon.com

Goodreads

Christmas by Candlelight

You might also enjoy my other books:

The Promise
The Last Card
The Letter
The Locket
The Island Legacy
Chances

Runaway Summer: Polwenna Bay 1
A Time for Living: Polwenna Bay 2
Winter Wishes: Polwenna Bay 3
Treasure of the Heart: Polwenna Bay 4
Recipe for Love: Polwenna Bay 5
Rhythm of the Tide: Polwenna Bay 6
Catching Hearts: Polwenna Bay 7
Christmas by Candlelight: Polwenna Bay 8

Magic in the Mist: Polwenna Bay novella
Cornwall for Christmas: Polwenna Bay novella

Escape for the Summer
Escape for Christmas
Hobb's Cottage
Weight Till Christmas
The Wedding Countdown
Dead Romantic
Katy Carter Wants a Hero
Katy Carter Keeps a Secret
Ellie Andrews Has Second Thoughts
Amber Scott is Starting Over

Ruth Saberton

Pen Name Books

Writing as Jessica Fox

The One That Got Away
Eastern Promise
Hard to Get
Unlucky in Love
Always the Bride

Writing as Holly Cavendish

Looking for Fireworks

Writing as Georgie Carter

The Perfect Christmas

Ruth Saberton is the bestselling author of *The Letter, Katy Carter Wants a Hero* and *Escape for the Summer*. She also writes upmarket commercial fiction under the pen names Jessica Fox, Georgie Carter and Holly Cavendish.

Born in London, Ruth now lives in beautiful Cornwall. She has travelled to many places, but nothing compares to the rugged beauty of the Cornish coast which never fails to provide her with inspiration for her writing. Ruth loves to chat with readers so please follow her author pages on Instagram and Facebook You can also follow her on Twitter.

Twitter: @ruthsaberton

Facebook: Ruth Saberton Author

Instagram: Ruth Saberton Instagram

Head over to Ruth's website for more information about her and her writing. You can also sign up for her newsletter where you'll receive updates on any new releases and other exciting items.

Web: www.ruthsaberton.com

Printed in Great Britain
by Amazon